Someone had been murdered . . .

Diane stopped dead, then laughed, feeling stupid. What had that man said about the hotel providing dead bodies for guests to investigate? Someone must have decided it would be fun to get the mystery writers in on the game.

Feeling better, Diane began walking closer to the body. Beyond it was a heavy brass candlestick like the one in her suite. Someone had gone to a lot of trouble getting blood all over it. And there was a mask, crumpled in the victim's hand.

At that point, another definite clue came to her. She'd been thinking of the victim as one of the hotel staff pretending to be dead, since it obviously wasn't a dummy. But it suddenly came to her that the body wasn't breathing. . . .

ABOUT THE AUTHOR

Haunted House is well-known science fiction author Sharon Green's first venture into the field of romantic suspense. A longtime lover of spooky stories and strangeness, she decided to turn her talents to writing a story that would take advantage of those elements. Sharon says she's always wanted to stay at a hotel like the one she described in *Haunted House,* but she thought a real murder would be more interesting to investigate than a fake one. Since providing real dead bodies is too antisocial to be fun, she's limited herself to creating fictional ones and letting her characters and her readers be the lucky ones to enjoy them. Sharon lives in Edison, New Jersey, with two of her sons and her five cats.

Haunted House

Sharon Green

Harlequin Books

TORONTO • NEW YORK • LONDON
AMSTERDAM • PARIS • SYDNEY • HAMBURG
STOCKHOLM • ATHENS • TOKYO • MILAN

Harlequin Intrigue edition published December 1990

ISBN 0-373-22152-5

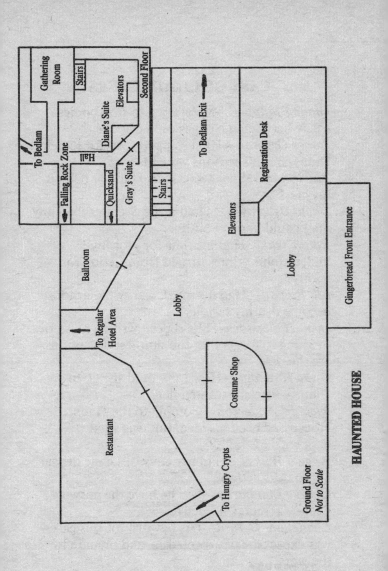

HAUNTED HOUSE

CAST OF CHARACTERS

Diane Philips—She preferred to find bodies solely between the pages of her books.

James Grayson—He'd stepped forward to help Diane, but his reasons were his own.

The Pirate—What secrets were hidden behind his mask?

David Bellamy—He had more enemies than any man could hope to outlive.

Ralph Teak—Had his flair for plotting undetectable crimes turned from fiction to reality?

Bill Raglan—Had his mock war with authors become deathly serious?

Lynn Haverstock—She'd been writing mysteries too long to forget that the simplest deceptions are the best.

Anita Rutledge—How far would she go to get Diane where she wanted her?

Richard Anderson—Coming to the Haunted House had been his idea, but was what happened his fault?

Angela Wilkes—Had her envy of Diane driven her to destruction?

George Lombardy—Did he have the answers Diane's rescuers needed?

Lieutenant Gerard—His byword for this case was expect the unexpected . . . and prepare for the worst.

Chapter One

James Grayson had been east before, but those other times he'd been lucky enough to find it warm. Southern California tended to spoil her natives, making them believe there was no such thing as really cold weather. This time Gray had had to buy an overcoat, and he couldn't get beyond considering the purchase as blackmail by Mother Nature.

It was business that had brought him east—personal business as grim as the winter lifelessness he saw outside the coffee shop window, although not nearly as depressing. But, after months of digging and checking and questioning reluctant or uninformed people, Gray had finally gotten a break. He had a lead on the people he was certain had framed his brother, and he would follow it to the end.

"Thank you for sitting where I'd be able to see you, Mr. Grayson." The soft male voice came from somewhere behind him. "Now, if you don't mind, let's move to a booth in the back, where other people won't be given the same opportunity."

Rather than answering in words Gray took his cup of coffee, got to his feet and followed his unknown contact to a booth that had no window beside it and wasn't easily seen from the door. They slid into opposite sides of the booth, all the way to the wall, then studied each other in the dimness.

"Do you think you were followed?" the stranger asked, his thin, sallow, mid-fortyish face an inadequate setting for his sharp, dark eyes. He wasn't Gray's size but he was still tall, and more skinny than slender despite his overcoat.

"It isn't possible to be absolutely certain, but I don't think so," Gray answered, leaning back in his seat. "How about you?"

"I made the effort to be absolutely certain," the man who'd asked to be called Jack answered with a faint smile. "None of the clothes I'm wearing are mine—including the underwear—so I can't have been bugged, and I chose this place at random out of the phone book. I also watched you for three blocks on your way here. If you have a tail, it's long and loose."

"And you know I'm who I say I am because of the picture I faxed ahead," Gray added with a nod. "That's a lot of precaution for one simple meeting."

"You should know better than that, Grayson," the man said, his voice sharpening despite the lack of volume. "You may have spent the last few years in a peaceful law practice, but before that you were Naval Intelligence. Your background is the main reason I agreed to talk to you, but if you don't start using what you learned we're wasting my time and risking your life."

"I know exactly how dangerous those people are," Gray answered, his own voice as mild as it had been all along. "That fact's been obvious from the beginning. I have to say I admire your sources, to have given you as much background on me as they did. My service record was supposed to have been classified."

"It probably still is," Jack said with a wave of one finger, dismissing the comment. "My source in this instance is a personal friend, who had the information and owed me a favor. For instance, your colleagues in the legal profession think your nickname, Gray, is just a shortening of your last name, Grayson. I happen to know it dates back to your service days, and refers to the kind of personality you can project when you're investigating. You can be so quiet and unassuming, no one notices your being there or considers you a threat. I decided that if anyone can break through on this it has to be you, and that's why I'm here. But I need to know more about why *you're* here."

"My brother was convicted of murder and sent to prison," Gray answered, his pleasant, handsome face turning expressionless. Only his light, innocent blue eyes showed his emotions, and those eyes made the man speaking to him feel shaken.

"The evidence against him was all circumstantial," Gray continued, "but taken as a whole the jury couldn't help but convict. He had motive and opportunity and an alibi that didn't hold up, but I know him better than anyone else alive. He isn't a murderer, and no one will ever make me believe he is. Someone set him up, and I'm going to find out who that someone is. Our mutual acquaintance led me to believe you know what's going on."

"Only to a limited extent," Jack said with a sigh, making sure part of his attention was on those who came and went in the coffee shop. "I used to be a cop. I got retired on a disability pension after being shot in the line of duty, then decided to open my own private investigations firm. I handled the easy stuff, background checks, consultation on security procedures, wide-range information retrievals, things like that. And then my old partner from the force, a man I'd worked with for nine years, suddenly turned up dead."

The man stopped talking while a waitress came over with a cup of coffee for him and a refill for Gray. Once the woman was gone, Jack continued.

"Now, Ed was a good cop," he said, using a spoon to stir the sugar he'd added to the coffee. "The department claimed he'd been gunned down by some crazy, hopped up on drugs. They made a real effort to find his killer, but when they came up empty I wasn't surprised. Ed would have known better than to get caught by a freak, so it had to be something else."

Jack paused to sip his coffee, then shook his head.

"About a week after the funeral a package was delivered to my office, sent by some out-of-state info storage service with if-I-die-do-this instructions. The file inside was sealed for privacy, and when I opened it I found newspaper clippings from all over the country and four from right here in the city. They all covered the same kind of story, a murder leading to an arrest and usually then to a conviction, with only two unimportant exceptions.''

''*Unimportant* exceptions?'' Gray interrupted after having sipped at his own coffee. ''What do you consider unimportant?''

''In one instance, the accused killed himself before a verdict of guilty could be brought,'' the man answered with a grimace. ''The reporter writing the story—and probably everyone else—decided he couldn't face paying for what he'd done. The other was a woman who got off on a quirk— her lawyer found a technicality and used it. But all he saved her from was doing time. She'd been some high corporate exec, but being brought to trial for murder killed her career good and proper.''

''Why do I get the feeling that was an acceptable alternative?'' Gray asked, one finger moving on the side of his cup as he frowned.

''Ed worked on two of the New York cases,'' Jack said with a faint humorless smile, confirming Gray's suspicions. ''He felt there were suspects in each case who might have had really good motives, but who were passed over in favor of the suspect who had it all. He did some quiet checking around to see what became of the overlooked suspects, and in every case someone was better off than they had been. Either they suddenly had a lot more money to spend, or they got the job spot vacated by the victim or the convicted murderer, or they inherited a business, or they were unexpectedly married to someone they shouldn't have had a chance at. Finding that out really made Ed wonder.''

''I'll bet he was wondering if those people benefited two ways instead of one,'' Gray said, his eyes suddenly glinting. ''Not just from someone's death, but also by having someone specific blamed for it. How many clippings did you say he had?''

''Enough to convince him the cases here in the city weren't coincidences or flukes,'' Jack returned. ''As ridiculous as it sounds, he suspected an organization of some sort, one that operates all over the country. You choose your victim, choose your patsy, pay over your money, then sit back and wait for the windfall."

"That's not my idea of ridiculous," Gray said without looking away. "It's my idea of good police work. But I have a tough question for you. You and your friend Ed were partners for nine years, and you say you continued to be close even after you left the force. If he didn't feel he could trust you, he wouldn't have had his file sent to you. Why you didn't turn it over to anyone official is clear—why you aren't following up, yourself, to find his murderer isn't."

"Would it be clearer if I said I can't trust my own body not to betray me?" Jack asked in turn, pain and shame evident in the dark of his eyes. "I had to face the unpleasant fact that if I tried going up against this organization they would probably have very little trouble stopping me. I almost did it anyway—until I heard that someone connected with one of those clippings was putting out feelers for information in a number of directions. I did my own background check on you, and then I got in touch."

"But not just to tell me you already knew my brother was innocent, and to forget about it because we can't prove it," Gray said, speaking with utter conviction. "You have something more, don't you? Something you can't do yourself, so you want me to do it."

"You're right, but I'm not planning on just tossing you out on your own," Jack answered, smiling at the hope and controlled eagerness he could see growing in Gray. "I can't back you up physically, but my specialty is information and that I *can* give you. You'll pick out the players, and I'll build the scorecard."

"That's why you went to such lengths to make sure we weren't seen talking," Gray said with satisfaction and a nod of understanding. "The way I've been poking around might just have gotten our opponents' attention, and you didn't want me to lead them to you."

"It's a little more involved than that," Jack said, his dark gaze still steady. "As Ed's ex-partner and best friend, it's likely I've been watched since he was killed. If we can keep them guessing about you long enough we may surprise them. But you'll really need to watch your back. If they do spot you and understand who you are, they'll try to take you out.''

"They will if they don't overlook me," Gray countered with a grin that was pure devilment. "Don't forget, being overlooked is my specialty. And if that doesn't work, they'll have another surprise coming— I'm not all that easy to take out. Now, what have you got, and how can we use it?''

"I have a lead Ed picked up, but I'm still working on where he got it," the man answered, leaning forward a little. "I'd be happier if I knew what it was all about, but since it's all we've got we'll have to go ahead with it and hope it takes us somewhere. It looks like something is scheduled to go down, but what it is and which players are involved isn't part of the info. Are you ready to do a little traveling?''

"Where?" Gray asked, also leaning forward. "I'm supposed to be on vacation, so I can go pretty much where I please, but if it's someplace no one ever heard of, I'll have to lay some groundwork to make it look natural.''

"That, at least, is one thing you won't have to worry about," Jack said with a narrow-faced smile. "It's in Connecticut, but more and more people are hearing about it. It's a resort hotel called the Haunted House...."

Chapter Two

"Oooh, look at *that*!" one of Diane Philips's fellow passengers in the hotel's shuttle van gushed, pointing toward the front windshield. "When you get close enough not to be able to see the upper floors, it looks exactly like a *real* haunted house."

"Brooding gingerbread," the woman sitting beside the gusher pronounced, her tone filled with satisfaction. "I've always *loved* brooding gingerbread, especially when it's garnished with gargoyles. If it's half that good on the inside, they're going to have to throw me out to make me go home."

Diane heard the sound of agreement from the woman's companion, and was only just able to keep herself from shaking her head. She would have bet any amount named, that the woman who loved gargoyles with her gingerbread was the sort to investigate spooky creakings no matter what, even if the dead bodies were piled so high she had to climb over them. It was nice to have hobbies in life, but dedicating oneself to pestering the unknown was a little beyond Diane's range of interest.

But the thought of a pile of dead bodies wasn't. Diane smiled to herself as she realized something like that *would* be in her range of interest, provided it was the normal and everyday rather than the supernatural that had done the murders. Picking up clues, following false trails to discover the true ones, questioning witnesses and finding the flaws in their stories—the things the detective characters Diane created most loved doing—that was the best fun.

Diane stirred restlessly in her seat, feeling the remains of her depression start to lift, a depression caused by a memory named Richard Anderson.

"Call me Rick, Richard sounds too stuffy," she mimicked to herself, feeling the hurt when she remembered that. It was the first thing he'd said when they'd met, and the charming grin that went along with the words had hit her hard. She'd given up expecting to ever meet anyone like him—charming, handsome and very interested—and then, almost literally out of the well-known blue, there he'd been.

It had happened at one of those wine and cheese booksigning parties held by a New York bookstore, and Diane had been there with some of her fellow mystery writers to do autographing and mingling. With all those people around it was hard to remember just who had introduced them, but that had been the start of it all.

"The start of not noticing that the world had other people besides him and me," Diane said to herself. She'd had dinner with Rick that night, found out all about the executive position he held with a small but high-powered ad agency, heard about the failed marriage he painfully admitted was mostly his fault, and agreed to see him again.

Not long after that they were taking turns visiting on weekends; either she went into the city to stay at his apartment, or he came out to New Jersey to stay at her house. They had gone everywhere that sounded like fun to them, and if the outing turned out not to be fun after all, it hadn't mattered in the least. They were still there *together*, and that was what counted.

Or at least it was what had counted until last week. Two months ago she'd been invited to a small convention of mystery and horror writers being held at a new hotel in Connecticut, and when Rick had heard about it he'd considered it a great idea.

"Come on, Diane, they say the place is great," he'd coaxed, his beautiful brown gaze holding hers. "It's out in the country all by itself, and it's been built to look like a haunted house. They have costume parties every night, the staff walks around dressed like the Addams family, and you can even reserve a suite that looks like an old mansion apartment complete with secret passageways. Didn't you ever want to spend some time in a haunted house when you were a kid?''

''Not without a large number of extremely well-armed bodyguards,'' she'd answered with a laugh. ''I was practical even as a kid, and never could understand why all those women in horror movies *always* found it necessary to investigate the strange, creaking noise coming from the basement or the attic. As far as I'm concerned, if something wants to creak it can do it. You won't find *me* creeping around trying to make it stop.''

''But that's just the point,'' he'd countered with an answering laugh. ''You don't have to worry about the creaking, because you'll already know who's doing it. And as far as needing a bodyguard goes, you now have one who's *extremely* dedicated.''

At that point he'd taken her in his arms, and she hadn't even had the chance to point out that conventions run by outsider amateurs—like the hotel people who, after all, were probably just looking for publicity—often turned into disasters. Writers and editors weren't told when to show up where, fans were given misinformation, books weren't available to be bought or signed, and utter chaos usually reigned.

Right then it had been an awareness of Rick which had reigned, and it hadn't taken him long to talk her into agreeing to go to the convention. They'd even requested one of the trick suites that were in the ''full party'' area, and Diane had begun looking forward to the time. After all, even if it did turn into a complete disaster, she would still be with Rick.

And then one of those strange times of calamity and catastrophe had chosen to hit. One of Diane's copy-edited manuscripts came in, late enough to need immediate attention. That same day she'd gotten the page proofs of a short story she'd done, thirteen thousand words and thirty pages that needed to be proofed and returned yesterday. And it had to happen when she was in the middle of rewriting a proposal being considered by a publisher she'd never before dealt with, and was trying to prove that when rewrites were necessary she wouldn't be three months getting them done.

She'd sat looking at the mess for about five minutes, juggling working times in her head, and then she'd reached for the phone to tell Rick she wouldn't be able to make it to the convention. It was already Friday, and if she'd continued with the plan of leaving the next Friday, she'd have had to give up sleeping and eating.

"And I actually expected him to understand," Diane thought with the pain still strong. "I thought he'd *know* I wasn't doing it because I wanted to."

But Rick hadn't understood, and had refused to hear what he began calling her excuses. He'd started out trying to laugh off the work load, telling her it would survive her being away for three short days.

But this time she simply *couldn't* give in to Rick's coaxing. People were depending on her to do her part so they could get on with doing their own, and she couldn't let them down. It wasn't in her nature to ignore others in favor of herself, not when they were relying on her.

Halfway through Diane's stumbling explanation of how she felt, Rick had interrupted. He'd said that going to the convention wasn't the point; whether or not she really cared about him was the point. If she did, she would put him ahead of everything else in her life. If she didn't, well, maybe they would be better off not seeing each other anymore.

Diane sighed over the memory of finding herself sitting and holding a phone that had gone dead when Rick had hung up. It had taken a few minutes before she had been able to hang up herself, and after that she'd dived into the work waiting to be done, drowning herself in fiction to avoid reality, and when she finally surfaced she discovered she'd come to certain conclusions.

The first was that making decisions during emotional turmoil was worse than tossing a coin to get an answer. With a coin you had a fifty-fifty chance of coming up with the right choice, but the other way— No, the memory of sitting and listening to a dead line was still too fresh, and it was perfectly all right to put off thinking about it.

The second conclusion was that fiction was fiction and real life was real life, and never the twain shall meet. Diane had always considered herself too practical to believe in storybook romance, but when Rick had come along she'd let herself be talked into changing her mind. It looked like the time had come to change it back.

"And how about that heavy gate they had to buzz open before we could drive through?" the woman who liked gingerbread went on with relish, her comments distracting Diane from her memories. "It looked as if that high, spiked fence circled the property completely, so there's no getting out if they don't *let* you out. And these trees along the drive look like they're contemplating the tortured spirits wandering among them."

"The tortured spirits of those who couldn't pay their hotel bill, and therefore got kicked out," another woman on the other side of the van said with a derisive laugh. "Or maybe they're the spirits of those who ordered meals in the High Hat Room at the top of the hotel, then died of shock when they were handed the check. This place may be in Connecticut, but I'm told its prices are pure New York City."

"So what?" the first woman asked lightly, having only partially enjoyed the second woman's comments. "If you're being given exactly what you want, shouldn't you be willing to pay for it? People who come here want to have fun being scared, that's why they haven't gone to the mountains or the seashore or Hawaii or Puerto Rico. If all you came for was to complain about prices, you're wasting your time *and* your money."

"Bravo!" a man agreed, turning in his seat to smile at both women. "All you have to do is be willing to join in the spirit of things, and the hotel people will make your stay one you won't easily forget. Not only do they have costume parties every night, they also have theme games running during the day. For instance, at least once a day a dead body is found in some part of the hotel, and guests who are interested can try to figure out which member of the hotel staff did the murder. Sometimes the guilty party is human and is only *pretending* to be a ghost or a malignant spirit, but other times . . .''

The man let his voice trail off in a very supernatural way, and everyone in the van chuckled their appreciation. It was obvious the man had been there before, and in spite of herself Diane found she was being hooked. There would be *murders* to investigate, and guests were *expected* to join in . . . ?

After her trouble with Rick, Diane had worked hard for the next few days. The only distractions she'd had were the telephone messages Rick left on her machine. The first one had come on Monday night, and had simply said, "I miss you. Don't you miss me?" The answer to that was an aching "Yes!" but she'd been able to keep herself from using the phone and giving it. She still couldn't abandon her commitments just to please him.

On Tuesday she was glad she hadn't called him. The message he left spoke about how disappointed he was in her. That was the point at which Diane had realized Rick hadn't said a word in apology.

Rick had spoken only of himself, how *he* felt and how *he* saw things. Diane had sat down with a cup of coffee to think, and the first thing that occurred to her was that Rick had always been like that. He'd never *ordered* her to do things his way, but she suddenly realized that he would have been more honest if he had. Whenever she had suggested they do something he hadn't been interested in, he'd either laughed at the idea or coaxed her into a preference of his own. If she ended up bored or unhappy, that was perfectly all right; *he* was happy, and that was all that mattered to him.

And all that closeness he spoke about. They had spent more than four months seeing each other on weekends, but during the week he had only called her on Wednesdays. In the beginning she'd tried calling *him*, wanting to talk to him when she realized how long it would be before she saw him again, but he hadn't let it continue. He often had to take work home with him, he'd explained, and if he spent the time on the phone with her, the next day he'd be swamped.

And now he'd had the nerve to complain when *she* was the one who had to work? Diane was doing a good job of trying to squeeze the life out of her coffee mug at that point, and her steaming anger had loosed even more memories. All the funny cards she had sent him, and the impulse gifts she had bought. Almost nothing had come back, and his gifts had been worse than cheap. A remembrance of something shared could cost very little, but be worth a fortune to the people involved. Rick's gifts had been almost anonymous, meaningless tokens grudgingly supplied as if to an acquaintance of little importance. And she'd thought he simply had no taste!

By Wednesday night, the usual time Rick called her, Diane's frame of mind had changed a lot, and she sat listening calmly to the message he left on her machine. It had finally occurred to him that apologizing might help, but all he'd apologized for was losing his temper when she'd acted foolishly. He'd given his solemn word not to do that ever again, and had tried once more to coax her into calling him.

Diane had spent some time thinking about it and then she'd gone back to work. She was really tempted to tell him exactly what she thought of him, but that wouldn't have helped anyone but the telephone company.

Thursday afternoon had arrived with a shock. Diane had found herself coming from the post office, having just sent off the last of her projects. She hadn't had much sleep during the week and she'd missed a good number of meals, but she'd actually managed to wade through the whole ocean of work. All she had left was the book she was in the middle of, and she was comfortably ahead of schedule on that despite the week's delay.

It took Diane until she was seated at her PC, her chapter file on the screen in front of her, to understand that rewriting and editing weren't the same as straightforward writing. In order to write you have to leave your mind free to wander the world of your creation, and turning her thoughts loose meant they flew immediately in one and only one direction.

Had she been too hard on Rick? Had she lost her temper and misjudged him? Was she throwing away her chance to be happy by refusing to listen to him? Did he really have to be perfect to be the right man for her? Would she be able to stand the loneliness of solitary weekends after all the time she'd spent with *him*?

Diane had always been extremely grateful that her Atari didn't have a blinking cursor, the kind that seemed to be demanding she start being creative *now*, simply because it was waiting. Her own cursor sat quietly at the bottom of the file, waiting for her to write or not as she pleased. But it *wasn't* as she pleased.

And then she remembered something else: under normal circumstances, the upcoming weekend would be one where Rick came out to *her* house. If he decided to show up in an attempt to prove nothing had changed, she didn't feel ready to handle it. She needed time to think about what had happened, without misery and without anger—but most of all without Rick.

Her patient cursor sat there and waited while she got up to pace, her mind searching frantically for a way out. She couldn't simply not answer the door, especially with her car parked right in front of the house, but she also couldn't picture herself driving it around the block to hide it. Rick would know she was hiding.

No, her best bet would be to actually go somewhere, but where could she go? If she went to stay with any of her friends Rick would never find her. He had never bothered to get to know any of her friends. He had never introduced her to any of his, either, but Diane had been so happy being with *him* that she hadn't noticed.

But if she stayed with one of her friends, she would end up discussing the problem rather than thinking about it. She didn't want to be told to lose the bum, or to have it pointed out that she was twenty-nine rather than nineteen, and she shouldn't be so choosy. She needed to think about how *she* felt, for or against, without pressure from any direction.

That was why she had taken a train, heading for a convention she'd never wanted to attend but had still committed to. She'd forgotten about her commitment, an important factor for her. And it had only recently come to her that she hadn't canceled her reservations. Not only would she be keeping the word she'd given, but the convention would certainly be the last place Rick would think to look for her.

So, when the van pulled up to the front of the hotel, Diane joined the others in getting out and looking around. Since the Haunted House was really a modern hotel there should have been some sign of a parking lot, or guests going in and out, or bellmen rushing out to help with the luggage.

In actual fact there was nothing like that, nothing to show that the small group she stood with weren't the only living beings for miles around.

The van had stopped in a stone-paved front courtyard of sorts, empty of everything including snow, two stone benches to either side of the door the only decorations offered. Beyond the paving was a small surrounding field of snow, the drive they'd come up slashed through the field in an ugly, intrusive way, the winter-dead trees both too far away and much too close. Diane wasn't the only one who shivered while looking around, and the reaction had nothing to do with the light but very cold wind knifing by.

The driver of the van had gone up to the curtained front door of what looked like nothing more than a very large, very old-fashioned and darkly brooding Victorian house. He used the ornate brass knocker set in the middle of the door. Instead of metallic knocking, what they heard was a low-register boom, a sound that echoed slowly throughout the emptiness of the landscape and resonated in their bones and nerve endings.

"Maybe nobody's home," someone muttered behind Diane, sounding as though they were having second thoughts about staying. "We can't go in if nobody's home, so why don't we—"

The suggestion ended abruptly as the curtained door began opening slowly, accompanied by the sound of hinges being tortured to death. It was so melodramatic it should have been laughable, but instead of laughing Diane found herself taking an involuntary step backward—right onto the foot of the person standing behind her.

"Oh, I'm sorry!" she exclaimed, turning in embarrassment to look over her shoulder. "That was stupid, and I'm really terribly—"

"Don't worry about it," the big man behind her interrupted with a small, warm smile that made him not only handsome but attractive. Then he glanced up and began to grin. "Look what's coming out to get our luggage."

Diane turned back immediately, then couldn't help laughing along with everyone else. The three *people* coming through the door with a hand truck were zombies—dead-looking, staggering instead of walking, arms stretched out in front of them—dressed in bright red bellman uniforms.

"The check-in desk is straight ahead and to your right," the van driver told everyone with a grin. "Please go ahead while the bellmen get your luggage, and we hope you enjoy your stay."

"What do they do if someone dies of heart failure during this routine?" one woman asked as everyone began moving forward. "Just bury the body and forget about it, I suppose."

"This isn't really the front of the hotel," the man who had been there before was explaining to the first woman and her companion. "The real front is glass and steel and looks out at the parking lot and tennis and handball courts. They also have the stables built in that direction, and the place where they keep the sleighs and carriages. If you don't like the indoor fun, you can always try the outdoor stuff."

By that time they were entering the hotel, but Diane saw nothing of the modern hotel front the man had been describing. The registration lobby was moderately large, but its bright wallpaper was covered here and there with dust and cobwebs, the imitation gas lamps on the walls were set low and flickering, the heavy, awkward furniture positioned around the room was covered in sheets, and there was low, chill-making horror-movie music in the background. The staff members behind the registration desk were all either corpses or demon-spirits, and their smiles of welcome were on the gruesome side.

"Ladies and gentlemen, if any of you are convention participants, please go to the line on your extreme left," one of the corpses announced pleasantly, pointing in the direction of a ghoul. "We have a special block of rooms reserved for the convention, and after you've checked in we'll direct you to convention registration."

The woman from the van who had been worried about high prices, sighed and headed for the ghoul's line. Diane followed the woman and someone else followed her. A quick glance showed her it was the poor man she'd stepped on outside. It almost made her smile wryly. The way her luck had been doing lately, the man would probably turn out to be her biggest fan—and after having been stepped on, he would give up buying her books entirely. It would serve her right, of course, for actually showing up at this convention. If she'd had any sense, she would have gone to the mountains, or the seashore, or Hawaii, or—

"That's right, Rutledge, Anita Rutledge," the woman ahead of Diane was saying to the ghoul, who was checking a noticeably dust-free computer terminal. "If you can't find my reservation there, no trouble at all. I'll just turn right around and go back where I came from, and more than happy to do it. If I was senior editor in my department I wouldn't have had to come in the first place, but rank does have its privileges. One of them being, of course, the choice of which conventions to attend and which to wish off on..."

"Ah, here you are, Ms. Rutledge," the ghoul interrupted happily. "Your room is ready and waiting for you, and if you'll just sign here...?"

The ghoul handed over a room registration/credit slip along with a pen, and the woman took both with a sigh and signed her name. She was fairly tall and slender, with shining dark brown hair and brown eyes, dressed comfortably but in very good taste. Diane recognized the woman's name as soon as she heard it, so she stepped a little closer.

"I see John is taking advantage of his exalted position at Phoenix Books again," she said to the woman, drawing her attention. "If we do have a miserable time, we'll have to lie like crazy and tell him we had a ball so he'll regret not having come. We've never met, but I've heard John mention your name. I'm Diane Philips."

"Diane Philips, of course!" Anita Rutledge exclaimed, coming up with a startled-looking smile. "You made it. And I thought I'd be the only real member of civilization at this thing. John has told me he's trying to convince you to write something for us, but so far you two haven't agreed on what. Once we drop our things off in our rooms, I'd like to buy you a drink."

"Right about now I think I could use one." Diane returned Anita's smile and opened her coat against the warmth of the room. "Especially if Phoenix Books is paying for it."

"Oh, don't worry, they'll be paying for it," Anita assured her with a laugh. "If I have to be here—and John insists my job, if not my life, depends on it—then it's all going on the expense account. I'll spend my own cash for a *good* convention, but this?"

She shook her head with a grimace, turned back to the ghoul to exchange her registration card for a card key and the rest of the paperwork hotels enjoy handing out. Then she stepped aside to give Diane access to the ghoul. Thinking about it that way made Diane smile, and with that smile came the realization that she was feeling a good deal better. She now knew at least one of the people at the convention, which made the thought of facing it more pleasant than it had been. The weekend just might work out well after all.

GRAY WAITED until the two women had stepped away to claim their luggage and find their rooms, and then he moved up to take his turn with the desk clerk. The smile he was getting was a bit on the gruesome side, and if he hadn't been there on important business he would have already begun enjoying himself.

"I have a confession to make," he told the clerk, a warm smile accompanying the words. "I'm not registered with the convention and I don't have a reservation, but it's not entirely my fault. I didn't hear about the convention until I got to New York City, and when I did, I decided to take a chance and came straight up. If they'd ever learn to advertise these things properly... Am I out of luck, or is there some small part of the mother lode left?"

"Well... you *are* in luck, but just what sort is for you to decide," the clerk said, tapping keys on the console. "All of the regular rooms we blocked for the convention are reserved, but there are still a few of the suites left. That's because the rate for suites isn't reduced for the convention. If you don't care to take a suite, the only thing you can do is wait to see if there are no-shows among the reservations, or book a room in the non-con section. If you book another room, it should at least be quieter."

"Because it's out of the way," Gray muttered, quickly running possibilities through his mind. "No, that won't be any fun at all. I guess I'll have to go with the suite."

The clerk was horrifically delighted with his decision, and immediately began putting the paperwork together. Gray was equally delighted for a different reason, and as he handed over his Amex Gold Card he was hoping hard that his luck would continue.

His greatest stroke of luck so far had been finding out about this convention. It was a perfect cover—better than anything he'd hoped for—especially since it was flexible. If he pinned on the badge, he'd be an accepted part of the membership crowd; if he took it off, the rest of the hotel would be open to him. Whichever way the action went, he could go with it.

And the action just might be going in the direction of the convention. Gray intended to keep an open mind on the matter, but the thought had come that he was there to search for anything unusual he might find. Conventions weren't all that unusual, but they were hardly the norm, and they were always scheduled well in advance. If something was going to happen at that hotel, it would probably either happen at the convention or the group would be used as distraction for the sake of confusion.

But he couldn't afford to be confused, not with his brother's future at stake. So he would have to keep his eyes wide open. He signed the form the ghoul handed him and gave it back with a smile, but he felt no trace of that smile on the inside. He had come to this resort to hunt, and didn't intend to leave again until he had a nice big head as a trophy for his wall.

Chapter Three

"Oh, sure, we all get a kick out of this," the zombie bell-man told Diane as he led her out of the elevator and toward her suite. Anita's room was on another floor, and they'd arranged to meet in twenty minutes at convention registration. "I guess most people are kids at heart, so it isn't surprising that we enjoy dressing up for work. It beats a shirt and a tie and a grey pinstripe."

"Some people would think the same about a blinding red uniform and death-pallor grease paint," Diane said with a chuckle, as she inspected the "decorated" hall they were moving through. This time the dust and cobwebs were painted on. Diane found out by stopping and touching. The hall looked like a cold, sparsely decorated castle or great house corridor that probably had ghosts.

"The suites here are only a couple of corners away from the convention area," the zombie continued, using his chin to gesture ahead. "You walk in *that* direction, and in a minute or two you'll be there. The main gathering room is where they've set up their registration, and it looks like a very large Victorian drawing room. The room itself has a number of secret passageways that lead to various hotel functions, like the terror maze and the wax museum and the bedlam and the Hungry Crypts. And if you intend visiting the bedlam, expect to spend some time. They take you on a tour to look at the crazy people, just the way they did it when there really were insane asylums called bedlams. You don't want to be in and out of a place like that in five minutes.''

"No, I guess not," Diane muttered to herself, wondering what something like that would be like. She knew that method had been used to get people out of the way, kidnapped and committed to bedlams so others would have control of their money and estates. It usually hadn't taken long before they *had* gone insane, and the writer side of Diane wondered if there was some way to use that plot in modern fiction.

"And here's your suite," the bellman announced, stopping at a pair of doors on their right. He put one of her bags down so he could use the card key, opened the right-hand door, then stepped aside to let her walk in first.

Diane was confused. The room was fairly large with heavy, old-fashioned furniture standing around under dust sheets, all except the tables, of course, two of which had vases of dead flowers. Three of the walls were paneled in dark brown squares that looked framed, and the fourth, opposite the door they'd come in by, had high windows that were heavily draped in dark gold. There were gas lamps on the wall, which had been turned on when the bellman pressed a small panel, and to the right was a big, ponderous desk with a thick brass candle holder. Decorative cobwebs hung wherever they wouldn't be in the way, and the carpeting was a somber dark gold and brown.

But there wasn't anything to suggest doorways to other rooms. Diane looked around again to be certain, then turned to the bellman.

"The last I heard, the word *suite* wasn't defined as 'a single room resembling a study,'" she said, wondering if the zombie was trying to hold back laughter. "If the next thing you intend to say is that the couch opens out and the bathroom is down the hall, don't bother putting my bags down. I feel a previous commitment coming on, and I never back out of commitments unless I have absolutely no choice."

"I think that's the best I've heard it put," the bellman said with the laugh he could no longer hold back. "Some people get a trapped look, others start demanding to see the manager, but you're the first to threaten the onset of a previous appointment. If you'll hold off checking your appointment book for a moment, there's something you need to see."

With the hall door already closed he carried Diane's bags to the wall on the left, opposite the position of the big desk, where he put one bag down. His hand went to one of the panels at about shoulder height, pressed, and part of the wall slid aside out of his way.

"This is a haunted house, remember?" he asked, picking up the bag he'd put down. "The rest of the suite is through this secret passage. If you'll follow me...?"

Diane couldn't help chuckling as she did exactly that. The secret passage entrance was as high as a regular door, and led into a dim gray area that was on the narrow side but was also carpeted and decorated with fake cobwebs. The passage had nothing but two hooklike objects on the wall to the right—rather widely spaced—and one on the left fairly close to the entrance. The bellman went to the first hook on the right, twisted it, then went through the doorway that appeared in front of him.

"This is the suite's first bedroom, and the second is behind the wall near the second lever," the man said as Diane followed him into the room. "Your bedroom phone is in that round commode next to the bed, and that picture standing on top of the commode is really a clock. Your television set is in that chest-on-chest, behind the top doors, and you can, of course, use it for speed check-out when you leave. In order to close or open the passage door from inside the bedroom, yank once on that heavy bellcord."

Diane looked at the various items as the man mentioned them, but she was also examining the rest of what the room held. The bed was as large as the beds in a good hotel usually are, but this one was also curtained and canopied in true horror-movie style. The closet was a free-standing wardrobe, the doors of its dark-wood face carved into the features of monsters and demons, and the low dresser and chest-on-chest doors matched it perfectly. The room itself was painstakingly clean, but the positions of the sparse, old-fashioned furnishings suggested everything was being kept exactly as it had been when its previous occupant had died under mysterious circumstances.

"And what happens if there's a power failure?" Diane asked, the practical side of her nature still refusing to be lured into the game. "If I'm in the room I have to decide between waiting and chopping the wall down, but if I'm outside I get to sleep on that desk?"

"If there's a power failure, all interior doors open automatically," the bellman said, polite but still amused. "If something goes wrong with an individual door, there's a switch in the wall next to it that will cut the power and open it that way. I'll show you where all the switches are, right after I show you how to get to the bathroom."

Once shown, Diane had to agree the switches were easily managed. She followed the bellman back out into the passage, was led through the wall into the big, bright and totally modern bathroom, then was shown the second way back into the study. Another secret passage door, to the left of the first, led directly into the bathroom from the study and was opened the same way as the first. The outermost edge of the fifth square from the right opened the bedroom-passage entry, and the fifth square from the left did the same for the bathroom.

The bellman then showed her the study phone, which was hidden in the desk, and the room's wet bar, in a cabinet that looked as if it had belonged to someone named Caligari. Also in the desk was another clock, but "in" was a literal description. The lefthand corner of the desk showed numerals that looked like wisps of mist, and every time a minute or an hour changed the mist writhed like a tortured spirit.

"There must be more people in this country who like to be frightened than I thought," Diane remarked when the tour was over. "For this place to stay in business, there would *have* to be."

"Make that 'in the world' rather than 'in this country,'" the bellman answered. "We haven't been open all that long, really, but we're already beginning to draw tourists from other countries as well as this one. An interest in the supernatural seems to be universal. We hope you enjoy your stay.''

"Oh, wait just a minute," Diane said, suddenly realizing she'd left her coat and shoulder bag in the bedroom. "I'd like to give you something."

"That isn't really necessary," the bellman said with another gruesome zombie smile. "It's part of my job to show you how your suite works, and you pay for the lecture in your room charge. That's why you weren't given the chance to carry your own bags up."

"That doesn't change the fact that you made the lecture enjoyable," Diane countered firmly. "You wait right there."

Using the secret passage Diane went back to the bedroom, got a tip for the bellman from her bag, then returned to the study with it. The man was warmly polite in taking it, and then he was gone and she was alone. The last thing he'd done was give her the card key, so she took it back with her to the bedroom to put it in her shoulder bag. Once she had hung up her coat and glanced at herself in the mirror, she was ready to leave the suite. Unpacking could wait until later.

Diane followed the corridor in the direction the bellman had shown her, but the walk took longer than a "minute or two," and it wasn't simply a matter of keeping at it until she reached the meeting area drawing room. More than once Diane faced a choice of which way to go, with nothing like wall signs to guide and advise her. Twice she went the wrong way and *then* there were signs, but not the sort that guided and advised.

"Straight ahead for the bottomless quicksand," the first sign had announced, a florid arrow under the words. Sure. Quicksand. On the second floor of a modern resort hotel. They probably had a janitor's closet at the end of the hall, but wouldn't have been caught dead simply saying so. The second sign had told Diane she was in the middle of a falling rock zone. Diane shook her head and retraced her steps in the proper direction.

By the time Diane reached her destination, she was more curious than annoyed. It had come to her that the signs hadn't been "haunted house" signs, and that wasn't logically consistent. It was possible those corridors led somewhere other than dead ends or broom closets, and if the convention turned out the way she expected it to, she would certainly investigate the question personally. Right then she had to ignore the itch of curiosity; Anita Rutledge was waiting for her, and it wouldn't have been fair to keep her waiting longer than necessary.

The main gathering room that held the registration tables was fairly large, but it wouldn't have been big enough to hold the members of an ordinary convention. For this group it seemed just right, though, with the tables set up to the far right of the doorway and a large number of sheet-covered couches and chairs to the left. Vampire waitresses were moving among the seated people, taking orders for drinks and delivering them. The walls were the same kind of brown paneling that comprised Diane's study, and the faux gas lamps hanging there cast more light than real gas lamps ever could.

Diane examined the people in the registration area as she walked toward the tables, but Anita Rutledge wasn't among them. Since a lot more than the agreed-on twenty minutes had passed, she wondered if Anita had given up on her. If she had she would probably be over in one of the chairs having a drink, and Diane could find her once the initial convention business was taken care of.

There was a separate table with a Pros Only sign on it. The man apparently in charge of it was busily engaged in reading a book. He glanced up when Diane stopped in front of the table, did a double take, then put his book aside with a grin.

"I know, I know, you're Diane Philips," he said before Diane could introduce herself. "I'm more into horror than mystery, but you're one mystery writer I never miss. Let me get your packet and badge."

He reached to a cardboard box that held about half a dozen medium-sized manila envelopes, flicked through

Look what we've got for you:

...A FREE surprise mystery
gift that will delight you

3 FREE GIFTS

...PLUS a sampler set of 2 of the best
MYSTERY LIBRARY "whodunits"
ever published.

The Mystery Library proudly introduces, for the first
time in paperback, the mystery writers America can't
wait to get their hands on. Read the books the critics
have raved about from our award-winning authors

AWARD WINNING MYSTERY

Once you've read your free books, we're betting you'll
want more of these GRIPPING mystery stories
delivered right to your home. So, unless you tell us
otherwise, we'll send you 2 more suspenseful
books from the Mystery Library every month to
preview! If you decide to keep them you'll pay
only $3.50 for each book with the added convenience
of Free home delivery!

PLUS MORE FREE GIFTS FROM TIME TO TIME!

You must be completely satisfied. You may cancel at anytime by
saying so on your shipping statement or by returning a shipment to
us at our cost. You're not required to buy a single book, ever. The
free gifts are yours to keep no matter what. It's a super "Get
Acquainted" deal if ever there was one. Try us and see!

Mystery, Intrigue, Suspense!

The plot thickens with every page . . . the clues seem crystal-clear, yet the outcome is always a surprise! That's the suspense and drama you'll find in every novel from The Mystery Library—each a thrilling read! So treat yourself to hours of riveting, thoroughly enjoyable reading with each and every Mystery Library story!

If offer card is missing, write to: The Mystery Library, 3010 Walden Ave., P.O. Box 1867, Buffalo, NY 14269-1867.

them until he came to the one he wanted, then carefully pulled it out. Along with the envelope was a plastic-encased preprinted name badge, already decorated with a long, dark blue ribbon that read Program Participant in gold letters.

"There's a separate list of your panels attached to the program book, and also the time your autographing session is scheduled for," the man told her as he handed over both envelope and badge. "If there's a problem with any of it, just come back and talk to someone with a yellow ribbon. The conference rooms for the panels are through that door, opposite the one you came in through, and they're all marked. Thanks for coming, Ms. Philips."

"My pleasure," Diane lied with a smile, not about to take out her unhappiness on someone who was working hard to make the convention a success. She pinned on the name badge and turned away to open the envelope and indulge her curiosity. Too often panel topics were the same old hogwash with a thin coating of whitewash as disguise, and Diane wanted to see if she'd gotten lucky or stuck.

The sheet of paper was folded in half and clipped to the program book, and at first it was difficult to tell the separate sheet from the book. The program book looked as if it had been run off on someone's printer, then photocopied for the quantity needed. Doing it that way was cheap and fast, but it was also totally unimpressive. As a convention program book it made a good throw-away leaflet, and thumbing through it didn't even reveal any publishers' ads.

"Would you like me to check to see whether they've spelled your name right?" a dry, mocking voice said suddenly, surprising Diane. "I know how much trouble you have with difficult chores like that, and since *someone* has to help it might as well be me."

"Yes, you're famous for the 'help' you give, aren't you, David?" Diane responded, fighting to keep her voice even despite the painful blush she could feel rising in her cheeks. David Bellamy always affected her like this. He understood and delighted in it. If Diane had known David would be here, she would have chosen to risk facing Rick rather than show up at the convention.

"Of course I'm famous for my help, sweet dear," David purred, his malicious blue eyes twinkling with enjoyment. "That's what editors and reviewers do best, after all—help the clumsy and inept to see exactly where their failures lie. You have so many I scarcely know where to begin, but by tomorrow afternoon I'll probably have settled on your latest fiasco. What was it again? Oh, yes, *The Circle Murders*."

"What are you talking about?" Diane asked, more repelled by the greasy little man than she could ever have put into words. Physically David Bellamy was neither greasy nor small, and was in fact generally considered attractive by those who hadn't yet gotten to know him. To Diane he was sickening, slimy and petty and small, and her revulsion had always put her at his mercy during their cutting exchanges.

"What I'm talking about is the panel we're scheduled to share tomorrow afternoon," David said, speaking the words slowly and carefully, as though he considered her mentally deficient. "I'll be reviewing *your* book after Robert Sims burbles over Angela Wilkes's latest garbage, and then you and Angela will have the chance to either explain or defend the position we've put you in. It should be quite entertaining."

"Do you think I'd ever appear on a panel with *you*?" Diane demanded, hearing the way her voice shook but helpless to stop it. "You aren't a reviewer, you're a vindictive little destroyer. Editing that magazine lets you do a review column, but everyone *I* know calls it the assassination column. You grind up the work of good writers just to hurt them, but you aren't going to hurt *me* again. If it becomes a choice between appearing on that panel with you and leaving, I'll leave."

"Oh, that would be even better," David said with a small laugh, brushing unnecessarily at the sleeve of his suit jacket. Everyone else at the convention wore casual clothes, which was probably the reason David had worn one of his very expensive suits. "If you don't show up for the panel now, I'll simply be able to say you can't argue my assessment of your book. I'll embarrass you as usual if you do show up, and simply cut you down if you don't . . . in front of what promises to be an unexpectedly large audience. Doesn't this weekend promise to be fun?''

He stood there laughing at her with his eyes, while those few people who overhead their conversation tried to pretend they hadn't. Diane was trembling so hard she was certain she would be sick. She hated David Bellamy more than she had ever hated anyone in her entire life, and it was that very hatred which made her so helpless against him. The thought of what her hatred might someday make her do terrified her.

Then, just as David parted his lips to say something else, there was an interruption that shattered the deadly confrontation.

''Excuse me, Ms. Philips, but I just had to tell you how much I enjoy your books,'' a calmly quiet male voice said. ''I just finished *The Circle Murders*, and it's fairly clear that only an imbecile could miss how good a writer you are. Speaking for readers everywhere, we're awfully glad you're around.''

By that time Diane had turned to look at the man speaking. At first his dark-haired attractiveness was totally unfamiliar. Then she saw his eyes—light blue eyes that were completely unlike David's eternally malicious ones—and she suddenly recognized him as the man she'd stepped on when she'd first arrived at the hotel. She started to respond to his comment, but David interrupted.

''How appropriate that you would be one of *her* fans,'' he remarked to the newcomer, controlled anger underlying his pretense of boredom. ''I'm sure even the *concept* of good manners is beyond you, so I'll try to make this as simple as possible. Ms. Philips and I were in the middle of a conversation, and your small-town exuberance is crushingly inappropriate right now. Go away, and come back some other time.''

''That's your idea of *good* manners?'' the man asked mildly, barely glancing at David as he continued to smile at Diane. ''Telling someone to leave when they weren't even talking to you? If you ever get to be as important as you

think you are, I have a piece of advice for you—hire someone to make public appearances in your place. That way
your importance might actually get to impress somebody.
Would you do me the honor of letting me buy you a drink,
Ms. Philips? Since you have nothing better to do.''

His smile warmed as he took Diane's arm, and the next
thing she knew he was guiding her around a furiously red-
faced David.

Diane was still too upset to be amused by the turnabout.
She let herself be guided to a sheet-covered couch, sat there
while her companion gestured for a vampire waitress, then
ordered a glass of wine. When the woman had gone on her
way, Diane took a deep, slow breath.

"Thank you," she was finally able to say, looking at the
man who had been studying her with faint worry in his eyes.
"You rescued me from a very awkward situation, and I'd
like you to know how much I appreciate it."

"Actually, the imbecile you were talking to should be the
one thanking me," the man responded, his warm smile back
again. "I've seen people go pale the way you did on other
occasions, and afterward they tended to do one of two
things. Either they fainted dead away on the spot, or they
tried to kill whoever they were talking to. For some reason,
you don't strike me as the fainting type."

"Does that mean David may owe you his life?" Diane
asked, fighting to keep her tone light. "If you did *that* sort
of favor for him, I don't think you and I are going to be
friends. That man doesn't *deserve* to have his life saved."

"But you do," her rescuer said, his words sure and firm
despite their mildness. "Throwing away your own life just
to end his doesn't make much sense. If you don't let him get
to you, he'll get tired of wasting his time and go looking for
another victim."

"No, no, I'm afraid he won't," Diane denied, leaning
back against the couch as she looked down at her hands. She
was still clutching her program book with the panel schedule attached, so she thrust it all back into the envelope it had
come from, then discovered she had nothing to do with her
hands.

"Why don't you tell me why you think he won't leave you alone," her companion suggested, the easy words in no way intrusive. "Since I'm an attorney, if you like you can even make it a privileged communication. No one else will ever know if you don't want them to."

"That's one of the problems," Diane said, accepting her drink from the waitress as she turned her head toward the man again. She was beginning to feel soothed in spite of herself. "Everyone already knows, and David will never forget that I'm the one who told them. He was humiliated . . . I'm sorry, but I don't remember your name."

"That's because you haven't heard it," the man said with another smile. "I'm James Grayson, and my friends call me Gray. Just on the off chance that we do get to be friends after all, why don't you call me the same."

"As a just-in-case?" she asked with a smile of her own, one that didn't have to be forced. "Well, I usually like to play it on the safe side, but why not? You see, Gray, David was once a senior editor at my major publisher, and that was when this all started. I only had two books in print at the time, so I was one of the new kids and he thought he could get away with anything. It didn't turn out that way, and he was ruined."

"But I take it the ruining didn't quite stick," Gray said, running a finger over the glass he held. "You mentioned something about his being a magazine editor and a reviewer. How did he manage that?"

"No one knows for certain," Diane answered with a shrug. "The magazine was started by a foreign investment group, and when it opened, David was managing editor. I've heard it said David went to them and talked himself into the job before they were in a position to have heard about what he'd done. His background and credentials were impressive, and if all they did was check with personnel departments to verify his employment record . . ."

When she shrugged again, Gray nodded in understanding. There were some types who asked only if you'd done the job you said you'd done, caring nothing about the quality of your performance.

"So he's been blaming *you* for what happened instead of himself," Gray said. "And you can't ignore him, because you're not the kind to dismiss people the way he does. But something else bothers you about him, and I'm curious to know what that is."

"It's hard to explain..." Diane groped for words, suddenly less comfortable than she'd been. "I've disliked people in my life, just like everyone else, but I've never felt such hatred and disgust. I usually have a choice about the things I do, but every time I come face to face with David I feel myself losing the choice. He makes me want to..."

"Do something you'd have trouble forgiving yourself for," Gray finished when she didn't, nodding again with that calm understanding that seemed so much a part of him. "I've known people like that, but I've always been able to find the strength to keep them from ruining my life. I have a hunch you've got the same kind of strength."

His warmly confident smile made Diane find a smile of her own, and she realized it wasn't the first time. The man was so comfortable to be with, as though she'd known him and liked him for years and years.

"Ah, there you are, Diane." She looked up to see Anita Rutledge standing next to their couch. "I'm sorry to say you missed it, but now I get the chance to tell you about it. When John hears, he'll laugh his head off."

"Hears what, Anita?" Diane asked, seeing the other woman's amusement. "What did I miss?"

"David Bellamy tried his knifing on Angela Wilkes, and she cut him down to millimeter size," Anita answered with relish, just about rubbing her hands. "When he told her he was going to trash her latest in his column, she laughed and thanked him in advance for the help. No one remembers what a reviewer says, she pointed out, they only remember they've heard of the book, so they buy it. She also said he was getting simpleminded if he thought he could get a rise out of her the way he does with—"

Anita broke off abruptly and looked trapped, but Diane just smiled and shook her head.

"Don't worry about saying it, I know she mentioned me. Angela and I don't get along at all. She seems to think I'm doing her out of her due. I've never understood what her problem is, but she's always disliked me."

"No, she hates you," Anita corrected with a shake of her head. "John told me her books aren't quite as well crafted as yours. That's why Phoenix has been after you for a proposal, but turned down two of hers. I understand that happened at another house as well, and they were indiscreet enough to put it to her just that way. She thinks you're stealing her market, and in a way she's right."

"Her problem is that she's lazy," Diane said with a grimace. "She's trying to get by with 'good enough,' when everyone knows she can do better. Someone told me that that's why she's being turned down—she hands in a manuscript that's almost great, then gives her editor a hard time over rewrites. What she needs is to be rescued from herself. Oh, and speaking of rescues, Anita, I'd like you to meet—"

Diane's words broke off when she turned to Gray, because he was no longer there. She had no idea where he'd gone, and was surprised that she hadn't seen him go. He must have felt that he would be intruding between Anita and her, and had simply gotten out of the way.

It was strange that he would do that after saving her, but maybe not all that unexpected. He seemed to be a shy, soft-spoken man who went out of his way to be considerate.

"Yes, I've heard that Angela gives her editors a hard time," Anita said, moving two steps to sit on the couch beside Diane. "You, on the other hand, have a reputation for cooperation, so let's discuss the point you and John are having trouble with. Maybe *I* can come up with something that will satisfy the two of you."

Diane wasn't really in the mood to discuss proposals, but that was better than thinking about David Bellamy and the decision she had to make about appearing on the panel with him. Everything inside her was urging her to turn around and leave, but she'd been running from David for years, just as though what he'd done really had been her fault.

But it hadn't been her fault, and it was time she began acting as if she believed that. She might discover she didn't have the necessary innards to face David Bellamy and give as good as she got, but at the very least she had to try.

Anita called a waitress and placed her drink order, then turned back to Diane. By that time Diane was ready for her. If she was going to face David the next day on the panel, she had no qualms about facing an eager editor now.

GRAY SLIPPED out of the meeting-registration area without anyone noticing him. The medium-blue shirt and gray slacks he wore helped him blend into the background almost anywhere he went, and his quiet personality made him fade even more.

He could have stayed in the room and moved from group to group listening, and no one would have remembered his presence ten minutes later, except for the fact that he had mixed himself up in the confrontation between that imbecile and Diane Philips.

He still didn't really understand why he'd done it, except that the woman had touched him on a level he hadn't been guarding. That she was a storybook redhead with green eyes and a pretty face was only a part of it, and not the most important one. More to the point was the direct way she tended to look at someone, and the way she'd apologized for stepping on him. Really meaning it, rather than just saying the words...

And that jerk had gone after her with everything he had, knowing she wasn't able to strike back at him and loving the idea. She wasn't the weak and helpless sort, Gray had been able to see that easily, and it had infuriated him when Bellamy had tried making her that way. He'd had no choice but to step in...

And now he had no choice but to step out again. He paused just outside the doorway, watching the Rutledge woman take his place on the couch, then forced himself to move on again. He wasn't at the hotel to meet women but to find something that would clear his brother, and it was almost time for his ex-cop partner to call him. Gray already had a list of names for Jack to check, but it was on the short side, and he meant to correct that as quickly as possible.

Something definitely didn't feel right at that convention. There were a lot of hatreds being trotted out for show, and Diane Philips was right in the middle of them. Gray couldn't picture the woman being involved in murder knowingly, but for his brother's sake he couldn't afford to dismiss anyone. He would keep an eye on Diane Philips, a distant and impersonal eye, and if the problem should be cleared up sooner than he expected, and she turned out to be innocent the way he believed, maybe . . .

Chapter Four

Diane was talked into an early dinner, but Anita didn't do the convincing. Bill Raglan and Ralph Teak saw them on the couch and came over, and Ralph's plea was pitiful and touching.

"We are, after all, sibling writers, my dear Diane," Ralph said with a faint air of helplessness that combined with his white hair to make him look frail and old. "Bill is a heartless, conscienceless editor intent on ruining my weekend, and Anita is the same, with *you* marked out as her victim. If we combine forces, we might be able to hold off the assault. Without you, I'm certainly lost."

"Oh, you poor thing," Diane said with a laugh while Bill and Anita chuckled. "You're helpless on your own, so you need *me* to lean on. That's so touching, I think I'm going to cry. By the way, Ralph, do you still run twenty miles every morning, then chew up publishers at tea-time? It seems to me I heard something about the last contract you negotiated, and without an agent, too."

"Now, now, child, we all know how ugly gossip can get," Ralph answered blandly, leaning down to take Diane's arm and urge her to her feet. "I never run more than five miles in the morning, and if you make a habit of having anything with your afternoon tea, you'll soon get fat. Are you going to deny an old man the sight of your pretty face over dinner? If I go with Bill alone, I'll end up courting indigestion."

"Why are you so down on editors today, Ralph?" Anita asked, getting to her feet with a grin. "If Bill isn't treating you right, John and I would love to discuss publishing the next Daniel King puzzler—the next twenty Daniel King puzzlers."

"You only think you would," Bill responded, amused and not at all worried. "Publishing Daniel King whodunits means having to negotiate with Ralph, and if your eye teeth don't end up in the bargain, he's having an off day. I wish he would get an agent."

"Oh, Ralph," Diane said with a laugh, seeing the twinkle in Ralph's eyes. "If I agree to have dinner with you, will you give me some lessons?"

"Gladly, dear child, gladly," Ralph answered with a chuckle, patting her hand. "It's simply a matter of knowing your physiology. The murderer is always aware of the area best suited for the death blow, but the writer must learn how to strike close *without* ending it. And if we intend being on time to the costume bash tonight, I suggest we eat downstairs rather than in the High Hat Room. I understand meals up there take a minimum of two and a half hours."

"That's what I heard," Anita agreed with a nod. "I'm glad you're here, Ralph. It's always handy having someone around who has all the dirt and details five minutes after he arrives. But I'm surprised. Do you really intend to go to the costume party tonight? Won't you feel silly with all those people in costume around you?"

"Why should I feel silly?" Ralph asked, beginning to lead the way toward the broad staircase that would take them down to the main floor. "I intend to be in costume right along with them, and Bill's going to be joining me. If there's one thing I've learned in life, it's to enjoy the fun times when they come along. If you're worried about a costume damaging your dignity, you don't understand what real dignity is."

Diane nodded her agreement. No matter what she did she was going to have trouble, so why not have a little fun first?

Dinner in the large restaurant that looked like a haunted mansion's dining room was the beginning of that fun, thanks primarily to Ralph. He was somewhere close to seventy with the white hair of his age group, but with few of its other characteristics. His tall body was completely unbent, his face was weathered and still handsome, he moved like the athlete he was and always had been, and his mind was still as sharp as ever.

Bill Raglan, on the other hand, was short, barely taller than Diane and a couple of inches below Anita. He was somewhere in his forties, his hair was thinning on top, and he had the sort of round face women considered friendly but not attractive. In another man, that, combined with a beginning roundness of body, would have been the picture of a man with self-image problems, a man who was unsure of himself. In Bill it was just what he happened to look like, having nothing at all to do with the inner man. Ralph teased him unmercifully and he pretended to injured sensibilities, but the two of them had worked together for fifteen years and were firm friends.

"You can't paint editors as innocent lambs, Bill, so save your breath," Ralph said, buttering another roll. "We writers know better, don't we, Diane? If your editor is always pleasant to you, that's the way you know he got you cheap. Writers have to stick together—but just for this one weekend we'll have to let you editors join us. If we don't, we'll be outnumbered by the horror group."

"Yes, there does seem to be more of them than us," Bill agreed. "All told there are scarcely more than a dozen of us, and all the rest are them. I know maybe five of the horror editors, and about the same number of their writers. And most of the fans are theirs, too, I think."

"Which is a pity," Ralph said, serious for once. "There's no greater thrill for a writer than to hear someone say he or she appreciates your work. The money is nice as well as necessary, but honest praise—there's no way to beat that, or even to match it."

"How about the other side of the coin?" Diane asked, surprising herself by speaking her thoughts. "Can anyone ever be paid enough to compensate for the terrible things said by someone who *isn't* a fan? Isn't it easier to give it up and walk away?''

"Do you mean, let yourself be run off?" Ralph asked, his dark eyes directly on her. "I heard that little exchange between you and David, child, and there's something you seem to have trouble understanding. No one pays any attention to David Bellamy except his victims, and even they're beginning to see the truth. He's not expecting to ruin your name in the field, he's only intent on terrorizing you. If you ever began ignoring him, he'd be helpless to do anything about it."

Diane returned Ralph's stare without saying anything, remembering someone else who had tried to give her the same advice. That pleasant man Gray, who had walked off after helping her. Well, she *had* made up her mind to face David on the panel, so it looked like all that advice had done some good.

"Ralph, you're absolutely right," she agreed, reaching for her coffee cup. "In a very short while David Bellamy will no longer be a problem, and then I can forget about him. What kind of costumes did you and Bill bring for the party?"

"Oh, we didn't bring costumes," Bill interjected, apparently pleased to have the subject changed. "We're going to rent them from the hotel. They have this incredibly large selection in most sizes, and if we don't like what we pick tonight, tomorrow we can be something else. I told Ralph he really should go as a devil. It matches his personality so well."

"Who, an angel like me?" Ralph demanded, managing to look thoroughly insulted. "Leave it to an editor to make a mistake in judgment like that. They simply don't understand us, Diane, and never will."

Bill's response made Diane and Anita chuckle, and the meal continued on with the same fun. They agreed to look at costumes together when they were through, and even Anita let herself be talked into promising to choose one. She hadn't intended to go to the costume party, she insisted, but if everyone else was going...

They asked their corpselike waiter for directions before they left their table, and were sent to an area across from the dining room. The costume rental place was disguised as a cloak room and as they stopped outside it and looked around, Diane saw something a bit farther along that surprised her.

"Why, that section looks like a normal hotel," she said, stopping to point it out to her companions. "It has a lobby area, and a souvenir store, and a snack shop and—isn't that a real front entrance beyond the desk counter?"

"It's a token ten percent," Ralph informed her. He glanced briefly at the area, as though he'd already been through it and knew it thoroughly. "It's there in case someone ends up here accidently and doesn't want to play, or if they come deliberately because they need to be in this area but don't need the games, that's the part of the hotel they stay in."

"I suppose they also use it for anyone who gets cold feet," Anita commented, "shifting them there rather than losing them early."

"That section is where the pool and sauna are, as well as another expensive restaurant," Ralph added. "It's all available to everyone in the hotel, so it's possible to have the best of both worlds.

"And it has its own bank of elevators, so the normal folk don't have to mix with the freaks." Ralph started walking toward the cloak room again. "For which, speaking as a freak, I'm profoundly grateful. I wonder if they have a costume to make me an axe murderer."

"But, Ralph, why would you need a costume for that?" Anita asked very innocently, leaving the rest of the comment unspoken. Bill and Diane chuckled, but all Ralph could do was give Anita a haughty, disapproving look. After all the comments he'd made about editors, Anita had finally gotten him back.

The costume shop itself wasn't very large, but its selection was just as wide as Bill had suggested. Most of the choices were in the cheap range: pirates, Robin Hoods, monks, witches, princesses and harem dancers. All of the basics along with more ornate skeletons and devils and angels and Frankenstein monsters. The medium-priced outfits came with an accessory or two, like wands or swords or daggers, or crowns. The expensive costumes were complete, and were made from good material with credible detail. All the costumes, in all the ranges, also came with masks.

When Ralph saw the devil outfit in the expensive category, complete with cape and horns and tail and a formal suit and red skin dye, he immediately adopted Bill's earlier, joking suggestion. Bill said something about hating typecasting, but for once he would go along with it. His choice was one of the French Louis costumes, a king's outfit with powdered wig. When they all stopped laughing Anita decided on the pink tulle and wand and halo of a guardian angel, and then it was Diane's turn.

Which brought her something of a problem. There were any number of practical costumes to match the practicality of her nature, but for once Diane was tempted by something else. The harem queen's costume they offered was beautiful, all sequins and veils in varying shades of gold, and it looked as if it bared everything even though it didn't. Like most people, Diane had worn bathing suits that were skimpier. It was simply the idea of the thing....

"Oh, go ahead," Ralph urged, when he saw where her gaze was lingering. "You can't say you don't have the figure for it, and it will make the party so much more interesting for the rest of us."

"But consider your dignity," Anita countered from Diane's other side. Her words seemed overly simple and much too sweet. "How will it look for a respected author to run around in an outfit like that? How will you look at yourself afterward? How will the rest of the women at the party look, standing there all by themselves while the men swarm around *you*?"

"And people think the devil has ulterior motives," Ralph said while they all laughed. "Take the costume, child, and enjoy yourself for once."

Knowing Anita had been teasing her made Diane feel better, but it still took the other three a few minutes to talk her into going for the harem outfit. It fit her character no more than the devil costume fit Ralph's, and everyone was bound to know it.

Some measuring got them the costumes closest to their proper sizes, and the four separated in the elevator to go to their respective rooms to change. They arranged to meet later, at the party which most of the people in the hotel would attend.

GRAY HAD an unprofitable conversation with Jack, passed on the names of his still very short list, then went to have a solitary dinner. Most of the people in the dining room were enjoying themselves, including Diane Philips and her friends, but Gray was feeling depressed. How many solitary meals had he taken since his brother had been arrested? How many more would he have to face before it was all over?

He leaned back in his chair and sipped his coffee, no longer interested in what was left on his plate. He'd put a lot of time and effort into this investigation over the last few months, reverting to the habits he'd developed in Naval Intelligence. He knew his partners in the law practice had understood. Terrance and Lorraine had backgrounds similar to his own, and in his place they would have reverted just as quickly.

But Terry and Lorraine also had each other, which made Gray luckier than them. He'd had no one to leave behind when he'd left to pick up the trail, no one to wonder where he was and worry over how he was doing. Under the circumstances, he was relieved that he'd never found just the right woman, a woman who would appeal to his mind and emotions as much as to his eyesight...

Right then his eyesight was resting on Diane Philips, watching the way she laughed and spoke with the people at her table. For a pretty redhead she was on the restrained side, and Gray couldn't help wondering again how she would fit into whatever was going on. He still wasn't certain she did fit into it, but that sixth-sense feeling he'd developed years ago was sending up flares in all the colors of the rainbow.

"Which means I'll have to force myself to stick close to her," he muttered softly, making sure his grin showed only on the inside. Diane was a legitimate lead. That she was more than just a pretty face was a bonus. Of course, he wasn't likely to be as close to her again as he'd been that afternoon, but it would certainly be no hardship to take whatever he could get.

Gray watched Diane and her friends leave the dining room, waited a moment or two before following, and came out just in time to see them disappear into the costume rental place. So, they intended to go to the party that night, and they were going in costume. Gray also intended to make an appearance, but not in a costume rented from the hotel. He'd had a couple of days in New York before he came out to Connecticut and he had made certain preparations. If only he could get a *little* lucky...

Chapter Five

Diane closed the door of her suite behind herself, went through the secret passage into the bedroom, then sat down on the bed with the box containing the costume in her lap. During the solitary walk from the elevator she'd almost gotten cold feet, but she'd had an interesting thought. There were a lot of men at that hotel, and she wasn't there with an attention-demanding Rick. There was no reason for not tossing out a little bait, just to prove to herself that he wasn't the only fish in the sea.

"And don't forget you're also learning a lesson here," she lectured herself aloud. "Running away can complicate your life, and if you don't believe that, just look at the situation with David."

She nodded at the thought, knowing she had to settle that point along with the rest—but first she was going to take a bath.

Thoughts of Rick came to Diane while she relaxed in the delightfully warm water, and this time she let them echo around in her head rather than trying to push them away. During dinner she'd been thinking that she was missing Rick, but was it him she was missing—or someone to share something deep and important with?

Ralph was a widower who had shown no true interest in women since his beloved wife had died, Bill was happily married with three kids, and everyone knew Anita's greatest love was her work. The others all had what they wanted or had had it, while she...

She was beginning to see through the clouds of depression. Missing someone in general was not the same as missing a particular individual, and that's what Diane wanted, someone she would really miss when he wasn't there. What she'd had in Rick was someone she'd begun having to make excuses for, someone who had rationed his time with her to suit his own convenience. That wasn't her idea of love, and when she got home Sunday night she would call Rick and tell him so.

Even if she wasn't nineteen any longer. One day she might wake up to find she was seventy-nine, but she didn't think she would look back and regret the decision. She wanted someone she would be completely in love with, and that someone was worth waiting for. She sat up in the tub and nodded her head firmly, then reached for the soap. She had a costume waiting to be put on, and who knew? Maybe the man of her dreams was already at the party, needing nothing but her entrance to draw him over to introduce himself. It was at least worth a try.

It wasn't long before Diane was ready, and she couldn't help looking at herself one last time before leaving the suite. The full-length bathroom mirror showed her the beautiful golden costume with matching slippers and, all modesty aside, she had to admit it suited her.

The top of it was a low-cut sequined bra with dangles, which matched exactly to the girdle belt around her hips. Flowing down and out from the girdle was a smoke-sheer skirt of veils which reached her toes, and matched exactly the veil that was held to the top of her head with a flat sequined comb.

The head veil was full enough to circle her shoulders and flow all the way down to merge with her skirt, and there was even a golden necklace that matched all the rest.

Diane smoothed her long red hair, deciding she had been right not to pin it up. Leaving it loose made the veil look even better, and when she put on her golden mask its side pieces were hidden by the hair.

It was clever making the mask fit like glasses, better than a head band or a lorgnette-type handle would be. With the mask self-elevating, the only thing she had to worry about was her card key, and a tuck in the lining of the girdle took the card and some money easily and neatly. She was ready to go.

Rather than walking through to the gathering room and using the stairs, Diane went back to the elevators and got down to the ground floor the easy way. The elevator was fairly full of people in costume, and only people in costume. Nonparticipants were obviously either staying in their rooms or had gone off elsewhere, but Diane couldn't decide whether or not to be uncomfortable. She wasn't the only one dressed up—or, more accurately, dressed down— but all those stares...

The elevator ride was very short and as soon as the doors opened in front of her, Diane went straight to the ballroom. The very large room was decorated in keeping with most of the rest of the hotel, with tessellated walls and small plaster carvings near the ceiling, and huge, cobweb-festooned chandeliers. Ghouls, zombies and corpses were selling drinks and snacks at various stations around the room, and pleasant, unintrusive music was playing.

Some of the people were wearing convention badges, but the rest were obviously just guests at the hotel attending a hotel function. Diane realized she had forgotten her own badge, but since this party was open to everyone she was sure it wouldn't matter.

The bar they'd arranged to meet at was to the right of the door, but the only one of Diane's former companions standing near it was Bill. The king looked completely at ease even when two of his subjects stopped to bow and curtsy to him with giggles. He raised his glass to them in acknowledgement of their homage, his smile below his mask wide and full. When he caught sight of Diane he gestured her over.

"Yes, there you definitely are," he said when she reached him, making no effort to hide his approving appraisal. "Ralph can be a bit overbearing at times, but it's impossible to fault his eye. You should dress like that more often, Diane.''

"People who dress like this on a regular basis usually get locked up, Bill," Diane answered with a small laugh, her cheeks warming. "And since that comment applies to two or three different groups, I'll leave it to you to figure out where that locking up takes place. Where are Ralph and Anita?''

"Anita rang my room to say she's running late because of a phone call," Bill answered. "She said she tried your suite first, but got no answer. Ralph is over there with the rest of the writers, sitting under the sign with his name and supplying autographs.''

Diane followed Bill's gaze to the back corner of the room, where the autographing setup had been arranged. She couldn't see any sign of available books, so it was possible fans had either had to bring their own, or planned to get their autographs on a piece of paper.

"I don't remember hearing the phone ring, so Anita must have called while I was in the tub," Diane said. "But I suppose one of those signs has my name on it, so I'd better get over there. They don't have anything planned for us after this, do they?''

"Not as far as I can tell," Bill answered, shaking his head. "And I think I've figured out the three lock-up places you were talking about. One has padded walls, one has harem guards, and one has bars on the windows and cell doors. How'd I do?''

"Fine, Bill, you got it just right," Diane said with a slight shake of her head. She'd forgotten how Bill loved to figure things out. "I'd better get over there and join my fellow writers.''

He raised his glass to her as she went past, a wordless salute of some sort that made Diane faintly uncomfortable. Bill was nice but he was also a little odd, and there were times Diane couldn't follow his thinking. Ralph would probably have said all editors are like that, but Bill *was* different.

AFTER DINNER Gray spent a little more time trying to become familiar with the complexities of the hotel, and then he went back to his suite to get ready for the party. That hotel was just about the worst stalking ground it was possible to imagine, and he was beginning to think he'd never catch anyone in the act of anything unless someone was murdered right at his feet.

At that, he'd been in the inner lobby earlier in the day when a "dead body" had been found, and he'd nearly made a fool of himself rushing over to see who it was and if there was any sign of who had done it. The "victim" had turned out to be a small man in a shirt reading, "unfortunate intruder." Remembering, Gray chuckled as he went through the secret passage to his bedroom. The number of clues left around the body, including "fingerprints" in dark black on the body itself, were so overdone and obvious that half the people who had rushed over with him had booed, shaken their heads, and walked away again.

Most people thought they liked subtle clues, Gray mused as he took his costume out of its place in the hidden compartment of his luggage. The biggest problem with subtle clues was that they could be overlooked or misinterpreted, and then you had trouble. And anything could be a clue, anything at all....

He took himself into the bathroom for a shower, still thinking about clues. Another problem with them was that you sometimes had to be right on the spot to pick them up, otherwise they were passed over with no one noticing.

There *was* such a thing as a perfect murder, but only if the murderer planned carefully, hit once, then never did it again. Repeated actions allowed more opportunities for mistakes. And, although the group Gray was after tried to make every hit a separate effort, they *were* actually repeating themselves. One of these times they were going to make one, large, visible mistake.

It didn't take Gray long to get into his costume, and disguising himself in the costume required only a small amount of effort. Stage makeup darkened his fading tan on face and hands and other exposed parts of his body, and a longish blond wig covered his dark hair. The colorful bandanna around his head kept the wig secure, and added flair to the rest of the costume. He didn't want anyone recognizing him or finding it possible to spot him later, not when he intended snooping openly while in the costume. One obvious snoop for them to worry about, one not-so-obvious watcher they should overlook and ignore. Gray intended to outnumber his opponents, a ploy that would hopefully catch them unprepared.

When he was finished he examined himself critically in the bathroom mirror. Everything seemed to be all right. He was dressed like a movie pirate, knee-high black boots, tight black trousers, a wide-sleeved white shirt open to halfway down his chest with a heavy bronze medallion showing in the opening of the shirt. He also wore a cutlass in a scabbard at his side, and the blond wig and headband bandanna.

Gray was a big man who kept himself in excellent physical condition, something his costume accented rather clearly. His broad shoulders and deep chest were usually camouflaged behind loose shirts, his narrow-hipped trimness hidden by trousers that were less than fitted. With his practiced tendency to fade into the background, no one should be able to link *him* with this sleek and dangerous rover fresh off the pirate ship he captained.

"And just to be certain, we have this," Gray murmured to his mirror image, lifting his mask and tying it on around his head. It had started as a perfectly ordinary mask, but he'd glued small pieces of special foil over the eyeholes. Now he could see out without any more trouble than a mask usually gave, but anyone trying to see his eyes would see only silver.

With the mask in place he was ready to go, so he resettled the leather sword belt around his hips, tucked his card key down into his boot next to the tiny flashlight and tool kit he expected to need, then left the suite.

The elevator took him down to the lobby level with others in costume, and he joined them in entering the ballroom. Once inside he took a look around, and immediately saw something that made him draw in a soft, sharp breath.

Diane Philips. It had to be her with all that red hair, but what a change! Earlier he'd thought of her as restrained, but the word certainly didn't fit what she'd become. A gorgeous creature of sequins and veils, her least movement seemed to be followed by half the men in the room, including the one she was talking to. A French king by his costume, Gray thought, and someone she knows. I wonder if I could . . .

Gray was about to turn away in disgust with himself, but a sudden line of logic came to erase all thoughts that he was losing sight of what he was there for. Yes, he wanted to go over and speak with the vision that Diane Philips had become, but it had suddenly struck him that it might be a good idea rather than a bad one. He needed to know how effective a disguise he was wearing, and approaching her should tell him that. If she recognized him, the enemy might well do the same.

He nodded to himself with a faint smile, waited until her conversation with the French king was over, then made his way through the crowd to intercept her. When he stepped out in front of her and bowed she stopped short, then looked startled when he took her hand.

"I would gladly leave off roving to sail in the name of a queen such as you, Your Majesty," he said in a raspy whisper as he bent to kiss her hand. "Would you grant me pardon if I attempted such a thing?"

"I'd have to take the matter up with my advisors," she answered with an embarrassed laugh that was also genuinely amused. "May we meet later to discuss this further?"

He bowed again to show that he would do as she bid, then stepped aside with a sweep of his arm to allow her to continue past him. She gave him a regal nod and another smile, then used the aisle he'd created for her. He'd certainly made an impression on her, he thought as he watched her go, and she obviously hadn't recognized anything about him. It was what he'd wanted, but in a way he felt vaguely disappointed.

Gray drifted after her, making sure she didn't see him doing it, and that way found out about the autographing session. Once Diane was settled behind her table she would probably stay for a while. He decided to circulate a little more widely.

The French king finished his drink and got another, and then was recognized by a small group of people wearing convention badges who seemed to be acquaintances rather than friends. When he joined them they all stood speaking for a little while, and then the entire group merged with the ballroom crowd.

Gray moved through the crowd himself, smilingly refusing offers to dance put forward by three or four rather attractive women, all the time watching for something out of the ordinary. Most of those people were innocent vacationers, there for a good time and nothing else, but *some*—

A distraction came when an old woman began pushing through the crowd, telling every fourth or fifth person she passed that they were going to die horribly; that the house would never let them leave alive. She was small and bent and had straggly gray hair over a severe black dress with a torn lace collar. It wasn't until people saw the heavy makeup on her pinched-in looking face that they began to understand she was on the hotel staff.

That was when she really started to embellish her predictions. Before very long the woman was surrounded by laughter, and quite a few members of the crowd followed her to see if they could get her to insult them. It seemed obvious she was a professional comedienne, doing her part of the hotel's version of a floor show.

Gray hadn't let the show distract him from watching the room, and a couple of minutes later he was glad of it. He saw a small door open in the back of the ballroom, and a man dressed like a staff zombie stepped through, paused to straighten his uniform, then moved off into the crowd.

By itself, the man's appearance was nothing unusual, but Gray happened to know that that particular door should have been locked. He'd learned earlier in the day that a shortcut corridor lay behind it, an alleyway of sorts to another part of the hotel that was used only during the day for one of the hotel's guest games.

So what was he doing in it now, and why didn't he relock the door? Gray thought to himself as he immediately began moving. "Let's take a look and find out."

DIANE WAS STILL smiling as she lost sight of the very attractive pirate in the crowd, half regretting that he'd let her go so easily. The encounter would undoubtedly be the highlight of her day—if not of the entire weekend—and she would have to thank Ralph for talking her into taking that costume. She smiled as she walked past his table, catching his eye.

"Ah, me, it's now quite clear my life has been wasted," the devil, Ralph, announced to those who stood patiently waiting for his autograph, his flexible voice filled with sorrow. "If I'd spent my time writing adventures of some sort, I'd be well within my rights to throw that tasty morsel over my shoulder and carry her off to her fate. Shall we discuss cross-genre investigations after the signing, Diane?"

"That's a really good idea, Ralph," Diane agreed over the chuckling of his audience. "I've been thinking about doing one of those dismember-everyone-who-comes-past kind of horror novels, and I think I spotted the perfect weapon for it out in the lobby. A nicely sharpened, two-handed broadsword..."

"On second thought, I think I have a conference with my editor scheduled for after the signing," the devil answered hastily, over the increased laughter of their audience, trying not to grin. "I'm sure you'd find the time boring, so do feel free to make other arrangements."

Diane laughed as she gave him a regal nod, and then was able to continue on to her own place. This really was starting to be fun, and in more ways than one. Angela Wilkes had been in line a few places over from Ralph, wearing a full witch's costume, but she hadn't done more than glare at Diane.

The writer on Diane's left was named George Lombardy, someone she didn't know, but on her right was Lynn

Haverstock, sitting at a small table like the others, but not in costume. Despite the fact that Lynn hadn't done anything new in three years, the line in front of her was as long as Ralph's.

"Diane, dear girl, how good to see you again," Lynn said at once, pausing to reach over to squeeze Diane's fingers. "It must be eight months since the last time, and that's much too long. How have you been?"

"The same as usual, Lynn," Diane answered with a very warm, very real smile. Lynn Haverstock was the closest thing their genre had to royalty, but the woman never stood on ceremony with people she liked, and she liked almost everyone. That feeling was returned, at least among those to whom Lynn hadn't shown her pointed, very undiplomatic disapproval.

"'The same as usual' is not an acceptable answer, dear girl, but we'll wait until later before going into details," Lynn proclaimed comfortably, going back to signing books. "I heard about your little face-off with David Bellamy, and my doctor would have been very unhappy with the way my blood pressure behaved. That sick-minded leech should be dealt with once and for all."

"Don't worry, Lynn, I fully intend to deal with him," Diane assured her, reaching for the book a young man had brought to her for autographing. She had to gently pull the book out of the young man's hands; his attention was so firmly fixed on Diane's costume, he'd apparently forgotten why he was there.

"The best way to deal with someone like David Bellamy is the way we deal with his sort in the pages of a manuscript," Lynn stated, her light eyes looking hard in the usually-gentle collection of wrinkles that was her face. She cheerfully admitted to being older than Ralph Teak, but she was just as cheerful in refusing to say exactly how much older. "If he were one of *my* characters, I think I would have to come up with something exquisitely horrible to account for him. The only problem is, if it were really fitting it would undoubtedly make everyone ill."

"It would also make for another problem," Diane pointed out as she handed back the signed book. "Whoever did the murder would have to get away with it, which wouldn't do much for the image of your detective. But, since the murder would be justified, finding and disclosing the culprit would be even worse. It isn't fair giving your characters a problem like that."

"Dilemmas of that sort can be worked around, dear girl," Lynn assured her, a smile having returned to her fragile old face. "Just consider how sweet the end result would be, and there you have your motivation."

Diane chuckled at the comment, also amused by the expressions on the faces of those in Lynn's line who were close enough to have heard what she'd said. With her white hair and dowdy clothes, Lynn was the picture of your average sweet little old lady. On the inside, though, she was as clinically bloodthirsty as any mystery writer. Calmly discussing murder and dismemberment was everyday to them.

The signing went on for long enough to make Diane wish she had a drink, but her line wasn't as long as some of the others. Most of the people coming to them had program books to be signed rather than individual books, and Diane suspected they were primarily horror fans who were taking the opportunity of getting the autographs of those mystery writers whose names they recognized. Angela had been one of the first to leave, and despite her normal preference for being charitable, Diane had been secretly pleased to see it.

"Don't forget that we're getting together some time during this weekend," Lynn reminded her as Diane whispered that she was going for something to drink. "I want to hear all about what you've been doing since the last time we talked, most especially including anyone of interest you might have met—or are in the process of meeting, like that pirate who walked by a few minutes ago. Or didn't you see him?"

"Lynn, are you accusing me of being three days dead?" Diane asked in the same low voice, grinning over being able to speak to the older woman in a way she couldn't with others. "If you're thinking about matchmaking, in case I can't manage to recapture his attention myself, I offer my heartiest approval and wish you the best of luck.''

"I always knew you were a sensible girl," Lynn said with calm satisfaction. "Since being old lets you get away with the most shameless things—like walking right up to a young man and introducing yourself— I'll be sure to be successful. Just you make sure to be available.''

Diane chuckled her agreement, then moved off toward one of the refreshment stations in the room. She didn't expect to meet anyone there. Bill was long gone, Ralph was still signing, and Anita had come past the line a couple of times and waved, but was right then lost in the crowd somewhere.

"Probably with *my* Mr. Right," Diane muttered to herself as she walked. Anita had looked beautiful in her guardian angel costume, and had drawn her share of stares. Wouldn't it be just like the way the rest of the weekend was going, for Anita to attract someone she wasn't interested in, while Diane— "Excuse me, ma'am, but someone would like to speak to you," a zombie said, interrupting Diane's thoughts. The man was really into his part, speaking in a deep, toneless, drawn-out accent, and staggering more than walking. "He asked me to deliver his message when you were free. Please walk this way.''

Diane refrained from making any of the standard comments about walking *his* way, and simply followed the man's stagger toward one of the smaller doors out of the room. She wondered who it could be who wanted to talk to her, and then the thought came that it might be a Mr. Right— like the pirate—Anita hadn't distracted.

The idea was so silly it made Diane laugh to herself, but it was fun to think about. It would certainly turn out to be an agent who wanted to know if she was represented, or someone on the hotel staff who had a question about the registration form she'd signed.

"Right through there, ma'am, near the telephones and rest rooms," the zombie directed her, pointing toward the door before staggering off into the crowd. Diane was surprised he hadn't waited for a tip, and then she remembered what she was wearing. It was fairly obvious she couldn't have much in the way of cash with her, and he must have already been tipped by whoever had sent him.

The identity of that whoever had really made her curious. She pulled the door open and went through, hearing the crowd noise cut off as the padded portal hissed closed behind her. She was in a featureless corridor, which was supposed to look like stone, and the make-believe torches on the wall let her see the way the corridor curved away to the right.

Diane began walking toward the curve, but her step was suddenly slowed by the thought that it might be Rick who was waiting. It would have taken more imagination than she'd given him credit for to find her here, but it wouldn't have been impossible. If it *was* him she would just say what she'd planned for Sunday night, and simply hope that he didn't make a scene. She'd already had enough of scenes, and she still had the one with David scheduled for tomorrow.

Diane rounded the curve and suddenly stopped dead, her heart beginning to thud. There on the floor, not ten feet ahead of her, was what looked to be a body. The torchlight wasn't really torchlight, and it was strong enough to show what had to be blood on the floor beyond the body. It was horrible. Someone had been murdered.

And then Diane laughed, feeling stupid enough to be glad no one was there to see her. What had that man in the van said, about the hotel providing dead bodies for guests to investigate? Someone must have decided it would be fun to get the mystery writers in on the game, and they had chosen her to be the first one on the scene. Well, she'd try not to let them down, assuming they'd left enough clues to work with.

Feeling a lot better about things, Diane began walking closer to the body. The part of the corridor where the body lay had a couple of darkened arches on either side, but no sign of telephones or rest rooms. It also soon curved away again out of sight. About three feet beyond the body was a heavy brass candlestick like the one in her suite. Presumably all the suites had ones like it and possibly the rooms as well, but it was definitely an important clue. If it wasn't the murder weapon, someone had gone to a lot of trouble getting blood all over it.

There was a mask, crumpled in the victim's hand. It seemed to match the costume he was wearing. It was a hood with eyeholes cut in it, the sort of hood executioners wore during the middle ages. The rest of the man's costume went along with it, buckle shoes and hose, knee pants and linen shirt, a long vest that reached down past the victim's waist. The only thing missing was the executioner's weapon, the usual ax or rope.

At that point Diane stood very still and swallowed hard, as another very definite clue came to her. She'd been thinking of the victim as one of the hotel staff playing body, since it obviously wasn't a dummy. It isn't hard to lie in one place pretending to be dead, but if you're only pretending you still have to breathe. It suddenly came to her that the body *wasn't* breathing...

A lot of what Diane had considered fake blood had splashed on the victim's face, and being busy looking for clues had kept her from studying his features before now. Right then all she wanted to do was run for help, but she forced herself to look at the face. It was distorted with shock and probably pain, the eyes wide and staring.

They were pale blue eyes that usually looked quite different. Diane put a horrified hand to her mouth and quickly backed away with a sickened gasp. The dead man was David Bellamy.

As she turned to run, hands touched her shoulders from behind.

Chapter Six

Sauntering over to the door and then through it got Gray into the corridor without being noticed by the party crowd, and once the door had closed behind him he eased his way toward the bend up ahead.

At first glance there was nothing to see in the undecorated stretch of walls, floor and ceiling, but that held true only until he had moved soundlessly around the curve.

There, on the floor, little more than ten feet away, lay the body of a man. This time Gray was certain the body was no joke. A quick glance showed him no one but the dead man, and nothing but two darkened archways to either side of the corridor near where the body lay.

The archways had something to do with the daytime game, but when Gray used the pencil flash he'd brought with him to get a better look at their interiors, he saw nothing but two small alcoves empty even of furniture.

Satisfied that he wasn't turning his back on a hidden enemy, Gray then looked down at the body. The man had apparently been killed by a heavy blow to the head, and the murder weapon seemed to be the brass candlestick lying not far from the body.

Gray didn't know how the hotel's amateur detectives would see it, but that murder weapon was a little too obvious for his taste. Either the man had been killed by something else, or the candlestick was supposed to point to one, carefully chosen suspect.

Gray's questing thoughts broke off when he examined the victim's face, distinguishing the features through the heavy screen of blood. He knew that face, he'd seen it recently. Then he realized who it was and his thought became, but how can she be framed for it if she isn't here? She has to be seen in the area by legitimate, uninvolved witnesses.

Or something on the body has to suggest she *was* here, he quickly corrected himself, glad the second option had occurred to him. The real game was started and it had almost happened at his feet, which was too bad for the true murderer but pure luck for Diane Philips. If they'd left anything on the body to implicate the woman, he would see that it was never found.

Gray was beginning to bend down when he heard the sound of muted footsteps coming from the direction of the ballroom. It didn't sound like the zombie coming back, but there was no sense in taking any chances. He straightened again, moved quickly and quietly into the dark of the alcove to the right, then waited.

But not for long. A moment later he heard the sound of a gasp, a few heartbeats worth of silence, and then a small, very relieved laugh. Right after that the newcomer moved close enough for Gray to see her, and he almost groaned aloud. Diane Philips was now at the scene of the crime, and he suddenly knew exactly what she was doing. She thought the body had been provided by the hotel, so she had started to look for clues.

The truth came to her rather quickly, but when she gave a horrified gasp and began backing away from the body Gray was ready. It hadn't been hard to make up his mind not to let her end like his brother, convicted of a crime she hadn't committed. He had to get her out of here as fast as possible. When he put his hands on her shoulders she made a strangled sound and whirled to face him, and then he had her by the arms.

"You have to get out of here and report this," he told her in a whispered rasp he'd practiced that sounded nothing like his normal voice. "You're being set up to be blamed for his murder, and the only way you can avoid it is to jump in a direction they aren't anticipating."

"What are you talking about?" she demanded in a whisper of her own, her green eyes wide behind her mask. "Who are you, and who do you think is framing me? Did *you* kill him?"

"Of course I didn't kill him," Gray rasped. He was faintly annoyed by her suspicion, but had to admit to himself he admired her courage. "I can't tell you who's framing you because I don't yet know who they are, but I intend to find out. Now, will you get out of here?"

"But who *are* you?" she insisted, those green eyes looking up at him, trying to see through his mask. "Why should you care what happens to me?"

"Isn't it enough that I do care?" he countered, and then he couldn't keep from grinning. "If you like, you can consider me your secret admirer."

Her eyes widened again at that. Later Gray couldn't understand what came over him right then. One instant he was looking down at her, and the next he had pulled her close and was touching his lips to hers. It was supposed to have been the lightest of kisses, no more than a brief, gentle reassurance, but without warning it became more than that. Gray's soul came through in the blazing passion of that kiss, and after the first breath he wasn't acting alone.

Sanity returned almost soon enough, and when he let her go she was looking nearly as dazed as he felt. Of all the stupid things to do, right there not five feet from a dead body.

"And now I want you out of here," he rasped, giving her a gentle push before letting her arms go. "Give me about thirty seconds, and then make as much noise and fuss as you can manage."

"But what about you?" she whispered even as she backed away a few steps, one hand to her mouth. "When can I talk to you about what's—"

Gray had already turned and gone to one knee beside the body, his hands reaching for the vest the corpse wore, but he never got to complete that search. Diane's words stopped abruptly, and then another, obviously male voice came at full volume.

"Aha, pretty harem queen, now we'll find out what you're up— Hey, what's going on here? What are you doing, mister?"

The French king Diane had been speaking to earlier was approaching quickly, in the company of a number of other costumed people. One glance was all Gray took the time for, and then he was up and running toward the other end of the corridor. He had to keep his pirate character free and unidentified to keep it useful, which meant he needed to get out of there. But one thing was certain, as soon as he got his pirate untangled from this mess, he'd have to go back as himself to find out what he could.

"DIANE, what's been going on here?" Bill Raglan repeated. "Are you all right? Who's that on the floor, and what was that pirate doing to him?"

Diane wanted to answer Bill's questions, but suddenly she discovered she was trembling too hard to do it. And what was she supposed to say? That the pirate had told her she was being framed? Who would want to frame *her*, and what earthly reason could they have to try...?

"Oh, good lord, it's David Bellamy," someone said in horror, and Diane looked up to see that one of the men who had come along with Bill had gone over to the body. "If he isn't dead, we'll never see anything closer. Somebody had better call the police."

"Diane, what were you doing in here?" Bill asked in a lower voice, through the exclamations of the others. He put his arm around her shoulders in a concerned, protective way. "Did you see that man commit the murder? Who was he, and what was he doing here?"

For some reason the words still refused to come. That pirate's my secret admirer, Diane wanted to say. Of course he didn't kill David. What he did was kiss me, something a murderer would never do just to cover his tracks, so of course he's innocent. He claims he's going to prove that I'm innocent, too, so how could I suspect him? It's all very sim-

ple, Bill, possibly as simple as he thinks I am, but once I
explain it you'll understand completely.

"You poor thing, you're in shock, aren't you?" Bill said
in a kindly way, helping her toward the door to the ballroom. "We'll find some place for you to sit down, and then
you'll be all right."

Of course I'll be all right, her numbed mind agreed as she
was led away. I'll be just fine—until the police get here.

BY THE TIME the police arrived Diane was ready to talk to
them. Someone with a less practical nature would probably
have still been dazed by the bizarre thought that she'd fallen
into one of her own books, but Diane didn't have time for
the hysterics of fancy. She knew she was in trouble even if
she wasn't covered in blood. And if she didn't stay fully in
touch with the real world she might never get out of trouble
again.

"The lieutenant would like to see you now, miss," a uniformed police officer told her politely, interrupting the furious workings of her mind. She sat in the lobby outside the
ballroom, in a chair Bill Raglan had taken her to. She'd been
in the perfect place to see the police arrive. It hadn't taken
long once they'd been called but, between their arrival and
the time Diane was called, more than a little time had
passed.

"Miss Philips is still rather badly shaken, officer," Bill
said immediately. "I think I should go along with her."

"Are you her lawyer?" the officer asked, letting himself
inspect Bill's costume.

"No, I'm just a friend, but I should be there," Bill answered. "I'm one of those who found the body and called
you fellows, so. . ."

"Then you'll certainly have your turn, sir, if the lieutenant hasn't already spoken to you," the man said with a politely formal smile. Then he turned back to Diane. "Would
you like me to give you a hand, miss?"

"Thank you, officer, but I think I can make it on my
own," Diane said with a sigh. "No sense in putting off the

inevitable, and at least I'll be able to see how accurate I've been.''

The man gave her something of an odd look, but didn't comment as he led the way into the restaurant across the lobby. One of the tables near the door had been appropriated by an average-looking man with dark hair and eyes. He wore a brown suit, his shirt was rumpled, and his tie hung around his collar like a noose. He was somewhere in his middle years, looked as if he could have used a shave, seemed surrounded by paper, and had a small, open notebook not far from his right hand.

''Miss Philips? I'm Lieutenant Gerard,'' he greeted her as she approached the table, standing to offer his hand. ''I know this must be a terrible shock for you, so I'll try to ask my questions as quickly as possible. Please sit down.''

''Thank you, Lieutenant,'' Diane said with a faint smile, briefly taking his hand before sitting in the indicated chair. Either the man was really good at putting suspects at their ease, or he wasn't up to handling a murder investigation properly. Time would tell, and not very much time, either.

''I've read the statement you gave my man, and there are just a couple of points I need to clarify,'' Gerard went on, sitting back as he consulted his small notebook. ''You said you were told by a member of the hotel staff that someone wanted to talk to you. Can you describe the man?''

''Certainly,'' Diane said with a sinking feeling. ''He was a six-foot-tall zombie in a blinding red uniform. I take it you can't find anyone of that description who's willing to admit he delivered the message.''

''What makes you say that?'' Gerard asked mildly, bringing his dark eyes to her face.

''The fact that you're asking me about it again means you can't verify it,'' Diane answered with a sigh. ''If I'm telling the truth, the lack of verification means someone is trying to frame me. If I'm lying, the lack means I'm trying to divert suspicion from myself. Knowing which is which will tell you what path to follow in your investigation.''

''That's very good,'' Gerard acknowledged with a nod and a tired smile. ''I've always wondered how well mystery

writers would do if they didn't start out already knowing
who the guilty party was. And *are* you lying?''

"I almost wish I were," Diane couldn't help saying,
finding it impossible to return the man's smile. "A writer
learns how to tell a logically consistent story with all the
loose ends tied up, one that doesn't leave an innocent character's innocence in doubt. I'm afraid this mess doesn't
manage to do any of that."

"No, I'm afraid it doesn't," Gerard agreed softly, almost compassionately. When he spoke next the compassion was gone. "When you found the body, you also found
a man dressed as a pirate. We checked with the costume
people here, but they don't have a costume that fits the de-
scriptions we were given. Was he standing over the body
when you first saw him?"

"He must have been in the small alcove to the right,"
Diane said. This lieutenant *was* good, and all she could do
was hope he was good enough. "When I realized it was an
actual dead body and not part of the hotel's entertainment,
I was ready to run and call for help, but he stopped me."

"He tried to keep you there?" Gerard asked. "Did he
threaten you?"

"No to both," Diane answered, still bothered herself by
that part of it. "The first thing he said was that I had to get
out of there. He said someone was trying to frame me, but
when I asked who, he said he didn't know yet. When I asked
if he'd killed David, he claimed he hadn't."

"Claimed," Gerard echoed, looking directly at her again.
"Did he say or do anything that made you believe he was
lying?"

"Only the fact that he seemed to expect I *would* believe
him," Diane said, fidgeting in annoyance as she tried to put
her impressions into words. "I mean, most people understand that if they're found near someone who was murdered, it's only logical to expect that they'll be suspected of
having done it. He said something like, 'Of course I didn't
do it,' just as though I should have known he was innocent.
Do you understand what I'm saying?"

"I think I do," Gerard murmured, writing something in his notebook before returning his full attention to Diane. "I'm told you knew the murdered man. Just how well did you know him?"

"Entirely too well," Diane answered. "But I would have enjoyed never knowing him at all, and now that he's dead I won't pretend I'm sorry."

Gerard nodded. "There doesn't seem to be anyone here who liked the man even as an acquaintance. If this was a train instead of a hotel, I'd be tempted to arrest every one of you. Would you tell me why you didn't like David Bellamy, and what the argument you had with him this afternoon was all about?"

Despite the question asked, Diane couldn't help smiling to herself at the lieutenant's reference to Agatha Christie's *Murder on the Orient Express*. The villain in that story *had* been murdered by everyone involved.

"David Bellamy was an editor with my major publishing house when I was only beginning as a writer," she said after the slight hesitation. "When I turned in the manuscript for my third book, he... suggested I had to do something else as well, or he'd see to it that my brand-new career died. He wasn't the sort of man who would bluff about ruining me, and I knew it."

"So you did what he asked?" Gerard prompted, the look in his dark eyes veiled but still hard.

"I'd rather have let my career die," Diane said, the words stiff with distaste. "What I did was go to my publisher and tell him everything, then I supplied another copy of my manuscript. My publisher gave it to another editor, and when David tried to send through his butchered version of what I'd written, he was caught in the act. It was pointed out to him that his little game would have cost the house he worked for quite a lot of money, and for that reason, if no other, he was being fired and blacklisted."

"Served him more than right," Gerard muttered, the look in his eyes now open and approving. "And then what happened?"

"He managed to talk himself into the job of managing editor of a magazine owned by foreign investors," Diane said. "He made it very clear that he considered his previous trouble to be all my fault. He never missed an opportunity to embarrass me or badmouth my books, and that was what our argument this afternoon was about."

"And you decided this would be the last time," Gerard said, his direct stare fixed on her again. "He tormented you for years, but you finally decided you'd had enough. You even told people he would soon no longer be a problem, and you said it more than once. Can you tell me it is just a coincidence that David Bellamy will never be a problem for anyone again?"

"It can't possibly be a coincidence, but I didn't kill him," Diane said intensely, in an effort to force the man to believe her. She'd expected the accusation, but her churning stomach proved that expecting something and coming face to face with it just wasn't the same. "I'd decided to stand up to David, just the way everyone told me I should. *That* was what was supposed to make him leave me alone. I'd have to be an idiot to kill him under circumstances like these."

"Or completely desperate," Gerard said, unmoved by her words. "You claim you meant to stand up to the man, but we have no more than your word for that. If you had..."

"Excuse me, Lieutenant, but you *do* have more than just the lady's word," a mild, male voice interrupted, startling them both. "I can bear witness to her decision, because I was there when she made it."

"Who the hell are *you*, and how did you get in here?" Gerard demanded while Diane stared at Gray in surprise. "How did you get past the officers at the door?"

"Well, I certainly didn't overpower them," Gray answered, looking privately amused at the thought. "Your men probably just didn't notice me going past them. I'm James Grayson, and I walked in here because no one told me I couldn't."

"We'll have to see about that, Mr. Grayson," Gerard said, still obviously annoyed. "You say you're a witness to Miss Philips's intentions, that you know she meant to do nothing more than confront the victim. Even if she told you that in so many words, how could you possibly know what her actual intentions were? Do you claim to be able to read minds?''

"What I claim to be able to read is character," Gray answered mildly, coming forward to stand not far from Diane. "In my line of work I get a lot of practice doing it, and I'm seldom wrong. If Ms. Philips ever decided to murder anyone, she would make certain she didn't have the best motive in sight. She's a gifted mystery writer. Even spur-of-the-moment, there's no doubt she could do better than this."

"And here I was waiting for you to tell me how you really knew, in your deepest heart, that she couldn't possibly be guilty," Gerard said sourly, leaning back in his chair as he gazed up at Gray. "Instead you tell me she would have killed him smarter if she'd decided to do it. Are you a lawyer, Mr. Grayson?''

"It so happens I am, Lieutenant," Gray admitted, his brows raised in mild surprise. "I'm not admitted to the bar in this state, but I can still act in an advisory capacity on Ms. Philips's behalf. Why do you ask?''

"Just a little hunch," Gerard answered with a faint smile. "Very well Mr. Grayson, you may remain for now. Ms. Philips, think back carefully and tell me what you saw when you approached the body.''

Diane was nearly shaken by the question. It was so abrupt. She'd been starting to enjoy the feeling of no longer being alone, of having someone there who was on her side, and had almost forgotten that the inquisition wasn't yet over with.

"There wasn't much to see, Lieutenant," she answered, taking a moment to rerun the events in her memory. "I saw the man's mask, which was off, and the brass candlestick, which looked like the murder weapon, and I didn't see anything in the way of the weapon that ought to go with his costume. Have you found out if he was missing part of his costume?''

"If I feel that's something you ought to know, Ms. Philips, I'll be sure to tell you," Gerard said, giving her his faint smile again. "If you asked the question hoping for an affirmative, intending to point out that you could hardly be the one who carried the missing weapon away, please don't bother. *Your* costume may be unsuitable for hiding things, but if that pirate was your accomplice, he could very well have carried it off. It's not . . ."

"Accomplice?" Diane demanded, voicing her outrage without thinking. "Now I'm supposed to have an accomplice?"

"Please, Ms. Philips, there's no sense in getting upset," Gerard began, the smoothness of his voice suggesting that upset was exactly the way he wanted her. Diane couldn't keep from obliging him.

"I'm sorry, Lieutenant, but you just can't have it both ways," she plowed on, letting him see exactly how angry she was. "If I had an accomplice, then the murder was premeditated. If it was premeditated, then I actually put myself in the position of being the prime suspect with lots of circumstantial evidence pointing to me, and no alibi whatsoever. If it wasn't premeditated, then I couldn't possibly have an accomplice even if I did do it, which I didn't. If you're going to accuse me, you have to at least be logical about it."

"The law tends to have a similar requirement, Lieutenant," Gray put in, his calm even more obvious in contrast to Diane's anger. "Could she have murdered the man in anger, just before a large group of witnesses arrived? If she did, then she didn't have the time to get rid of anything by way of evidence. If she didn't, then why did she go back, just in time for people to find her standing over the body? To retrieve something that would implicate her? Then why isn't it still there on the scene?"

"It's odd that you mention that, Mr. Grayson," Gerard said with sudden, very close attention, as though he'd just closed the jaws of a trap. "There *is* something on the scene that implicates Ms. Philips, and it couldn't have been removed in front of witnesses without their noticing. I intended to mention the matter myself, but now you've saved me the trouble.''

"There was something there?" Diane asked, feeling the churning of her insides again. "What was it?"

"The murder weapon," Gerard said with what was becoming his usual expression, a faint smile, dark eyes fixed directly on Diane's face. "The brass candlestick came from your suite, I'm told, even though there aren't any fingerprints. Is there anyone else who could have had access to the thing besides you?"

"No," Diane answered, back to feeling stunned. "Even I haven't spent all that much time in the suite, and no one came to visit while I *was* there. Are you sure it was from my suite? How do you know?"

"There's a small number stamped in the base of the thing," Gerard said, looking the slightest bit disappointed. "The numbers correspond to the room and suite numbers. That's the way the hotel people keep track of them. When was the last time you saw the candlestick?"

"As far as I can remember, the first time was the last," Diane said, her fingers playing with the edge of her veil. Then suddenly her anger was back to replace the shock. "That has to be the lamest thing I ever heard of! I'm supposed to have been intelligent enough to wipe away my fingerprints, but too stupid to check the murder weapon for something else that might point to me? Are they picturing me as an idiot, or were they too rushed to do any better?"

"They?" Gerard asked softly, obviously trying not to interrupt her possibly informative outburst. "Who are you talking about?"

"The pirate was right," Diane declared, pointing one finger at the lieutenant. "I thought at first that he was trying to mislead me when he talked about a setup, but he was right. My walking in there alone to find the body could have been a coincidence, but what are the chances that the murder weapon just happened to come from my suite? What sort of coincidence would cover that?"

"A very, very large one," Gerard muttered, as though he were giving her the point only grudgingly, and then he raised his voice. "I'll tell you the truth, Ms. Philips. These coincidences are the only thing that's keeping me from arresting you right now. You *happen* to have been directed to the body by someone we can't find. You *happen* to have been discovered standing over it. And the corpse *happens* to be someone you had a motive for killing. On top of that the murder weapon *happens* to be from your suite, and the only thing we're missing to convict you is an accusation written in the victim's own blood."

"Thank goodness they didn't realize they were overdoing it," Diane said, breathing deeply. She felt like closing her eyes in relief. "Just a little more subtlety..."

"But that doesn't mean I'm dismissing you entirely," Gerard interrupted, his tone fractionally sharper. "Overdoing it could be a clever way of diverting suspicion from yourself, with the backup excuse that a professional mystery writer would never be that obvious. I still don't know where that pirate fits in, but he's another reason I'm not making any arrests. When I do find him, he should be able to supply answers to a number of questions."

"Are you through with her now, Lieutenant?" Gray asked. Diane realized that she'd almost forgotten he was there. Gerard didn't quite look startled, but he also didn't seem to have been expecting the interruption.

"For the moment, Counselor," he answered, giving Gray a sour look. "This convention is supposed to continue through the weekend, and Ms. Philips is being officially requested to stay as well. And since you're here, would you like to tell me why *you* weren't at the costume party? Or did you take the time to change before coming in here to interrupt?"

"But I *was* at the costume party, or at least on the fringes of it," Gray said, this time looking faintly surprised. "Since I hadn't gotten a costume I didn't try to mingle, but I was there long enough to look around a little. What made you think I wasn't?"

"As someone who had words earlier in the day with the victim, your name was on the list my men had," Gerard replied. "Everyone else involved was at the party, but no one could remember seeing you. Did you run into anyone you know, Mr. Grayson?"

"Since I don't know anyone here except for Ms. Philips, that would have been difficult," Gray said. "Do you mean I'm a suspect, too?"

"At this point everyone's a suspect," Gerard responded. "That official request about staying applies to you, too, Mr. Grayson. But you and the lady can go for now."

Chapter Seven

Diane had always thought that sort of interview with the police would be fascinating, even if she happened to be a suspect. She would use her brilliant, analytical mind to prove her innocence beyond all doubt, and then she would help them see what had really happened....

"Is something wrong?" Gray asked, guiding her around the uniformed officer guarding the way into the restaurant. "You look like you just stepped into something absurd."

"You could say I'm having an unpleasant reaction to a rude awakening," she answered, then looked at him with a smile. "It seems I owe you thanks again for rescuing me, and this time more than the last. Facing David's viciousness would have been a lot easier than facing a murder charge."

"I just seem to end up being in the right place at the right time," Gray said with an answering smile, dismissing her gratitude. "Why don't I buy you a drink. If you feel like talking about what happened you'll have a handy ear."

"I can use a drink, but we'll have to be sure not to make a habit of this," Diane said. "If I start drinking after every crisis, this weekend will make an alcoholic of me."

"You expect something else to happen?" Gray asked, moving with her toward the stairs leading to the second-floor bar. "With the police on the scene looking for a murderer?"

"What better time to give them something to find?" Diane asked in turn, brushing aside the faint impatience she felt over his having missed the point. The man wasn't used to thinking in terms of murder and detection, after all, so he couldn't be blamed for not seeing the obvious. "Since their first attempt to frame me didn't work—thanks to Lieutenant Gerard's scepticism—there's an excellent chance they'll try something else."

"You sound very grateful to a man who just gave you a pretty hard time," Gray observed. "I had the impression more than once that he really thought you were guilty."

"At this point, he'd be an idiot if he didn't," Diane said. "What I'm grateful for is the fact that the man can think, and he's noticed how very obvious all that evidence against me is. Someone else in his place might have taken it all at face value and simply arrested me. And it can still happen."

"Then shouldn't you be on the phone now, calling your lawyer?" Gray asked. "If there's a chance you'll be arrested, you should have someone on hand to give you legal advice."

"If it comes to that, having a lawyer won't do more than get me out of a cell," Diane said, shaking her head. There weren't too many people in the bar area, so they were able to reclaim the couch they'd shared that afternoon. "What I really need is to find out who's trying to frame me, preferably with hard evidence to back up the contention. In other words, I've got to get them before they get me."

"You don't intend to snoop around on your own?" Gray asked.

Diane thought she could see worry lurking behind his frown. "People who commit murder are dangerous, and if you get in their way they could kill *you* just as easily as they did Bellamy. If that lieutenant is as clever as you say, you can leave it to him to get to the truth."

"But what if he doesn't?" Diane countered. "What if something else turns up to convince him that I'm guilty after all? The more time the murderers have to plan something, the better it will be. And right now they have all the thinking time they need. If I sit back and wait for someone else to save my neck, I won't be able to complain if it ends up in a noose.''

"I still say it's too dangerous," Gray grumbled, rubbing at his face with one hand, and then his light eyes came back to her. "But if you insist on doing this, you have to let me work with you. If I don't I'll just be sitting around somewhere worrying."

"Of course you can help me," Diane said with an inner sigh, wondering how hard it would be to avoid his amateur "help." Gray was a delightful man and more attractive and interesting every time she saw him, but investigating a murder took more drive and push, and less worry about how dangerous it was. If she got lucky and he forgot to show up to help she would be relieved, but also somehow disappointed.

Her agreement seemed to reassure Gray. A vampire waitress came and took their order. Even after she was gone, Gray hesitated before turning to Diane again.

"Look, I owe you an apology and I don't quite know how to put it," he said, and Diane could see that he was embarrassed. "What I said when we were talking to the lieutenant, about incriminating evidence you might have gone back for . . . I had no idea that candlestick came from your suite, but I should have kept my mouth closed. I nearly gave them a solid basis for arresting you, and I'm really sorry."

"You did no such thing," Diane told him firmly, resisting the urge to pat his hand. "Since they already knew the candlestick came from my suite, the possibility of my having gone back to retrieve it must have occurred to them. If there are apologies due anyone, I owe one to you."

"For what?" Gray was honestly at a loss as to what she meant.

Diane gave a rueful smile. "I let David bother me so badly, you felt it necessary to come to the rescue. You heard what the lieutenant said—because of the words you had with David this afternoon, your name is now on the list of suspects. If that wasn't my fault, whose fault was it?"

"Mine and mine alone," Gray responded firmly. "You never asked me to help you with that creep, the decision was one I made on my own. And I'm not worried about being considered a suspect. They can't possibly build a case against me. I never met the victim before today, had never even heard of him, and came away the winner in our very brief exchange. Bringing charges against me would be an exercise in futility."

"Not if they discovered you were a hit man in disguise," Diane said in a stage whisper, leaning toward him just a little. "Go on, you can tell me if you are, I won't spread it around."

"Well, of course I am," Gray said with a laugh of delight at her joke. "I should have known you would see the truth, but Lieutenant Gerard isn't nearly as perceptive, so I'm still safe. And now that I've confessed, why don't you tell me everything that happened to you. If I'm going to help you investigate, I should have as many of the facts as possible."

Gray noticed that Diane hesitated very briefly, as though reluctant to go over it all again. If he'd had the choice he wouldn't have put her through it, but he had to get a cover for knowing things he hadn't officially seen. Diane Philips was really bright, and if he slipped he had no doubt that she would catch it.

It bothered him that she intended to snoop around on her own, but as their drinks were brought and she paused in her narrative to give the waitress a chance to leave, Gray realized he was also glad. He now had a pressing, legitimate reason to stick close to her, and if anyone tried anything he'd be right there to stop it.

There was a good chance he'd find out who here was in that murder ring. And if he didn't do it this weekend he never would. He'd never have the same anonymity he had right now. Even if he located another murder scene, there was too much chance that the people responsible would spot him immediately. He also wasn't about to desert Diane Philips. She needed help as much as his brother did, and clearing her might well end up clearing him.

"...and then Bill Raglan helped me out to the lobby area and into a chair," Diane finished with a small gesture of her wineglass. "The police got there fast enough, but they spent quite a long time questioning people in general and examining the death scene before they got down to questioning witnesses. Before the lieutenant called me in I thought I was tired of waiting, but after I was there I decided I could have waited a lot longer for the pleasure."

She grimaced to show him her opinion of the interview, then sipped at her wine. The man beside her had listened attentively to what she'd told him, as though he really did expect to pick up something she'd missed. He looked thoughtful.

"Now I can see more clearly why you weren't charged," he said, absently toying with the glass he held. "That pirate fellow—if they can't prove he was your accomplice and they can't find him, it can be reasonably assumed that he committed the murder. He was the one who ran, after all, and in front of witnesses. No, I think they'll have to leave you alone until they find him."

"But I can't leave *him* alone," Diane said in a murmur. She hadn't told anyone about the kiss, but that didn't mean she'd forgotten it. "I have to know where that pirate fits into all this, and if possible clear him of suspicion."

"But why?" Gray asked, brows raised. "As long as he can be pointed to as the main suspect, the police won't bother you."

"He knew I was being framed right from the beginning," Diane answered, staring down into her wine. "That means he knows what's going on, or at least knows more than everyone else. And I've been thinking about what he said. The very first thing he did was to tell me to get out of there, and if I'd listened I wouldn't even have been found standing over the body. That alone should mean he was on my side rather than the murderer's. If so, I'm obligated to clear him if I can."

"You certainly have a strong sense of honor," Gray said, and Diane could have sworn he was fighting a sigh. "All right, finding the pirate is part of our agenda, but what's the rest of it? How do you intend to go about your investigation?"

Before Diane could part her lips to answer, the hordes descended.

"Diane, are you all right?" "Dear girl, how badly were you hounded?" "Did they have the nerve to threaten you, child?"

Bill Raglan, Lynn Haverstock and Ralph Teak arrived together, the three of them all talking at once and making it seem as though there were three hundred rather than three. Diane flinched just a little, then gave them a reassuring smile.

"I'm still alive, in one piece, and unarrested," she said. "I've been told not to leave town, but so far that's all they've done."

"Lucky for them," Ralph said, still looking outraged. "I've accumulated a lot of friends and acquaintances over the years, and if they'd had the bad judgment to do any more, they would have heard from some of those people. Are you sure you're all right?"

"How all right can the girl be?" Lynn demanded with outrage that matched Ralph's as Bill pulled a chair over for her. "We all know they suspect her of murdering that useless lowlife, and if they can't find anyone else to blame they'll undoubtedly charge *her*."

"Then we'll have to find them someone else to blame," Ralph said, taking the second chair Bill brought without even thanking his friend.

"Ralph, this isn't a book or a game," Bill warned, finally able to get a chair of his own. "This is a real murder, committed by a real murderer, and the police won't look kindly on your interfering. By the way, is this gentleman one of ours or one of theirs?"

"He's wearing a convention name badge, Bill," Lynn pointed out without so much as a glance toward Gray. "He came here alone and he's on the quiet side, but he's certainly not shy. He also isn't with the police, or at least not with the Connecticut police."

"And his name is James Grayson," Diane put in. She was struggling not to laugh at his expression, which was more than startled. "Gray, this very observant lady is Lynn Haverstock, the angry gentleman beside her is Ralph Teak, and the voice of caution comes from Bill Raglan, Ralph's editor and friend."

"I'm pleased to meet all of you," Gray said with a nod, his expression still uncertain. "The name Lynn Haverstock tells me why the lady knows so much about me, but not *how* she knows. Have you been following me, Ms. Haverstock?"

"I haven't followed men around for thirty years," Lynn answered with a chuckle, her wrinkled face creased into a smile. "I knew you were here alone because, despite your convention badge, you're not in costume any more than I am. In my case I'm too old to consider changing clothes fun, but you obviously had no one to coax you into it or ask you to join them as a favor."

"The lack of costume also says you're quiet, since you passed up the opportunity to attract women with a flashy outfit," Ralph took up the explanation. "Shyness is ruled out through the fact that you're sitting with our Diane, and the same fact rules out your being blind. Do we need to go on?"

"I don't think so," Gray said with a laugh, while Diane's cheeks reddened. "I can see I'll have to watch my step with you and Ms. Haverstock around. If I were the murderer, I'd be feeling very nervous right now."

"Nervous enough to make a mistake, I hope," Ralph said grimly, settling back in his chair in a very deliberate way. "So far, we know that someone is trying to frame Diane, but he hasn't been able to yet. That means he has to try again, so *we* have to be ready for him."

"How do you know about the framing?" Gray asked, serious again.

"Diane told Bill what happened, and Bill told us," Lynn informed him, gesturing away the question. "We're not magicians, but we *are* able to think. Anyone who knows Diane knows she's incapable of committing murder, so she didn't do it. If it looks like she *did* do it, someone is trying to frame her. Since she hasn't been arrested the frame isn't as tight as they'd hoped, so they have to try again and this time make it stick."

"Even if they'd be smarter to just let it ride," Ralph put in thoughtfully. "Right now there doesn't seem to be anything that points to anyone else, so if they sit back and bide their time they just might get away with it."

"Unless for some reason they can't simply let it go," Bill mused, obviously weighing possibilities. "Is there a circumstance where they'd have no choice but to try again?"

"Certainly," Lynn said. "If you murder someone there's a reason, even if the reason happens to be insanity. We aren't dealing with that here, I'm sure, so there must be a more substantial reason buried somewhere. If the police aren't convinced of Diane's guilt quickly, they'll keep digging, and digging unearths things no matter how well they're buried. To keep from being found out, they have to be sure Diane is charged."

"And whoever they are, they have to know both David and me," Diane contributed. "That argument we had in front of everybody this afternoon was too convenient. Confrontations in the past don't do nearly as well as a brand-new squabble. They knew David would start in on me as soon as he saw me, and also knew I wasn't likely to simply shrug it off and walk away. How many people here at the hotel fit that requirement?"

"Our own people, certainly," Ralph answered at once, looking as though he were making a mental list. "The four of us here, Anita Rutledge and George Lombardy, Angela Wilkes and Robert Sims, John Fryer and Miles Henry. What about the editors from the other crowd, Bill? Do you know if they knew David at least?"

"One of them had heard something about him, but the rest hadn't," Bill said, rubbing his chin with the back of a finger. "I was asked during the party about the hullabaloo this afternoon, and when I mentioned who was involved only one of my listeners thought they recognized David's name. David seemed to make a point of not mixing with editors from other genres.''

"If he had no power or standing with people, he didn't waste his time on them," Ralph commented. "I'm sure a few of them know your name, Diane, but probably not much more. I think we ought to try eliminating those of our own genre first. If we eliminate them all, we can then spread out to the horror people.''

"I think the police are trying almost the same thing," Lynn put in with a chuckle. "Their method of elimination seemed to be those who didn't have a grudge against David, which means they didn't get very far. We writers detested him for those so-called reviews he constantly printed, and other editors disliked him for the bad name he brought to their profession. I doubt if they found anyone at all who was willing to say a good word for him.''

"Ralph might have been the exception to that," Bill leaned forward to say. "He's the only one I can think of offhand who never got blasted in David's review column. He must have been a fan of yours, Ralph.''

"Fans like him I can do without," Ralph answered with a grimace, ignoring Bill's bland look. "I told the police exactly what I thought of the man and, since there were no ladies present, I used the appropriate language. That lieutenant didn't seem surprised to hear it.''

"He was surprised when he heard it from me," Lynn stated, her smile now quietly devilish. "I asked why they hadn't charged me yet, considering the fact that I'd talked about killing David off in front of any number of witnesses. That man Gerard tried to tell me I was signing books when the body was discovered, and I had to laugh in his face. The time of death was being placed at about an hour to an hour and a half before discovery, and I hadn't even been asked where I was at that time.''

"Now how did you come up with *that*?" Gray demanded. "If that came about through deductive reasoning, I'm going to push for getting rid of Gerard and giving *you* his job.''

"Lieutenant Gerard is still young," Lynn said almost smugly. "He'll learn. And of course I didn't get that from deductive reasoning. I got it from a young officer who happens to be a fan of mine. The poor thing had no idea how much he was telling me. He was intent on impressing me with the importance of his position."

"So it was done some time before the signing started," Ralph mused, looking at Lynn with fond pride. "I'd been going to mention that Angela Wilkes left the signing before the rest of us, but now that's no longer significant."

"I noticed that too," Diane said with a nod. "And I have a feeling the time of death involves me somehow, too, only I can't for the moment think of how. Did you find out anything else, Lynn?"

"The way David died," Lynn said with satisfaction. "Bill told us about the blow to the front of the head, producing all that blood. Well, the medical examiner was fairly certain that that wasn't the death blow. The back of the skull was also crushed, showing he'd been hit more than once, but the medical examiner couldn't tell if the frontal blow came before the others or after."

"The autopsy should tell him that, but how do *we* find out when it does?" Diane asked, now sounding fretful. "Knowing which came first is so important, but the police will undoubtedly keep the information to themselves."

"Why is it important?" Gray asked, watching as the others nodded at what Diane had said. "As long as he died of the bludgeoning rather than from poison or a bullet or a knife, what difference does it make which blow came first?"

"The way the blows are arranged makes all the difference," Diane said, trying to be patient. "If he was struck from behind first, that most likely means there were two of them and they had a reason for adding the frontal blow. If he was struck first from the front, there didn't necessarily have to be two attackers."

"And if the frontal blow came first, he was talking either to someone he trusted, or someone he wasn't afraid of," Lynn added when she saw Gray's expression. "From the description we've had of that corridor, it isn't likely anyone would have been able to sneak up behind David while he was waiting for some unknown person to meet him. He had to be engaged in talking to that person in order for him to be surprised, and then it doesn't matter whether he trusted that person or not."

"But if he did trust the person he was talking to," Ralph took up the tale again, "or if he wasn't afraid of him or her, the unknown could have gotten close enough to stun him with the frontal blow, and then finish him off with the rest. In that case, an accomplice wouldn't be needed."

"And if the frontal blow came afterward, that means something, too," Diane resumed, trying not to show how the word *accomplice* disturbed her. "Either the murderers were counting on the M.E.'s being unable to tell that it hadn't come first, which would help with framing me, or someone hated David so much that they wanted to hurt him even after he was dead. Frankly, I can't decide which of those possibilities bothers me more."

"You're jumping to conclusions, Diane," Gray said when Diane's gaze went to the wine that was left in her glass. "There's nothing to say the murderer hates you just as much. Making you the prime suspect of this piece is probably only a matter of convenience, something that has to be done if they're going to get away with it. Now, how will we begin our investigation? By checking alibis for the time of death? And what will we do if some of the others of your group want to help us?"

"Ralph and Lynn can claim seniority and exclusivity," Bill suggested with a grin. "They'll tell them the one about too many cooks, and then charm the socks off them. But I think you all had better consider making Anita an exception to the shutout. If she hadn't been called in to talk to the lieutenant, she would have been right with us when we followed Diane up here."

"Wait a minute, I think that's it," Diane said suddenly, leaning forward. "Alibis and Anita. Bill, didn't you tell me she mentioned she'd tried to call me in my suite, but got no answer? I decided it must have been the time I was in the tub, but what if that call was somehow deliberately blocked?

If that was when the murder was taking place, I don't even have an unsupported alibi.''

"And I'm sure that man Gerard has the point out of her by now," Lynn said, just as suddenly vexed. "He may be young, but he certainly has talent and potential. He doesn't seem to have asked any of us for an alibi, but I'll bet he's been getting the information in other ways. And I'll also bet that checking alibis won't help us."

"Why not?" Ralph demanded. "Everyone has to have been somewhere— Oh."

"You see it now," Lynn said with a nod of approval. "I was taking a nap in my room, and you and Bill were undoubtedly in your own rooms, getting into your costumes. Or are you two sharing accommodations?"

"Unfortunately, no," Ralph answered sourly. "We're more comfortable having separate rooms when the rates are this reasonable, which means even we four can't account for our whereabouts. And at that time of day, it must be the same for everyone. A pity he wasn't killed during the night, when there might have been a few illicit assignations that would eliminate some of us."

"Are you saying everyone should sleep around, just in case there's a murder?" Bill asked Ralph with a grin. "If you intend to put that in the next Daniel King mystery, we're going to have to talk about it first."

"At this rate, there may not *be* another Daniel King mystery," Ralph came back. "We may be spending the next twenty years of our lives trying to figure out who was where when this murder was committed. After that we can tackle who might have done it."

"You youngsters may have twenty years to spend on this, but I have better things planned for my time," Lynn said very firmly. "If we don't get this figured out by the end of the weekend, our suspects will scatter and take all our clues with them. And if the police find themselves at a dead end, they may decide to go with the circumstantial case they have against Diane. If we don't want that happening, we'd better start doing some thinking."

"Then let's go with the usual breakdown—means, motive and opportunity," Ralph said, back to making lists. "Everyone in sight seems to have had the opportunity, so for the time being we'll eliminate that one. Everyone also seems to have had a motive, but there's a big difference between hating someone and hating them enough to kill them. We'll have to interview everybody, to see if we can find a reason for that extra slice of hatred. And means. Since someone had to have taken that candlestick out of Diane's suite, it might be possible to find out who."

"Especially if they were forced to bribe a member of the hotel staff," Lynn said with hopeful satisfaction. "We can work on those two lines of inquiry tomorrow, when everyone's available and most of the police are out of the way, and that just leaves tonight. Diane, dear girl, is anyone using the second bedroom of your suite?"

"Why, no," Diane answered, surprised by the sudden question. "I came alone. Do you want to take a look at it?"

"What I'd like is to use it," Lynn said, a definite sharpness in her gaze. "If the enemy is going to try something else to set the frame more firmly in place, what you need is someone who can give you an unshakable alibi."

"Having you there with Diane is the best idea I've heard yet, and for this company that's saying something," Bill said in a very dry voice, obviously speaking for everyone.

"We'll stop at your room to let you pack a bag, and then we'll escort you and Diane home," Ralph said with firm decision. "I think we'd all better check the suite before Diane goes back to it. If something incriminating has been left there in her absence, we don't want her finding it without witnesses around. That way no one can say it's a piece of evidence she was trying to hide."

"And there we have a second good idea," Bill said with an approving nod, "I'm going to suggest a third one. Since it's still relatively early we have time for a nightcap, which I think we can all make good use of. Once the investigating starts tomorrow, we'll have to keep our heads clear."

"It won't matter that much for you, Bill," Ralph said at once, a gleam in his eyes. "Everyone knows editors can't think—all they can do is take advantage of the creativity of writers. And draw obscure hieroglyphics with red crayons.''

''That's red *pencils*, Ralph,'' Bill corrected mildly while the others laughed, turning around to look for a waitress. ''And it happens to be copy editors who use them, not editors. We specialize in child care and infant psychology, and that way we can handle all the writers we have to.''

Diane joined in the laughter again, but only for forms' sake. On the inside she was suddenly cold and frightened, especially after Ralph's last suggestion. Was it possible the murderers had moved already? Would they really find something incriminating in her suite? Diane didn't want to think about it, but she really had no choice. She *had* to think about it—and face it—if she was going to help save herself from those who wanted to see her convicted of murder.

She'd been thinking how nice it would be to get back to her bed and lie down, but now couldn't help wondering if she'd be doing it alone. What if she got back to find another dead body?

GRAY LISTENED to the banter with half an ear while he lost the rest of himself in thought.

Those people were incredible. For all intents and purposes they were untrained amateurs, but they'd reached the same conclusions he had and probably just as fast. Or faster. He'd been thinking of them as nothing but a bunch of writers, people who were able to sound clever in books because they started out already knowing what was going on. It looked as if he'd been wrong. They saw what was going on around them and thought about it, then drew the proper conclusions.

And they used whatever sources of information came to hand. He and most of the rest of the world had enjoyed hours and hours of reading Lynn Haverstock mysteries. Her characters were always open, honest and honorable. He had never dreamed the old woman would stoop to pumping a fan for official information. And apparently the fan had been taken in the same way. It had saved Gray a good deal of trouble.

Ralph Teak was almost as sharp. The suggestion that they search Diane's suite for unexpected surprises had been a good one, perfectly in keeping with the sort of thinking found in his Daniel King mysteries. Gray had read a few of them, too, and although they tended to be so intricate they were hard to unravel, he'd also enjoyed them.

Bill Raglan hadn't contributed much, but his calm steadiness seemed to be keeping the others from getting overly emotional. Gray wondered if his suggestion of a drink had been for everyone else's sake, or simply for his own. He'd seen the man putting away a lot of alcohol that day, but it hadn't seemed to be affecting him.

But that could be bad rather than good. Was Bill *too* calm, using the drinking to steady his nerves? It was a point to keep in mind...

And last but not least, Diane. She'd kept right up with the others, and had even contributed ideas of her own. When he'd seen how upset she was he'd wanted to put his arm around her, but they hadn't "known" each other long enough for that. To her he was simply someone who had stepped in to give her a hand a couple of times, a virtual stranger who had insisted on helping even more...

As long as she was willing to let him help, he'd hear everything her group came up with.

And it would also let him steer her away from wherever "the pirate" might want to be. She seemed determined to find the pirate to learn whatever he might know, but that would just get her into deeper trouble. If it became necessary, the pirate would come forward to have a talk with the police, but first the weekend had to be put to use.

In as many different ways as possible...

WHEN THEY HAD FINISHED their drinks they all went to Lynn's room to let her get what she needed, and then headed for Diane's suite. Diane had taken the opportunity to admire Lynn's walking stick, a magnificent thing of gnarly black wood with a heavy grain, bound in silver both top and bottom. Lynn insisted the silver was just plate, which made sense. But Diane wondered. There had been a murder weapon just like it in óne of Lynn's books, and *that* stick had been bound in pure silver.

"Well, here we are," Diane announced when they arrived at the doors of the suite. She reached into her girdle belt to retrieve her card key. "In another minute we'll know if Santa Claus has been here."

"If the presence of a gift is that obvious, I'll be very much surprised," Ralph said, trying the doorknob before Diane put the card to the slot. "I can't decide whether or not I like the idea that these doors can't be left unlocked even if you want them that way. You have to push out the inner part of the night lock to keep them from closing completely and locking, which means you can never have anyone sneaking up on your hero or heroine because they forgot to lock the door."

"Right now I find that delightfully comforting," Diane said as she opened the door and switched on the light, her tone extremely dry. "Daniel King may enjoy showing off his prowess when he's jumped from behind, but some of the rest of us would rather let that opportunity pass."

"Opportunities ignored become opportunities regretted," Ralph said in a lecture voice that didn't quite match his grin. "If you're ready for anything, you can't be surprised. Let's take a good look at where that candlestick was standing."

Diane began to lead the way to the right, but stopped dead before she reached the desk. Ralph had been absolutely right; there was something here she *hadn't* been prepared for, and surprise was the least of what she felt.

"That can't be where the murder weapon was," Bill said in a mild voice, while everyone else stood silently and stared. "It's still there."

Chapter Eight

"Don't anyone touch it," Ralph cautioned at once, though no one had moved toward the candlestick. "Diane, where's the phone in here? I'm going to see if Lieutenant Gerard is still in the hotel."

"Thank goodness," Bill said in true relief. "I was sure the bunch of you would decide to investigate this on your own. We're much better off letting the police handle it."

"We're better off telling the police before they find out about it themselves," Lynn corrected, frowning at the innocent-looking candlestick. "If they came in here with a search warrant, what are the chances they'd believe Diane had no idea that thing had been put there?"

"Since they didn't see how she obviously expected *nothing* to be there, no chance at all," Ralph said. "Diane, the phone?"

"It's somewhere in the desk," Diane said, frowning at the candlestick the way Lynn was doing. "Apparently Santa Claus did leave his present right out in the open, but I can't make any sense of it. Why another candlestick, and where did it come from?"

"We'll look into the where as soon as Ralph is off the phone," Lynn said, watching as the search for the instrument ended in the deep side drawer to Ralph's right as he sat at the desk. "We'll have to be careful not to disturb anything forensics might be able to discover, but we can still look."

Diane nodded with a determination matching Lynn's. In a way it was annoying that things had taken such a strange turn, and that Lynn and Ralph were as confused as she was. If they hadn't been they would have at least ventured a guess as to why the thing was there. What could the murderers hope to gain by replacing the object that had been the murder weapon?

"The lieutenant was getting ready to leave, so we called just in time," Ralph announced as he hung up the phone. "They said he'd be right up."

"Good," Lynn said with a nod, then gestured to the desk. "Is there anything in there we can use to mark the candlestick's position?"

Ralph opened the center drawer of the desk, located two pads of paper with the hotel's logo on them, and pulled them out. Using the pads he built a square corner against which the candlestick's position was clearly outlined, and then he reached for the handkerchief in the breast pocket of his devil's tux. He touched no more of the candlestick than absolutely necessary even with the handkerchief, and was just able to lift the thing and peer underneath. As soon as that was done he replaced the object, removed both handkerchief and pads, and then sat back in the chair.

"Well?" Lynn demanded. "What did it say? Is it from a room, or does it decorate a more public part of the hotel?"

"It's from a room," Ralph answered, suddenly reaching for the phone again. "And it's heavier than I thought it would be— Operator, room 337, please."

Once again everyone stood silently as they waited, and at the back of the group Gray was privately amused. Ralph Teak hadn't had to be told that the hotel operator would never part with the name of the guest in room 337, so he'd simply called the room. If and when someone answered, he could make the effort to find out who they were. It looked like Gray might be able to sit back and put his feet up while these people did most of his work for him.

"No, Operator, I don't think I will leave a message," Ralph said after a moment. "I'll try again later or tomorrow. Thank you."

"Room 337," Lynn mused while Ralph hung up. "And whose ever room it is, they aren't there. Which rooms do you and Bill have, Ralph?"

"We're in 302 and 304," Ralph said, "so we don't even share a corridor with 337. Otherwise we might have seen someone we knew going in or out of the place. The lieutenant should have a list of everyone involved and their room numbers. I wonder if he'll be willing to share the information."

"Him, share?" Diane said with a short laugh, remembering her own efforts to get Gerard to answer a question. "He doesn't believe in sharing the wealth unless it's you sharing with him. He—"

A knock at the door interrupted her. Gray made himself useful by going to answer the knock. When Gerard stepped inside he wasn't alone. Two other men in suits and one in uniform followed him, and the lieutenant's expression was impossible to read.

"Mr. Teak," he pronounced, as though the name itself was highly significant. "The desk clerk said there was something you wanted to show me."

"Don't worry, Lieutenant, it isn't another body," Ralph said with barely restrained amusement. "We found something that seems to relate to the first body, so we called you immediately."

"It always does my heart good to meet civic-minded citizens," Gerard commented. "Have you, by any chance, found an accusation written in the victim's blood?"

"Not quite," Ralph answered with a grin.

Diane barely restrained her own laughter. For a policeman with a rather grim job, Gerard had an interesting sense of humor.

"We found something we shouldn't have, and therefore something you should know about. Diane tells us the murder weapon belongs there." Ralph's finger pointed to the intruding candlestick.

Four sets of official eyes were immediately locked on the object, and Gerard's, at least, were glinting. "And how did the group of you come to make the discovery?'' he asked, a bit more than curiosity in his voice.

"Merely doing our duty as civic-minded citizens, Lieutenant," Ralph returned innocently. "*We* happen to know that Diane couldn't possibly have committed the murder, so we decided to search the suite to see if anything incriminating had been planted here. We got no farther than this room and this desk."

"But we can't quite decide how a replacement candlestick would put Diane more deeply under suspicion," Lynn added, sounding like a sweet, slightly bewildered, little old lady.

"It could be argued that she thought the mere possession of a candlestick in her room would *clear* her of suspicion," Gerard said, watching as the other two men in suits made their way over to the intruding object.

Ralph's answer to that was a small laugh of absolute incredulity.

Gerard ignored the comment and watched intently as his two men dusted both desk and candlestick with fingerprint powder, but didn't seem surprised when one finally looked up to shake his head.

"No fingerprints on either desk surface or candlestick, not even ones that would turn out to belong to the housekeeping staff," Gerard interpreted, showing only faint annoyance as he moved closer. "And I was all set to find out the dead man had touched it last. Let's see who the thing belongs to."

He lifted it with less care than Ralph had used, checked the bottom and put it back, then got out the small notebook Diane had seen him writing in during her interview. He flipped through a number of pages, found the one he wanted, used a pen from his jacket to note something, then put the small book away again.

"Well?" Ralph said, now sounding friendly and reasonable. "In whose room does it belong?"

"It belongs in the room of someone at the convention," Gerard answered with equal friendliness and a matching smile. "Ms. Philips, since you were going to allow your friends to search your suite, would you mind if my men did it instead? Just to save us a second trip up here if anything *is* found, you understand.''

"And to save you the trouble of having to come back with a search warrant," Diane said, needing to show the man she did understand her position in this mess. "Please do, Lieutenant, but I think I ought to mention something first. When I left here earlier in the evening, there were no messages written in blood accusing me of David's murder."

"We'll be sure to keep that in mind," Gerard said with a quick grin. The candlestick, wrapped in a plastic evidence bag, was left in the possession of the uniformed officer, while the other three went about the chore of searching. Diane showed them how to use the "secret" passages, and then there was nothing to do but wait.

The sitting room was searched last, and Diane found herself a good deal more nervous than she'd thought she would be. There were so many things that could have been planted to make her look guilty beyond all doubt, things that would have been simple and easy to arrange. A chapter written in her style, describing David's murder, for instance, or— "Ms. Philips," Gerard said, interrupting her morbid thoughts, "We're finished now, and we thank you for your cooperation."

"You do have to tell us whether or not you found anything, Lieutenant," Gray put in mildly, saving Diane the effort of asking. "Since she did have a choice in the matter of letting you search now, the least you owe her is peace of mind—or a formal accusation."

"No accusation, Mr. Grayson," Gerard answered at once, glancing apologetically at Diane. "We found nothing that shouldn't have been there, and certainly nothing of an incriminating nature. I'll admit I was willing to settle for even a shopping list if it was written in blood, but some days you have no luck at all. I bid you a good-night."

He looked around to include everyone in the wish, seemed pleased at the faint smile Diane showed in response to his joke, then led his men out of the room.

"I have the feeling he knows we know what room that candlestick came from," Ralph said, staring at the closed door with an amused expression. "You'll notice he didn't ask us if we'd touched the thing."

"I would guess he's decided to treat us as though we were skilled professional criminals," Lynn said, smiling. "He's realized we have the expertise for it, so he won't waste his time or ours on nonsense. Which means, of course, we'll have to wait until the morning to find out about our clue. If we try again tonight and step on his heels while *he's* investigating, we may end up locked in a cell. Well, are we ready to call it a night, or is there something left for us to do?"

"There's one quick thing left," Ralph said, getting out of the chair to circle the desk. "Gerard said there was nothing in this suite that didn't belong here, but for him that's just a matter of opinion. I think Diane should take a quick look around before we leave you ladies to your rest."

"Ralph, you have one of the most devious minds I've ever come across," Diane said with a wry grimace. "I'll do your looking around for you, but if I find anything I'm going to call Gerard and confess. That way I should be able to get a little rest."

"Just a few more moments, and then you can have your rest *without* a prison uniform," Ralph said soothingly. "It's better to be safe than sorry, child, especially where murder is concerned."

Diane felt as though she'd heard enough homilies to last a lifetime, but she didn't say so aloud. She led the group from the bedrooms to the bathroom and back to the study as quickly as she could, checking through her things with the practiced eye of a convention-goer, knowing anything out of place or out of the ordinary would jump out at her. Since nothing jumped in any of the rooms, she was able to turn to Ralph with weary satisfaction.

"Since there weren't any bodies behind the drapes, let's take this up again after we've all had some sleep. A healthy mind can't do any thinking if its healthy body is falling off its feet."

"If you're going to rewrite perfectly good sayings, it certainly is time we left," Ralph said with a pretense of pain. Then he gave Diane a warm smile. "You get your rest, child, and try not to worry. Lynn will be with you for the night, and we others will rejoin you tomorrow. I give you my word they won't get you without a fight."

Diane yielded to the urge to give Ralph a hug and a kiss on the cheek, gave the same to Bill, then stopped to laugh awkwardly when it suddenly became Gray's turn. The big man grinned and offered a handshake to settle the problem, but she couldn't see being quite that formal with someone who was there only to help *her*. She leaned up and gave him his own kiss on the cheek, feeling odd as she did it, and then the three men were gone behind the closing door.

"Make sure it catches all the way, then double-lock and latch it," Lynn directed from her chair. "Once that's done we'll be able to sleep in peace."

"It's going to take more than a couple of locks before *I* can sleep in peace tonight," Diane said with a sigh, nevertheless doing as Lynn had suggested before turning back to her. "Can you think of any reason at all for that replacement candlestick to be there? I have the strangest feeling it should be telling us something, but I've suddenly gone deaf."

"That's not affliction talking, it's exhaustion," Lynn told Diane firmly, using her stick to help get herself out of the chair. "Since I'm speaking from the experience of a like condition, you can take my word for it. Tomorrow we'll all see things more clearly—and hear them as well."

"For the sake of my sanity, I think I'll accept that without argument," Diane acceded with a smile, then began looking around. "Where's your bag? I'll carry it to the bedroom for you."

"That's already been done by your young man," Lynn answered, for some reason walking a lot more slowly than she had earlier. "I'm not surprised that you didn't see him doing it. Most of his actions seem to be a whisper through the shouting of life.''

"He *doesn't* seem to attract attention unless he wants to,'' Diane agreed, smiling faintly as she remembered the way he'd suddenly appeared during her interview with Gerard. "But he's not *my* young man. He just seems to have picked up the habit of rescuing me from uncomfortable situations. Once this weekend is over, I expect he'll take his memories and go home.''

"You think his interest in you is only passing?'' Lynn asked, amused again. "If that's true, then you really are tired. What will you do if he doesn't go home quite as fast as you expect?''

"Why— I don't know,'' Diane admitted, surprised by the question. She hadn't had much chance to think about Gray. He was certainly nice, and attractive in a quiet way, and he did seem concerned about her....

But there was also someone who claimed to be her secret admirer, someone she felt a very great need to find out more about. Dreams may be silly, and a waste of valuable time, and only rarely work out the way you want them to, but there were times you just *had* to take the chance.

"Personally I think Gray is a fascinating young man,'' Lynn said, "but I tend to think that about most young men. I'm afraid I'm degenerating into a dirty old lady.''

"And I think you'd love being a dirty old lady, but just haven't the talent for it,'' Diane said with a laugh, leading the way through into the passage. "This is how you get into the bathroom. While you're making yourself comfortable in your room, I'll turn out the sitting room lights. If anyone wants to break in, they can do it in the dark.''

"Making it easy for them *would* be rather foolish,'' Lynn agreed, moving toward the second bedroom. "Except for necessities like closing doors and turning lights on and off, we'll save the tour for tomorrow. This really has been a very long day, even for night people like me.''

GRAY'S SUITE was only a short way down from Diane's on the other side of the hall, an arrangement that met with Ralph Teak's approval. He led Bill Raglan toward the elevators after insisting that Gray call them if there was any trouble.

The phone was ringing when Gray opened the door, and he had to race across the room to reach it before it stopped.

"Well, it's about time." Jack's sour voice came through clearly. "Nice of you to interrupt your good time to remember you're there for a reason."

"I'm having an even better time than you know," Gray responded, leaning back in the desk chair. "There's been a murder, and one of the people here is a prime, A-one suspect."

"It happened at the convention," Jack said at once, now sounding faintly excited, his words in no way a question. "I'm not surprised that it happened, only that it happened so soon. I was calling to tell you that it looked like Saturday would be the day."

"What have you found out?" Gray demanded, now leaning forward just a little. "The convention crowd *is* involved, but we've tentatively eliminated the horror people and are concentrating on the mystery group. They're the ones most closely connected to the victim."

"You know I got the name of that hotel from Ed's papers," Jack said. "But that was all we had, an ad boasting about how great a hotel it was with this weekend's dates written in by hand. My first thought was whether there was more, and if so, where would it be? That was when I called Ellie, Ed's wife, and asked her to go through his desk."

"And there was something there about the convention?" Gray asked, hoping there was more in spite of Jack's lack of enthusiasm. "Did the something name names, even if they were just Ed's guesses?"

"Only the convention was named fully, and with a flyer rather than a handwritten note," Jack said, drowning Gray's hopes. "It also had the Saturday date circled, all the mystery writers' names were highlighted, and in block letters near the circled date it said, 'D-day.' Was it one of the writers who got it?''

"No, it was a loudmouthed editor-type," Gray said, then told Jack everything that had happened, including all of his own actions. "After I left the scene of the crime I knew I had to get out of the costume before the police arrived, but I made one stop on the way to my suite. I thought it was worth the risk to search the victim's room before the police did it."

"Did you find anything we can use?" Jack asked, but he didn't sound terribly hopeful.

"Beyond a very expensive wardrobe, there wasn't much of anything there at all," Gray said, seeing the room again in his mind. "Everything was neatly put away. The only things on the desk were a copy of the convention flyer and two books. One of the books was written by Diane Philips, the police's major suspect in this thing, and the other was by Angela Wilkes, who's also here at the convention."

"Do you think there's anything in that?" Jack asked.

"He was supposed to be on a panel with them and another reviewer on Saturday," Gray answered. "If that wasn't the reason he had the books, it may be a while before we know the real one. But that isn't what's bothering me about all this. Everyone seems to have a better than average motive for offing the victim, which means it doesn't *feel* right. If a vote was held whether to convict his murderer or give him or her a medal, people would start freeing up their calendar to attend the medal ceremony."

"Maybe the organization we're after has decided to do a little pro bono work," Jack suggested dryly. "You know, handle a freebie that won't get anyone convicted, but will make a whole bunch of people feel good? If that turns out to be the truth, I'd be tempted to put together a short list of my own for them to consider."

"I'm not ready yet to concede that possibility," Gray said with a grin at Jack's sarcastic tone. "And if I ever need to put a list together, I can take care of it myself."

"I enjoy associating with capable people," Jack said, just as dryly as before. "Do you intend hanging around with the amateur detectives, or will you be doing some snooping on your own?"

"A bit of both," Gray said. "For amateurs these people are surprisingly good, and if they stumble into something dangerous I want to be there to pull them out again. But I'll have to pick my time carefully for wearing the pirate costume. And if it turns out to be the wrong time you may have to come to arrange my bail. Meanwhile, I have a more complete list of names for you to check, and you'll have to work as fast as possible. Come Sunday, everyone here will be heading home."

"Go ahead," Jack said, undoubtedly already taking notes. "But try to avoid my having to come out to arrange bail. With my health what it is I don't leave the city except for real emergencies. You'll just have to stay out of the hands of the police."

Gray chuckled as he went down the names on the mental list he'd made and said, "That's it for now. And be sure to continue using the automatic switchboard when you call. Punching in my room number after the beep puts you through without a live operator getting involved, and that's the way we'd better keep it. The police may decide to check all incoming and outgoing calls."

"I'll also sweep the line from this end," Jack promised. "If there are ears the next time I get you, I'll ask if you've decided to visit the city again before going home. If that happens, find a phone that doesn't go through the switchboard and call me back."

"Right," Gray acknowledged. "I hope it doesn't come to that."

"So do I," Jack agreed. "Watch yourself, and try to still be in one piece when I call back with your information."

"I'll try, but no promises," Gray said with another grin. "Have a good night, partner."

Jack muttered something that didn't sound very complimentary and then hung up, leaving Gray free to head for bed. His pirate's costume and body makeup were already back in the hiding place he'd prepared, so all he had left to think about was the next day and what progress they might make. And seeing again a redheaded harem queen, even though ordinary clothing would take the place of sheer golden veils and eye-catching sequins....

Chapter Nine

Waking up was a surprise for Diane, considering that she hadn't expected to be able to sleep.

"Which just goes to show how dumb your subconscious is," she muttered to herself as she checked the time. "You could have been attacked, framed or accused at any hour of the night. Wonderful sense of self preservation."

It was a lot earlier than she'd been afraid it was, so she felt slightly better as she got out of bed. There were a lot of things that had to be done that day, and a thought had come to her the night before about the original candlestick which had stood on the desk. She'd said no one had had access to it, and when she'd said it she'd thought it was the truth. But now she remembered something, and it might make a big difference.

It didn't take her long to dress. Her blue slacks and a white blouse with tennis shoes were perfect for the relaxed atmosphere of a convention where you walked around or stood most of the time. She thought Lynn might be awake by the time she was ready to leave, but there wasn't a sound behind the closed door to her bedroom.

"She did say she was night people," Diane reminded herself as she went to the desk in the study to find something to write a note on. "I usually lean that way myself, but not when there's the chance of a murder charge hanging over my head."

She used a piece from one of the pads of paper Ralph had found last night to tell Lynn she was going to breakfast and would see her later. Then she hung the note on the hook that opened the door to the bathroom. She didn't mention the digging she also intended to do. That went without saying.

Diane took the elevator down to the ground floor. Once she was settled in the restaurant with her breakfast ordered, she pulled out the schedule of panels and convention events. It was highly unlikely that anyone would be so broken up over David's death that they would cancel the scheduled offerings, so she'd better pay attention to where she was supposed to be when.

The ghoul who was her waiter brought the food out quickly, but not before Diane had found the two panels and individual talk group she was down for. The first panel was at two o'clock that afternoon, and had Lynn and Angela Wilkes as her co-panelists, with Anita Rutledge moderating. The topic was, "Mystery Women— How They Do Committing a Man's Crime," and Anita was also supposed to give her views as an editor on women who wrote mysteries. The usual thing wrapped up in pretty words that were supposed to tell people it was a brilliant new topic.

At eight-thirty that night was the panel David had told her about, the one he'd been so looking forward to. Diane put orange marmalade on her toast as she thought about it, then took a bite as she made her decision. If that panel wasn't canceled she'd be there, just as she'd promised herself she would be. Living or dead, David would no longer be stampeding her.

The individual talk group they'd come up with was scheduled earlier than the second panel, at six o'clock that evening, in one of the larger conference halls on the second floor. All the pro guests would be there at the same time, seated with their fans in different parts of the hall. What a fan would do if he or she wanted to be part of two or more groups was something the organizers obviously hadn't thought about, but they were certain to *hear* about it in no uncertain terms.

"But that's amateurs for you," Diane muttered to her scrambled eggs. It took a lot of hard work, intelligent thought, and some sort of experience to run a convention properly, but there were those around who thought they could do it simply by deciding they could. The best Diane could charitably find to say was that at least they hadn't scheduled her for anything on Sunday. Panels on the day you were going home weren't bad if you had a car and could make your own departure schedule, but when you had to use the train . . .

"Can I get you anything else, miss?" her ghoul stopped by the table to ask. "A refill on your coffee, maybe?"

"Yes, please," Diane agreed with a smile, then waited until the man had returned with the coffeepot. "I wonder if I could ask you a very silly question."

"Most people just go ahead and ask," the man said with a grin, carefully refilling her cup. "It's a part of the job we're told to expect, so don't feel as if you're intruding on anything private. Is it about the costumes and makeup?"

"Of course," Diane said with a grin. "What else? I was just wondering if the people who use the streets and highways around here have gotten used to the sight of the undead on their way to work. And what in the world do you do if you happen to get a flat when you're only halfway here?"

"We thank everything we hold dear that we don't put on our makeup until after we get to work," the man answered with a laugh. "I could just see myself ignoring screams and crashes as I sweated to change the tire in sixty seconds flat. Before the police or the guys from a funny farm got there to help me."

"Oh, that is lucky," Diane said with a chuckle for the picture he'd evoked. "It avoids headlines like, 'Ghoul, Zombie and Vampire Carpool in Connecticut.' So there's a place in the hotel where you change and put on makeup. With everyone on the staff commuting, that must make for a lot of relief."

"Not all of us commute, at least not all the time," the man said. "There are staff dorm rooms here, for those who report in early to avoid coming bad weather, or those who get stuck here because of the weather. They want to make sure they never have a hotel full of guests and only a handful of staff. They also offer a bonus of the weekend off for anyone who sleeps here the full week before.''

''That makes a lot of sense,'' Diane said with a thoughtful nod, and then she cocked her head to study the ghoul a little more closely. ''I suppose those of you who work here all the time get to recognize each other even through all that makeup. To tell the truth, I was having trouble telling you from the other ghouls waiting table here. You weren't just passing by, were you? I mean, if I leave you a special tip for being nice enough to answer my questions, you *will* be the one who brought my food and are therefore entitled to take money from the table?''

''Oh, yes, ma'am,'' the ghoul assured her with a big grin. ''I'm the one who served you, so I'm the one who gets to take any tips. And we *do* learn to tell each other apart. So anything you leave will not only be gratefully appreciated, it will also reach me for sure.''

He gave Diane a pleasant nod and then left, obviously intending to see if any more of those at his tables wanted their coffee freshened. Diane had had her thoughts freshened even more than her coffee, so she sat back to think about what her next move should be. She knew what she wanted to find out, but what she needed was a plan to get the information.

The bottom of her coffee cup brought with it a sound working plan, so Diane left a good tip in cash for her cooperative waiter, charged her meal to her suite, then left the restaurant. There was no sign of the police that morning, but that didn't mean one or two members of the force weren't lurking about in plain clothes, and it didn't mean their brothers in arms wouldn't be around later in force. If she expected to get anything done, it had to be right then.

There were only two people behind the registration desk, but one of them was a ghoul like the one who'd registered her. No one was checking in or out at this time of the morning, which made things much simpler.

"Excuse me, but are you the ghoul who checked me in yesterday afternoon?" she asked, then laughed a bit self-consciously. "I didn't think I'd have the nerve to ask the question like that, and now that I've asked it I feel like an idiot. I hope you know what I was really trying to say."

"Of course I do, miss," the man answered with a ghastly smile, "and the answer to your question is, yes, I probably am. I was on duty here yesterday afternoon until six."

"Oh, good," Diane said with innocent enthusiasm. "Then you should be able to answer a question for me. I did something silly yesterday, and it wasn't until this morning that I figured out how to undo it."

The man was paying her polite attention, and probably hoping that she wouldn't tell him her life story. Diane had a story, all right, but it had nothing to do with *anyone's* life.

"You see, I'm booked into a suite, and the nicest zombie went up with me to show me how it works," she burbled on. "He told me I didn't have to tip him for doing that, so I didn't. But later on I got to thinking that he'd only said that for form and I should have done it anyway. Is there some way you can tell me who he is, so I can give him that tip?"

She stopped then and waited for an answer, but made sure the desk clerk could see her bubbling and burbling just under the surface. If he refused to tell her what she wanted to know she would try to babble him into it, and that should do well enough for a man's version of a fate worse than death.

"Ah, well, let's see," the man temporized after clearing his throat. "There were four bellmen on duty yesterday afternoon, and I'm not quite sure I remember which of them did the suite instruction. Let me see . . ."

When his voice trailed off thoughtfully, Diane knew exactly what he was waiting for, but she didn't let herself catch on too fast. The character she was pretending to be was a little on the slow side, so she let a few moments pass before suddenly coming down with revelation.

"Oh, oh, do let me thank you in advance for whatever help you can give me," she quickly bubbled, handing over a ten-dollar bill. The tip was much too high for any legitimate purpose and too low for an illegal one, but that would just reassure the man. He would be certain Diane had more than a tip she wanted to give to the mysterious zombie, so there should be no reason to hold back his name.

"John Dixon must have been the one to go with you," the man said with a smile as soon as he made the tenner disappear. "There was only one other suite booked yesterday afternoon, and I happen to remember Alfie handled that one. But if you're looking for John, you may be out of luck. I think I heard him say he had the weekend off, so he's probably not in the hotel. Sorry."

Of course the man was sorry. He'd parted with information for a price, but the information would do Diane no good at all—or so he thought.

"Oh, how disappointing," she pouted, showing nothing that said she'd more than half expected it to be that way. "Well, if he's not here, he's not. Thanks again for your help."

Diane was sure there was a perplexed look on the ghoul's face as she simply turned and walked away, but it served him right. He could spend the rest of the day wondering why she hadn't demanded her money back, and would undoubtedly never consider the possibility that she'd gotten what she'd wanted.

Which she had. Armed with the name she needed, Diane visited the gift shop in the normal part of the hotel, bought a box of envelopes, then took one out and put John Dixon's name on it. The rest of the box she left behind a potted plant. After putting a ten-dollar bill in the envelope before sealing it, she headed for the elevators.

Diane got out on the second floor, but when she reached her suite she just kept going. Right then she was trying the shakiest part of her plan, the part that was pure deduction. She couldn't have asked anyone the location of the staff dorm area without arousing suspicion, but there was a definite possibility that she wouldn't need to ask. It had come to her that she might already know.

She retraced her steps toward the large second floor gathering room, but rather than go the entire way she took the lefthand curve that led to that sign claiming quicksand was ahead. She remembered how that arrow and the other sign warning about a falling rock zone had made her curious. Now she thought she had the puzzle figured out.

Beyond the quicksand arrow should be the staff area, there and not past the falling rock zone. Her reasoning for that was logical. Diane was sure that people who enjoyed dressing strangely for work would be more likely to consider their area a quicksand bog than a falling rock zone. Falling rocks were at the very least a nuisance, so Diane thought she knew what lay that way, too.

But her theory still had to be tested. There was a curve about twenty feet beyond the arrow, and once Diane rounded it and had gone another five paces, she let out the breath she hadn't realized she was holding. Just ahead on the left was a door marked Private that was standing open, and Diane caught just a glimpse of what looked like mirrors inside.

Moving up to the open doorway confirmed what the glimpse had suggested: here was where the staff members put on their makeup. Mirrors and counters lined three of the four walls of the large room; tubes, jars and bottles littered the counter; and straight-backed chairs stood side by side in front of it all. Strong fluorescent lighting was arranged at the top of the mirrors, but only the bank on the left wall was turned on just then, and there wasn't even anyone using those. As far as Diane could see, the room was empty.

"Everyone has already come on their shift or gone off it," she muttered, still looking around. She'd been hoping most of the staff would be elsewhere, but she did need someone to use her envelope on. How could she ask directions to where she could find the person named on the envelope, if there was no one around to ask?

"Now that sounds like a good reason for snooping if I happen to get caught at it," she murmured with a grin, stepping back out into the hall. "Honestly, officer, I was just looking for someone to ask directions from...."

She stopped the silliness at that point, a grimace replacing her grin. She was in enough trouble with the police. It would be best to find what she was looking for and then leave as quickly as possible.

Diane couldn't help noticing how quiet the area was as she began to look at the doors nearest the makeup room. There were other doors stretching all the way down the hall toward a small, private-looking bank of elevators, but the rooms nearest her seemed larger than those farther away. The first door on the left read Men and the opposite one on the right Women, but Diane had a sudden thought. It was natural to assume they were bathrooms for the staff, but just maybe . . .

Entering the door on the right, she took two steps into the room and grinned at what she saw. There were bathroom stalls to the left of the door, but to the right was a locker room. If there was a special place for putting on makeup, it stood to reason there was also a place for changing into costumes.

But that meant the locker room she had to check lay behind the door marked Men. Diane's grin died a second time, but her determination didn't vanish with it. She was a modern woman, after all, and above everything, practical. Walking into an empty men's locker room should be no harder than the women's. . . .

Right. Diane braced her shoulders, marched back out to the hall, looked around one last time in the vain hope of finding someone to ask other directions of, then had to give up. John Dixon could have slept in any of the dorm rooms lining the hall farther down, all of which were undoubtedly locked. Without someone to direct her, who might also be talked into giving her access to the room, the only hope she had left was the man's locker.

In some ways that was, after all, the better choice. If you share a room with people, hiding something you don't want them to find is a risky proposition. People tend to stumble over things by accident. If an alternate, more private place is available, why not use that instead.

"Okay, just open the door," she commanded herself in a mutter. "After you're inside, you'll see how easy it is."

Easy, right. She took a deep breath first, then turned the doorknob and opened the door a crack. A silence matching the one in the hall greeted her, which was as much encouragement as she could have hoped for. She slipped inside before something happened to make her change her mind.

The silence persisted as she moved to the right, the same direction the women's lockers had been in. Luck was with her in that the locker doors had personalized name signs. Even so, the dimness in the large room made some of them difficult to make out. But Diane wouldn't have used a flashlight even if she'd been silly enough to bring one. You can claim spur-of-the-moment bad judgment if you happen to get caught doing something you shouldn't, but not if you've come well prepared.

It took a number of minutes for her to make her way to the back of the large room, and by then her anxiety was increasing more than the dimness and heavy silence could account for. The windows in the room were way off to the left of the final row of lockers, and directly behind that row stood rack after rack of neatly hung uniforms and costumes.

Freshly cleaned outfits for the staff to claim when they needed them, Diane thought, moving to the left as she read name after name. There's nothing there but clothing, so why do I keep getting the feeling I'm being watched? Uniforms can't watch you, and costumes wouldn't want to bother.

The joke fell flat even as she thought it. She was spending as much time looking around as she was checking names, and because of that she couldn't help noticing that she was moving into the dimmest part of the room. It was now obvious John Dixon's locker was over there, where the light was poorest. As a dedicated amateur burglar she should have been pleased. Should have been, but wasn't quite.

Three lockers from the end she finally found it, thanks to the light green phosphorescent paint the name sign had been decorated with. The lockers around it were apparently empty, as there were no name signs and no locks on them. Some of the other lockers had had key locks, but Diane was pleased to see that John Dixon was one of the majority with a combination lock. There were excellent possibilities in *that* . . .

Like the fact that well-used combination locks were unbelievably easy to open. She'd researched how to do it for one of her books, taking lessons from an ex-thief turned security expert. He'd been a very good teacher, and she'd been a very good student . . .

It made Diane feel guilty to take advantage of something her research as a writer had taught her, but she was still more desperate than ashamed. If she didn't do something she would probably be charged with murder, and if *that* wasn't a good enough excuse to ignore proper manners, nothing was.

With determination, then, she reached for the lock, and that was when she heard the door opening. Someone was coming in, and the sureness of their stride said they belonged there. Diane froze where she stood, praying that the newcomer had a locker in front. But no such luck. His footsteps brought him toward the aisle she stood in, and if he came all the way back he couldn't possibly miss seeing her.

It isn't possible for other people to hear someone's heart pounding, but Diane discovered right then why so many of those who had pounding hearts thought it was. Her pulse was trying to deafen her as she slipped around the end of the bench and backed toward the last rack of clothes, praying that the shadows there were deep enough, that no one would turn on the lights, that whatever the newcomer was after would not be what she chose to hide behind . . .

She also prayed that he was a member of the staff, rather than one of the murderers coming to destroy evidence or steal something to help them in the next thing they tried. For some reason it hadn't occurred to her that she might actually run into one of the enemy, all alone in a place where she might see and recognize him and have him see and recognize her.

If Diane's pulse had been pounding to begin with, it was now thundering. She could feel her hands trembling from the noise as she tried to back up without sound, fear turning her mouth dry and her mind blank. Don't let him see me, she prayed, please don't let him see me . . .

And then her prayer was answered, but not in the way she would have chosen. Just as the rack of costumes hid her from whoever might be coming up the central aisle, her last step backed her into what couldn't be anything but a hard, broad body. She felt the blood drain from her face as she began to cry out and run. Neither action was allowed her. A wide palm came to cover her mouth and a metal bar of an arm circled her waist, and Diane Philips, no-longer-fearless investigator, was caught but good.

Chapter Ten

The first thought coming into Diane's frantic mind was idiotic, but nevertheless true. Although she was too petrified even to struggle against whoever was holding her, she hadn't fainted and wasn't likely to. That had to mean she could count on never fainting for the rest of her life; if this situation hadn't made it happen, nothing ever would.

Her second thought was that the man behind her and the one coming in weren't on the same side, whatever side they each happened to be on. It astonished her that she was able to realize that in the midst of pure panic, but it still didn't tell her what to do.

If she continued struggling, the newcomer would probably hear it and come to investigate, but she didn't know if she wanted to attract his attention. If he was a member of the staff she did, but what if he wasn't? And what if the man holding her was the enemy?

If she made the wrong choice she could end up dead, and it would be no one's fault but her own.

The newcomer had reached the rack and was slowly shifting hangers, apparently looking for something in particular. The hand over her mouth was keeping her from making any sound and the arm around her waist held her still, but aside from that she wasn't being hurt. Would that continue, or change as soon as they were alone...?

And then she noticed something she hadn't consciously noted before. Even in the deep shadow she was able to tell

the man holding her wore a long-sleeved, light-colored shirt.
That, in turn, made her realize the man she was leaning
against was wearing some sort of long metal necklace.

Like a medallion. In the opening of a white shirt. And a
single movement of her foot found a hard shoe, which might
be a boot. Could it possibly be . . . ?

But even if he *was* the pirate she'd wanted to find, what
if he wasn't as innocent as he had claimed? Even if he hadn't
killed her when they were alone in the passage near David's
body, did that mean he could be trusted? And what about
what he'd said, warning her she was being framed—and that
he was her secret admirer? Could *that* be trusted?

She heard the sound of a hanger being removed from the
rack and footsteps moving away. Her heart pounded again
at the realization that the newcomer was leaving, but that
wasn't the only reason. She was going to take the chance
that it *was* the pirate behind her and he really *was* on her
side. She *had* to know, she simply had to.

It wasn't long before the footsteps left the locker room
entirely, suggesting the man had either been picking up the
clothing for someone else, or didn't intend to wear it until
later.

"He's gone," a raspy whisper sounded from behind her.
"If I let you go, do you promise not to scream?"

She nodded as well as she could with his hand still over
her mouth, but as soon as she did the hand was no longer
there. She flexed her jaw just a little to get rid of the feeling
of being held, but otherwise didn't move.

"Do *you* promise not to scream if I ask a few questions?" she whispered back, feeling nowhere near as steady
as she was trying to sound. "I've been waiting for that man
to leave, and now that he has I'd like to take advantage of
it."

"You sound as though you knew it was me holding you,"
the man answered, a bit of skepticism and displeasure clear
even in his whisper. "What do you think you're doing here?
Trying to find a way to be killed?"

"What I'm doing here is trying to find some answers,"
she countered, taking a step forward before turning to look

at him—or at least at his shadow. "It so happens I *did* know it was you holding me, and that's why I didn't struggle. I need to know how you knew I was being framed, and where you fit into this mess. The police think you could be my accomplice, and I have to have some facts that will change their minds."

"What I know and what I'm doing here won't change their minds." His whisper contradicted her in no uncertain terms as he took his own step forward. "I have no proof about what's happening, so anything I could tell you or them is mere speculation. You have my word that I'll share any facts I come across, so why don't you go back to your friends and leave the snooping to me? I'd really hate to see you get hurt."

"I don't think I'd enjoy it much myself," she was able to respond. "But that doesn't mean it has to happen—or that I have to take your word about keeping me up to date. If you really mean to share what you find, tell me what you were after in this locker room."

He hesitated very briefly, as though trying to decide whether or not she was taking advantage of what he'd said, but then he realized it didn't matter. He was the one who had said he would share, so he couldn't very well resent being put on a spot.

"I'm here looking for the uniform worn by the bellman-zombie who directed you into the passage," the pirate admitted, folding his arms as he leaned a shoulder against the metal post of the rack. "I'm fairly certain I saw the man before he found you, and I happened to notice that his uniform had a small dark stain about waist high. It could have been ink, but it could also have been blood. And even beyond that I wanted to know if that uniform had been returned, or if it was still in the possession of the man who had used it."

"But if he'd returned it, wouldn't he have put it in with the dirty clothing?" Diane asked, trying at the same time to remember if she'd noticed such a spot. "I mean, that would get it out of sight and out of everyone's way, just in case the police—or someone else—came looking."

"But that would be the first place the police checked once you told them about the man," he pointed out. "Especially when they couldn't find him among the staff. Holding on to the uniform would also be dangerous, just in case the police got a general search warrant. Putting the uniform back on the rack would be the perfect camouflage and the perfect solution, so I was checking."

"Well?" Diane prompted, annoyed that he would stop before the most important part. "Did you find it?"

"As a matter of fact, I did," he admitted, but for some reason didn't sound as happy as he should. "I located it over here."

He moved past Diane toward the center of the racks, and she followed eagerly. Coming up with what could be a blood-stained uniform should help her cause with the police, especially since they ought to be able to tell all sorts of things about the man who had worn it. When the pirate stopped she hurried nearer, glad there was more light to see by over there.

"Which one is it?" she asked, reaching out to move aside the first of the bright red uniforms, but then she paused. There was a gap between two of them, as though something had been removed, and a sudden thought brought her a definite chill.

"Yes, that was where the uniform was hanging, so it must have been the murderer who came in to get it," the raspy whisper confirmed her idea. "I was afraid that was true when he left without putting it on, but by then it was too late to either stop or follow him. Now we have to wonder what he's going to be doing with it."

"And it happened because I was in the way," Diane said with a shiver, remembering how close she'd come to trying to attract the man's attention. "My timing isn't very good this weekend. Would it help if I said I'll try not to let it happen again?"

"Yes, it would," the pirate said as she turned back to him, now seeming faintly amused. "But it could help just as much if you tell me why you came here in the first place. What were you looking for?"

"I was looking for the locker of John Dixon, the bell-man who showed me how to use my suite," she answered. She owed him at least that much. "After he finished giving me the tour, I left him alone in the study while I went to get a tip out of the bag I'd left in the bedroom. It's possible he took the candlestick while I was out of the room, and if he did I thought there might be something in his locker to say who he took it for."

"And did you find the locker?" was the raspy question, this time definitely amused. "I won't ask how you learned the man's name or where the locker room could be found. I can't imagine anyone refusing to tell you anything you wanted to know."

"The locker's over there," Diane said with a gesture, glad the room was too dim for him to see the sudden blush in her cheeks. The way he'd said that—! "I found it just before our visitor got here."

She led the way, took the lock in her hands and noticed something she hadn't expected. She proceeded to move the dial slowly around the face until the lock clicked open. A moment later, the door stood open as well. The beam of a pencil flash reached across her shoulder and illuminated the darkness.

"How did you do that?" the pirate asked in his raspy whisper while shifting his light over the contents of the locker.

"We got lucky," she whispered back, pleased at the admiration in his tone. "John Dixon's apparently the lazy sort. He left his lock with all but the last number turned to, so he'd be able to open it faster when he got back. Instead, he made it easy for me to do the opening."

"Remind me to be partners with you more often," the pirate's whisper came again, definitely amused. "Do you see anything worth a closer investigation?"

Rather than answering in words, Diane ran her hand down the single shirt hanging from a hook; lifted a wooden bat to check the weight; then crouched to examine a standard-sized softball, an old left-handed mitt, and a pair of used high-top sneakers. Diane straightened to check the shelf at the top.

Once the beam of light had followed her, she found a bottle of men's after-shave that was mostly full, a ring of keys, an envelope with about fifty dollars in cash, and a small address book. The book contained nothing but names and phone numbers, mostly women's, none of them familiar. After putting the book back where it had come from, Diane turned to the pirate.

"Unless you see something up on that shelf that I missed, we're out of luck," she said with a sigh. "If he was involved and got paid he took the payment and any evidence with him, or else he simply wasn't involved."

"From its creases, that envelope looks to have held more cash than it does now," her companion mused. "If that more cash was there recently rather than some time ago, its absence would suggest John Dixon took it with him to spend. If he was paid for taking the candlestick, he probably wouldn't have had to dip into his own funds."

"If, probably, likely and possibly," Diane said sourly. "I can see we're making progress here in leaps and bounds. Well, at least it will give me something to think about once they lock me up and throw away the key."

"Don't spend time worrying about that, because I won't be letting them lock you up," the pirate countered. "I'll find the ones who are really guilty, you have my word on that."

"Why are you doing this?" Diane blurted, wondering if she had gone crazy and *that* was why she'd been trusting him. "You have to be involved in this mess somehow, but you won't tell me how or even let me see your face. Do you expect me to just take your word for the fact that you're not really one of the enemy, trying to ruin my life?"

"Yes, I expect you to just take my word for it," he answered, the amusement suddenly back. "Since I can't give you any proof, that's the only way. But I promise you won't ever regret trusting me, not even for a moment."

His arms went around her then, his face lowered to hers, and an instant later they were kissing the way they had the night before. But this time there was a difference. Diane was no longer in shock, which meant she couldn't blame her response on that. His lips were so gently soft and yet hard and demanding, his arms so strong and possessive, his body so alive against hers.

This second kiss lasted longer than the first, and its ending was all his doing. Diane felt that she could have stood there for hours, her eyes closed, her entire body tingling. It came to her that maybe she couldn't have stood there for hours, not the way she was feeling, and then she discovered she wasn't alone in feeling like that.

"Five minutes more, and I'd be throwing you over my shoulder to carry back to my ship," the pirate whispered with a soft, gentle laugh. "Promise me you'll stop poking around in places where you can get into trouble."

"I can't just sit still and let them frame me for murder," she protested, still held in his arms. "There are places I can go that you can't, things I can find out that you have no access to. I won't give up."

"Then at least promise me you won't go poking around alone," he rasped softly, compromising with a good deal of reluctance. "You have friends here who are anxious to help you. Stay with them. Promise me."

"I'll try," Diane said grudgingly. His concern seemed so real. It bothered her not to agree. "If I have the choice I won't go poking around alone again. Is that good enough?"

"I suppose it will have to be." Diane thought she could hear a sigh behind the words. "If I learn anything worth knowing, I'll get in touch with you. Right now I think we'd both better leave."

His arms opened with that final suggestion, and it was too sensible for Diane to argue with. She closed the locker and replaced the lock, used the pirate's pencil flash to see, and reset it to the number it had originally been on. Then the two of them made their way to the front of the room.

"You're the one who gets to leave first," the pirate whispered before Diane could put the question. "I won't leave you here alone."

"All right," she whispered back. She felt a silly smile building inside her. "But since anyone can see I'm bigger and stronger than you, and chances are I fight better, if you get into trouble and need my help, just yell.''

"I'll do that," he said with a chuckle as he looked down at her, obviously enjoying the idea of being protected by someone half his size. "Now, on your way."

She would have preferred to say something else to prolong their time together, but there was really nothing else to say. She nodded and turned from him, slipped to the door to check the hall, then simply left.

Diane kept her thoughts under control until she was back at the arrow sign, but that was as far as she could take it. Her ''secret admirer'' had kissed her again and shown how worried he was about her, but she still knew nothing about him.

Every time she met him he had no trouble talking her into believing him. Or kissing her into it. For someone who was supposed to be so interested in her, he didn't do much in the way of asking for a date. And he wanted her to trust him, but didn't trust her enough to tell her who he was.

"Yes, you've definitely lost your mind, and need help desperately," she muttered to herself as she walked back toward her suite. "The only question is, are you going to *get* that help or simply enjoy being crazy?"

Diane waited for an answer to come, preferably an intelligent answer, but her practicality seemed to have gone on vacation.

Checking the suite showed that Lynn was already gone, so Diane took the money out of the envelope with John Dixon's name on it and flushed the pieces of the envelope down the toilet. Then she went looking for Lynn and the others. She found all of them but Gray in the restaurant having breakfast, and went to join them.

"And what have you been up to?" Bill demanded as soon as she sat down. "Lynn told us you were already gone when she woke up, but she didn't know where. If you were out pricing truth serum to use on everybody, I'm going home."

"Why?" Ralph asked him, looking amused. "You know there's no such thing as secrecy where writers and editors are concerned. The word is out as soon as you turn around, including a detailed description of whoever it was you turned around *with*. What could you possibly have to hide?''

"The location of my fortune in gold," Bill replied promptly and primly. "You think I work with you for the money, but no one gets paid well enough for that."

Ralph went into a forced fit of coughing while Lynn and Diane laughed, and then Lynn shook her head.

"If you two don't save the vaudeville routines until next convention, Diane and I will carry on alone," she warned. "But first I want to hear what Diane's been doing."

"Mostly I've been wasting my time," Diane said. She paused to let their waiter bring a cup for her and fill it with coffee. It was the same waiter she'd had earlier, so she smiled and thanked him, then waited until he was out of earshot before continuing.

"I went looking for the bellman who took me to my suite yesterday," she went on after the break. "I remembered that he had access to the candlestick while I was out of the room, but it looks like he's off for the weekend. Unless he comes back unexpectedly, we won't be able to question him."

"You should tell that lieutenant about him," Bill said, reaching for another piece of toast. "The police can locate and question him, and if he knows anything they'll find it out."

"*Maybe* they'll locate him and *maybe* they'll find it out," Ralph said with a snort of derision, a typical Daniel King reflection on the abilities of the police. "The point is that *we* won't be able to question him. As it is, we'll have to stand in line to question our suspect in room 337."

"Have you found out who it is?" Diane asked at once.

"I found out this morning," Ralph answered, looking smug and satisfied. "I dialed through myself, then pretended I'd called the wrong number by mistake. She was annoyed, but decided not to be as sharp with me as she is with most people."

"She," Diane echoed, staring at the man. "Ralph, if you don't tell me who it is this minute, there's going to be another murder. Right here, at this very table."

"Save yourself the effort, my dear, I'd make a very dull corpse," Ralph returned with a twinkle in his eyes. "The person registered in room 337 is Angela Wilkes."

Diane sat with her mouth open for a moment, then closed it while she considered that. The replacement candlestick had come from Angela's room. But did that mean she was involved, or simply another victim. Diane knew Angela really disliked her, but did that emotion stretch far enough to cover murder and framing?

"We've decided that I'm to be the one to talk to Angela," Lynn said, breaking into Diane's thoughts. "I've never had the problem with her many people do. I think she may be a fan of mine. With that in mind I've been trying to decide how to go about the questioning, and that, together with Ralph's comment, has given me an idea we can all use."

Ralph raised one eyebrow at her, Diane looked at her eagerly, and Bill just sighed. Bill was obviously not at all pleased with the thought of digging deeper into the mystery, and that amused the older woman.

"We're going to ask all of our colleagues who *they* think did the murder," Lynn explained after sipping from her cup of tea. "As soon as we have their opinions, we'll ask what they've heard about the relationship between David and some of the others of us—not between David and the one we're talking to. Most people hesitate over giving out their true feelings about someone, but the stories they repeat and circulate usually show exactly how they feel."

"Of course," Diane said, delighted with the idea. "If you think someone is an angel, you'll believe and pass on stories proving the point. If you think they're pure evil, you'll believe and pass on that sort. It's human nature to look for support of one's own prejudices. And since, as Ralph said, nothing stays secret in our group, we should be able to learn who stands where."

"It's the easiest, all-around way of doing it," Lynn said. "So why are you scowling, Ralph? Do you know something we don't?"

"I was just wondering how effective that method would be," Ralph said. "Our colleagues should understand the point as thoroughly as we do, so one of them could use it against us by feeding us false information."

"That's the sort of plan that tends to backfire on the user," Lynn said with a small gesture of dismissal. "We'll be questioning more than one or two people, and I'm sure we've heard most of the stories going around as well. If someone comes up with something no one else has heard or can confirm, that's a strong clue in itself."

Ralph nodded distractedly as he returned to his food, and Diane sipped her coffee while she waited for everyone to finish eating. The plan should turn up something they could use, and when it did she could then tell them about her second meeting with the pirate. Until that time she'd decided to keep even the general details of that meeting to herself.

When the meal was over they left the restaurant together. Diane was about to suggest that they start in the gathering room on the second floor, but fate intervened.

"Well, good morning, Mr. Teak," came a pleasant male voice from their right. "My schedule tells me we're on a panel together later, and I'm looking forward to it."

"I don't know if I am, George," Ralph answered with a grimace as he shook hands with the newcomer. "When you've been to as many conventions as I have, discussing whether or not violence detracts from a mystery plot becomes very depressing. The fact that they have that panel topic at all makes you wonder if they've listened all the other times you discussed the point."

"I suppose you're right," George said with a laugh. "I've been going to every convention incautious enough to invite me, but it'll be a while before I have the experience you do. Oh, excuse me for interrupting. I shouldn't have bothered you while you were with friends."

"Not at all, George," Ralph said with a sudden smile. "Excuse me for not introducing you, since these are colleagues you should know. You've met Bill Raglan, but not the ladies. George Lombardy, this is Lynn Haverstock and that's Diane Philips."

When Diane heard the man's full name, she remembered the masked jester who had been signing autographs beside her the night before. George Lombardy was fairly tall and on the thin side, either in his late twenties or early thirties, with blond hair, gray eyes and a pleasant face. He shook hands with Lynn and then with her, then turned to Ralph with a sheepish grin.

"All right, I think I'd better confess," he said. "I came over to speak to you on purpose, hoping you would be kind enough to introduce me to the ladies. I'm a fan of them both, but I've never learned how to say that gracefully."

"There's really no ungraceful way," Lynn told him, smiling at the apologetic glance he sent her. "It's always a pleasure to hear from a fan, and a double pleasure when the fan is also a colleague. Would you like to join us for a while?"

"I'd love to, but I'm afraid I can't," George answered, looking crushed. "I promised to take one of the hotel's game tours and give my opinion of it later in a discussion group. The thing will be starting in just a few minutes, so I'm stuck. Say, maybe you folks would like to come along. It should be a lot of fun."

"I'm afraid that Ralph, Bill and I have other plans," Lynn returned smoothly before anyone could say anything, her smile the very picture of innocence. "But I do believe I heard Diane mention an interest in those games, so maybe she'll join you. It would probably be time well spent, dear girl."

Diane knew Lynn Haverstock too well to believe she'd commit someone to something without first asking them, and she also knew she'd never told Lynn anything about that kind of interest. Those facts told Diane exactly what the older woman was suggesting.

"Why, Lynn's absolutely right, George," Diane said at once, giving the man a smile. "I *would* enjoy trying one of the hotel's games, and trying it with a fellow writer would be even better."

WOW!

THE MOST GENEROUS

FREE OFFER EVER!

From the Harlequin Reader Service®

GET 4 FREE BOOKS WORTH $10.00

Affix peel-off stickers to reply card

4 FOUR FREE BOOKS **4**

4 FOUR FREE BOOKS **4**

PLUS A FREE VICTORIAN PICTURE FRAME

AND A FREE MYSTERY GIFT!

NO COST! NO OBLIGATION TO BUY! NO PURCHASE NECESSARY!

Because you're a reader of Harlequin romances, the publishers would like you to accept four brand-new Harlequin Intrigue® novels, with their compliments. Accepting this offer places you under no obligation to purchase any books, ever!

WE EVEN PROVIDE FREE POSTAGE!

It costs you *nothing* to send for your free books — we've paid the postage on the attached reply card. And we'll pick up the postage on your shipment of free books and gifts, and also on any subsequent shipments of books, should you choose to become a subscriber. Unlike many book clubs, we charge *nothing* for postage and handling!

"Oh, the pleasure will be all mine, Ms. Philips," George said eagerly, returning her smile. "I've read every one of your books, and I'm probably your biggest fan."

"Please call me Diane," she said easily, then turned to Lynn and Ralph. "I'll see you guys later, and tell you all about the game."

Lynn nodded regally, Ralph looked faintly disturbed, and Bill seemed mildly curious about what was doing on. Once she and George had left, the others ought to tell Bill. But maybe by then he would have figured it out for himself.

Diane had been given her first victim to question.

Chapter Eleven

"There's a gathering area for those who want to play the game on the other side of the restaurant," George told her. "We still have a few minutes, but if we're going to wait we might as well do it there."

"Sounds good to me," Diane agreed, following him in a direction she hadn't gone before. "Which game will we be playing?"

"Something they call the Hungry Crypts," he answered with a grin. "Doesn't that sound absolutely horrible?"

"I usually like mystery better than horror, but I'm willing to have my mind changed," Diane said with a small laugh. "As a matter of fact most of us feel that way, those of us who write mysteries, that is. How many books do you have out now, George?"

"Only the one, but it seems to be doing fairly well," he answered, apparently expecting Diane to know which one he meant. "I've been playing with an outline for my second effort, but so far it isn't going the way I want it to. Say, do you mind if I ask about what happened last night? I heard that David Bellamy was killed, but that's all I heard."

"I wish that was all I'd heard," she said with a grimace, privately pleased that George had broached the subject himself. "I'm one of those who found the body, and it was definitely not good horrible."

"I can imagine," he said with sober concern, stopping in front of a closed door that stood all the way to the left of the restaurant. "This is where we have to go. But tell me, what was it like to find an actual dead body? We write about it and see it all the time on television and in the movies, but what's the real thing like? Terribly shocking and awful?"

"Once you bring yourself to believe it," she agreed with a nod, walking through the door George had opened. Inside was a plain paneled and cobwebbed room holding half a dozen people. Those who were already there glanced at the newcomers, then went on with their conversations.

"You mean it's hard to believe the man is really dead?" George asked quietly once they'd chosen a private section of wall to stand beside.

"The problem is that at first you can't conceive of its being real," Diane explained, understanding that George was asking research questions, not being ghoulish. "You don't spend your life tripping over people who have died, things like that happen in hospitals or other places where they belong. And murder. Murder is found in the movies or books, not practically in your lap. Even if you don't like the person, it can't possibly be real."

"You know, you're not the only one who's said something about not liking him," George commented, folding his arms. "You'd think that if someone was dead—especially murdered dead—those who knew him would find *something* decent to say."

"You'd first have to think of something decent that would fit," Diane said with a grimace. "A job like that would do well as one of those impossible tasks given to heroes in old mythology. Didn't you know David yourself?"

"I met him a couple of times, but that's not the same as 'knowing' him," George said. "The first time someone tried introducing us, he ignored the introduction, me and the person doing the introducing. He let the man get started talking, and then simply walked away to speak to someone else. It makes you feel really important and significant when somebody does that."

"It was a favorite David Bellamy put-down," Diane said with a nod of sympathy. "It made him feel like he was really important. Who was the person trying to introduce you?"

"I don't remember," George said with a frown. "It was a few years ago, and conventions run together. The second time it was an editor introducing me, so he didn't pull the same trick. That time he asked me when I thought I'd be learning how to write."

"Definitely a David Bellamy type of question," Diane said. "And was it your own editor who introduced you?"

"No, as a matter of fact it was Bill Raglan," George said. "My own editor wasn't at that convention, but that reminds me. A very interesting story was circulating about David and one of the writers at that convention."

"Oh?" Diane said, trying not to show her sudden, deep interest. "Which story was that?"

"Well, it was the talk of everyone there, even some of the fans," George began. Apparently, he was more than willing to part with the details, but just then they were interrupted.

"Okay, folks, give me your attention, please," one of the hotel staff said in a moderately loud voice. The man was dressed like a vampire. "It's time to start the game."

Everyone including George perked up at that, and there was a general movement toward the man. Diane wished he'd waited another five minutes before showing up, but there was nothing she could do about changing his timing.

"Now, I'll need each of you to sign these releases," the vampire went on, gesturing with the clipboard he held. "As soon as that's done, I'll review the rules of the game."

He started with the man closest to him, directed that the name should be first printed and then signed, waited for the moment it took to be done, then moved on to the next person with a fresh sheet.

Diane hoped that she and George would be toward the end of the group—which would give her enough time to ask about the story—but had no such luck. They were approached quickly and given their own forms to sign, and then there were only three people left who hadn't signed. That didn't leave enough time for any conversation at all.

"Okay, folks, now we're set," the vampire announced as the last woman handed back his pen. "You may think you signed in red ink, but actually it was blood. We like to pay attention to details such as that.''

The man laughed evilly while everyone else either grinned or laughed with him, and his red-rimmed eyes looked pleased.

''We've got a good group here, I think,'' he said, looking around at everyone. ''Now, for those who don't know, the game works this way. You'll all be entering the maze of the Hungry Crypts, and all you have to do is find your way out again. The first one to do it wins the game, and the rest who get through earn honorable mention. That's easy enough, isn't it?''

Once again he looked around at everyone, but no one was fooled by the innocence of his expression. He'd left something out of his explanation, and the players were waiting to hear what it was.

''All right, all right, I can't get away with trying to trick you,'' he admitted after a moment, dropping the innocent look. ''There's one other *small* thing you have to worry about besides the maze. There are harmless spirits down there and malignant spirits, and if you're caught by one of the malignant ones, the Hungry Crypts get fed.''

His voice turned sepulchral with the last few words, and for an instant Diane could have sworn that his eyes glittered. A mutter ran through the small group, but for the most part the mutter was delighted. Naturally.

''How do we tell the difference between harmless spirits and malignant ones?'' George asked, clearly one of those who was delighted. ''And what can we do to protect ourselves? Also, what does feeding the Hungry Crypts entail?''

''One at a time, one at a time, please,'' the vampire requested, holding his hands up to fend off the other dozen questions that had been put along with George's. ''You're all asking pretty much the same thing, so let me give you some answers and then we'll see if you think I left anything out.

''The spirits can take any form, from fully substantial to mistlike, but their form doesn't matter. The harmless ones won't hurt you even if they're solid zombies, and the malignant ones can't be ignored even if they're ghostly outlines.

"As for how to tell them apart—well, there's one theory most of you should be familiar with. It says that evil spirits are so concerned with being evil, they don't pay enough attention to making sure whatever form they take is done right. In other words there will be something wrong with the way malignant spirits look, but you may have to check close to find the mistake. It could be something small and easy to miss.

"Now, the way you protect yourselves is easy, but the method has to be used sparingly. If you meet a malignant spirit you say, 'In the name of Good, begone!' That will make it run away or disappear, and you'll be safe.

"But if you happen to say it to a harmless spirit, something different will happen. The first two times they'll count at you—one, and then two—and you'll have lost two of your supply against the malignant. If you haven't gone far enough, there will be more malignant spirits than you have the power to banish.

"If you *have* gone far enough toward finding your way out of the maze, you'll be all right *unless* you say it to a harmless spirit a third time. At that point the harmless spirit will be so insulted, it will turn malignant and feed you to the Crypts. Does everyone understand?"

The man drew a collection of nods from the group, mostly on the thoughtfully intrigued side, but that wasn't the way Diane felt. By that time the thought had occurred to her that she might be wise to back out of the game, but their vampire entertainment director was going on.

"Now you have to understand just what the Hungry Crypts are," he said, speaking with a good deal of relish. "They're vaults to both sides of the maze path that were meant to hold bodies, but haven't been allowed to do so. Because of that they've grown very hungry for bodies, and they've made a deal with the malignant spirits. Whenever one of the spirits catches someone, he or she is fed to one of the Crypts. How long the crypt holds you depends on how well you've done against the spirits."

"Do you mean that if you make it through most of the way, you're held for only a little while?" one of the woman asked. "Or do you get held longer if you've given a hard time to the spirits?"

"The better you do, the less time you're held," the vampire answered, smiling toothily at the woman. "After all, someone who comes close to winning does deserve a reward. The Crypts aren't happy about that, but they have to abide by the rules, too."

"What does the winner win?" one of the men asked while everyone chuckled at the vampire's broader grin.

"The winner wins a dinner for two in the High Hat Room," was the answer. "Runners-up, if any, win themselves a lunch there. Are there any other questions?"

"What do you do if you've changed your mind?" Diane asked, thinking her question would be buried under someone else's. But it wasn't.

"Now, now, you don't *really* want to back out," the vampire assured her with a small chuckle. He began leading the way toward one of the walls. "Everyone who plays this game enjoys it, so give it a try. Follow me, please."

Diane was about to assure him that she really did want out, but the words died when she saw the way George was looking at her. She'd supposedly gone along with him to play the game, not to ask questions. If she turned around and walked out he'd begin to realize it was the other way around. And she hadn't heard that story he'd mentioned yet. Diane suddenly felt trapped, but it looked as if she would have to play the game.

"All right, everyone goes through here," the vampire said after opening a secret passage in the wall. "One at a time, please, and in the order you signed the releases."

Diane stayed close to George as they joined the loose line. It wasn't as if she would be alone, after all. And once the game was over she would get what she needed from George.

The vampire sent the first person through the secret door, waited about fifteen or twenty seconds, then sent the second person through. Diane thought that meant there was something to be seen as soon as you stepped into the maze, and those who ran the game wanted each player to have the chance to see it before the next player came through. She wondered what it could be, then shrugged. She'd find out soon enough.

Soon enough came all too quickly, right after George stepped through. The vampire held her in place the necessary seconds, and then she stepped through the wall to see a short, dark corridor stretching right. Diane walked to the end of it, looking for a hook to turn, but a hook wasn't necessary. A doorway slid open to her left, obviously controlled by those who ran the game, telling her that that was the way to go.

Moving through the doorway put her in a much longer corridor, one that had brooding dark gray lighting and very faint, very eerie music. The corridor was wide enough for two people to stand abreast, but each of the walls had what looked like vaults in them. There was also a faint smell of damp, which made Diane uneasy.

Then the front of the vault to the left began to open outward with the creak of unoiled hinges. Diane felt goosebumps rising on her arms, and that did it for her.

"Too bad about what George thinks," she muttered, very relieved to be making the decision. "Either he'll tell me the story anyway, or I'll try to find out about it from someone else. Whichever, I'm getting out of here."

She turned to retrace her steps—only to find that the doorway had closed silently behind her, and there was no longer any sign of where it had been. Diane stared at the blank wall, not understanding only because she didn't want to. Another scream of tortured hinges brought her whirling around with a pounding heart and a sick feeling in her middle.

There was no sign of anyone ahead of her in the corridor, and the door she'd come through hadn't opened again even though the time delay had more than passed. Somehow they'd arranged a lot more than one path through the maze, and Diane was all alone in hers!

Chapter Twelve

Gray gave Diane a head start out of the staff locker room, then slipped back as quickly as possible to his own suite.

Once he was back in his rooms, Gray returned his costume to its hiding place, then took a shower to get rid of all traces of the makeup. He spent the time trying to decide whether or not he should be cursing at himself. He'd made an assumption, and it had turned around and kicked him in the teeth.

He'd decided to go prowling that morning after deciding Diane would be late getting started. The second decision had been the assumption. Diane hadn't slept late, and if she'd gotten hurt because he wasn't watching her it would have been all his fault.

Or mostly his fault. He stood under the pouring water of the shower, still angry over the way she'd gone prowling on her own. "She's too damned good," he growled into the stream of water, wondering if any other woman he knew could have found the trail she had. Or would have had the nerve to follow it. That was what frightened him most. Her courage could lead her right into the hands of the murderers.

Hands. Arms. His arms. His anger dissolved and ran down the drain with the water. Another, better, memory of Diane took its place. He'd done it again, kissed her and held her close to him. She was so warm and alive, so shyly responsive to the touch of his lips....

Gray reached over to add a lot more cold to the stream of water pelting him, needing some kind of help to pull himself back. The more he saw of Diane Philips the less self-control he was left with. Something would have to be done. Maybe if he promised himself to try to get closer to her in his own persona, his head would stop spinning and he could get back to serious work. Lord knew he had to try something.

"Even though there's no guarantee that'll work," he muttered, turning the water off and reaching for a towel. "That kiss on the cheek she gave me last night—there was more heat and interest in what she gave Ralph Teak, and he's almost old enough to be her grandfather. Next time I *will* put an arm around her if it's called for, damned if I don't."

He began drying himself briskly, insisting to himself that he would *not* have any trouble. Just because his ability to go unnoticed was linked into his true character, didn't mean he was shy. He was a grown man, and grown men didn't have to put on costumes and masks before they were able to show interest in an attractive woman.

Gray was just about ready to leave when the phone rang. The ringing meant a delay in getting back to Diane Philips, and that made him answer the phone with a surly, "Yeah?"

"Yeah," agreed the sour voice on the other end. "What did I do, catch you at an indelicate time?"

"If it was nothing but that, I wouldn't be in this foul a mood," Gray told Jack. "Among other things, I missed a chance at one of the group this morning."

"You got that close?" Jack demanded, immediately diverted. "Who was it? How? Where?"

"You sound like you're doing a news report," Gray returned. "There was a spot on the uniform of the zombie bellman who set up Diane Philips last night. This morning I went looking for that uniform, and found it in the place it was most likely to be—in the middle of other uniforms just like it. Not dirty uniforms, but clean ones."

"That means they didn't want to be caught with it in their possession," Jack said with a whistle. "But it also means they probably intend to use it again."

"Not probably, definitely," Gray corrected. "I decided to hang around for a while to see if anyone came for it, and they certainly did. But I missed seeing who it was, because one of my amateur detectives showed up just before him, and tripped over me while trying to hide. I hadn't gone out armed, so I had to keep her quiet until the man had left. He could have been armed, and if he had been, the two of us might have been done."

"Damned bad luck," Jack grumbled, but said nothing against Gray's having chosen to protect an innocent rather than pursue the guilty. Jack had been a cop. He would have chosen the same. "If you could have followed the guy, you might have been able to crack the whole thing then. Now you'll have to be set for the next time they use the uniform."

"Hoping all the while that I won't be too late," Gray said. "Did you call just to check on my lack of progress, or do you have something to tell me?"

"Not all of us spend our time missing the bus," Jack said with the faintest hint of smugness. "Do you want to take notes, or just listen?"

"I can't afford to have notes that might be found," Gray responded, sitting a little straighter in the chair. "Go ahead and tell me, and if I need to verify I'll call you back to do it."

"Okay," Jack agreed, and there was the rustle of papers. "Here it is. Subject one is David Bellamy, the victim. Forty-three years of age, unmarried, well-stuffed bank account, nicely rounded portfolio. No close relatives or friends, no debts, no known contact with unsavory types."

"Neat to the point of compulsion and universally disliked," Gray added. "Who would benefit most from his death?"

"Aside from that vast multitude who hate his guts, no one as yet discovered," Jack answered. "If he has a will, it must be on file at an attorney's office. But something else occurred to me about him. You remember that note about D-day on the convention flyer? Well, how about the *D* standing for David? Maybe he was supposed to have been killed on Saturday, but something went wrong and it had to be moved up to Friday. If you can find out what went wrong, it may also tell us who and why."

"That doesn't sound like their usual smoothly run operation," Gray said with a frown as he considered the suggestion. "It almost sounds like panic, but why panic? Did he stumble onto something that told him what was being planned? And maybe who was paying for the job?"

"How about Ralph Teak?" Jack suggested, the papers rustling again. "Mr. Teak is seventy-one and a widower. He's the creator of Daniel King, a near legend in the world of mystery. With his sales as high as they are Teak should have no problems about money, but for the last couple of years he's been neck-deep in debt. His wife was sick for a long time, and medical debts are the worst. He spent almost his last dime trying to keep her alive, but she died anyway."

"What has that got to do with Bellamy?" Gray asked, frowning even more. "Someone said Teak was the only writer Bellamy never knifed in his column."

"That could be because of the argument they had a few years ago," Jack said. "Bellamy had just got himself set with that magazine he edited, and he ran into Teak at a convention. He told Teak he was going to give Daniel King a good going over. He said once he was through with the series, no one would have the nerve to get caught dead reading one.

"Teak is the sort to keep his cool, so he didn't blow up or anything. He just told Bellamy straight out that if he ever printed a word about his Daniel King books, he would take out a contract on Bellamy's life. There were a lot of people listening to that exchange, and the write-up reporting the incident said Teak wasn't joking, and everyone there knew it."

"Everyone, apparently, including Bellamy," Gray mused. "If he never printed a word, he knew doing it would be tossing away his life. But taking out a contract on someone costs, and right now Teak doesn't have the going price. Or so Bellamy thought. If he worked up his nerve to make his threat again, Teak could have jumped over the edge and made a deal with the ones we're after. Killing Daniel King right now would kill Teak's chances of ever getting financially straight again, so Bellamy had to go."

"And it isn't necessarily Teak who's footing the bill," Jack said. "Bill Raglan has been his friend and editor for years and, in spite of his family, he's been able to sock away a nice pile. *He* could be the one who did the hiring, to protect his good friend and meal ticket—with or without Teak's knowledge."

"And if one of them is involved, they not only know the identity of the people we want, they're deliberately trying to frame Diane Philips," Gray said. "That's the one part that's keeping this from coming together for me—framing the Philips woman. Teak seems genuinely fond of her, and I can't see him sacrificing her for his own safety. Raglan may be another story, but I'm not certain even with him. Unless—"

"Unless what?" Jack prompted. "Unless you remember that a lot of people play noble until they have to choose between somebody else's neck and their own?"

"No," Gray said, still distracted. "Unless Teak is only using the Philips woman as a diversion, and will clear her with the next part of the plan. Just the way he would do it in a Daniel King book."

"You're not trying to say this thing is plotted?" Jack demanded, sounding totally scandalized. "By someone like Ralph Teak? Most of the time it's hard figuring out exactly what was *done* in his books. Knowing *who* did it either comes as a divine inspiration, or doesn't come at all until Daniel King makes his explanations. I don't want to hear that that's what we're up against."

"It's just a theory, Jack, so don't spend any time worrying about it," Gray soothed his distant partner, wishing he could take the advice himself. "And too much time is going by, so we'd better make this march. If something else is going to happen, and I've got the strangest hunch it will happen soon. I want to be there."

"Right," Jack agreed resignedly, then went quickly through the rest of what he'd found out. Gray listened and filed the information away in his memory. By the time he hung up he was so anxious it was all he could do to walk to the door rather than run. He couldn't pin it down, but every instinct he had was screaming that he'd better find Diane Philips—and fast!

"OKAY, let's not panic," Diane said to herself very firmly, trying to ignore the screeching hinges of the opening crypt. "This is all a game. So, scary or not, we just have to remember it isn't real. All we have to do to get out of here is find the other end of the maze."

Getting out. Simply standing there staring wasn't going to make it happen. She had to play the stupid game; if she didn't, she'd end up being locked into one of those crypts. That was enough to set her moving.

She gave a wide berth to the opening vault but even with a few steps distance and the dim gray light, she could see what looked like a ghostly hand inside the vault, beckoning to her. Come on in, the dust and cobwebs are fine, she thought as she hurried away even faster.

The gray light and eerie music kept her company as she reached the end of the corridor and followed it left around a curve.

The first problem appeared just as Diane saw the first fork in the corridor. About thirty feet ahead she would have to choose left or right, she noticed—and then all directional choices were gone from her head. The dim light darkened perceptibly, there was a bright flare of yellow light—and a "spirit" stood there not ten feet ahead of her.

The thing was horrible, with red-rimmed, sightless eyes, the slouch of the painfully dead, the shuffle of the unnaturally living. Decomposing clothes hung formlessly over decomposing flesh, shifting as the thing advanced at her.

"Good grief," Diane breathed as she stared, for the moment her mind blank with fear, and then with a rush of memory blurted, "In the name of Good, begone!"

The apparition stopped, suddenly grinned as it pointed at her, said in a very deep voice, "One," and then vanished.

"Damn it, that's not fair!" Diane exclaimed aloud, suddenly feeling very much like a fool. The thing had been so horrible looking she'd been certain it was malignant, but that's what they'd wanted her to think. Now she'd wasted some of her ammunition against the real thing, which couldn't be the best way to start the game.

Completely disgusted with herself, Diane stalked toward the fork in the corridor. She remembered something a mathematician friend had told her years earlier. The best and fastest way to get out of a maze was to go right at every choice. That's what she would do.

Along with logic, hindsight told her the first spirit would certainly be harmless even though it didn't look it, just to panic her into wasting ammunition. That should mean the second would look innocent but be malignant, to catch those who were taken in the first time. Annoyance and overcaution would keep them from saying the phrase, and then—

And then one more chance and they would be fed to a crypt. Diane grimaced at the thought, but this time she didn't shiver. If they wanted someone to *really* play their game, they now had her.

Diane strode past creaking vault doors without even glancing at them, going right again at the next fork. Just past the fork the second "spirit" appeared, and this time she noticed that the faint background music went to terrified-violin sounds just as the thing appeared. They thought they had the game stacked against her, but they were wrong.

This time she looked closely at the female form that had wings, a long gown of white and a smile showing fangs. A nice touch that, scary-looking but not too scary, she thought, except for the hands. They were being held out in front of the figure and were bent clawlike, but they were *on the wrong way*. The thumbs were on the outside rather than inside where they belonged, and that was all Diane needed.

"In the name of Good, begone!" she said calmly, and was rewarded with having the thing disappear without counting at her.

Satisfaction eased her stride back down to a more comfortable walking pace, one which let her think. She now had to decide what the next spirit would be, harmless or malignant, and the challenge was beginning to appeal to her. Wouldn't it be funny if *she* ended up winning—the one who hadn't wanted to play at all?

Thoughts of the game stopped abruptly when she suddenly realized something, something she'd just seen and noticed because she was calm enough to notice details. The opening vault she'd passed only a few steps back—could that really have been bright red she'd seen in it? What would bright red be doing *there*, in a place were the game consisted of projections—?

Diane felt her heart beginning to beat faster, but she still forced herself to look over her left shoulder. She immediately wished she hadn't. A man dressed like a zombie bellman was trying to climb quietly out of the opening vault, but that wasn't the worst of it.

There was a small dark stain on the right side of the uniform, the stain the pirate had mentioned, and something even worse. In his left hand the zombie carried a silenced gun, and when he saw her watching he began to raise the gun.

That was all Diane waited to see. Panic might have frozen her in place in the presence of a spirit, but a murderer with a gun set fire to her feet. She took off fast, heading for the next bend in the corridor, and was just tearing around it when she heard the "ffft" of a silenced shot.

"Faster!" her mind screamed at her then. The shot had missed, but that might be because silenced weapons weren't as accurate as unsilenced ones. If she let the zombie find his range, he would probably be able to manage a hit.

Sheer panic kept her moving despite the way she was panting, that and the sound of pursuing footsteps. He was chasing her in the hope of getting a clear shot, she knew, and careened around a curve just before a second "ffft."

That run was more of a nightmare than anything the hotel people had been able to come up with. Diane stumbled into vault drawers, feeling the pain of contact, sobbing from it but not slowing. She had to get out, she *had* to, but where was the end of that horrible place?

Distantly she knew she'd run right through some of the projections and without thinking about it had also taken every righthand fork. Her hair was soaked with sweat, every part of her was trembling, and the greatest ache she felt was in her chest. Her lungs were going to burst, she knew they would—

And that was when she rounded a curve and slammed into a blank wall, one that wouldn't let her run anymore. She pounded at it as she panted and gasped for air, still hearing the footsteps behind her even through all the noise she was making. He was coming, the killer was coming, and *she couldn't get away!*

"Help me!" she tried to scream, but there wasn't enough air for screaming. She clawed at the wall, desperately seeking a way out. She didn't want to turn to see death coming at her—

And then she *was* screaming, fear overcoming her shortness of breath. There were hands on her arms, actually touching her, and she automatically fought them....

Chapter Thirteen

There was a voice shouting at her with words that slowly began to make sense. Then she realized the man trying to hold her wasn't wearing blinding red.

He was wearing a tan shirt and dark gray trousers.

"Diane, are you all right?" Gray demanded, his fingers unconsciously digging into her arms. "What's wrong? What happened?"

Diane paused just long enough to realize that the gunman was gone and Gray had come in through a doorway to the right of the end of the corridor. Then she collapsed against his chest. She was trembling too hard to speak, but that didn't matter. As soon as she stopped fighting, Gray's hands left her arms, and then he was holding her to him in a way that felt better than good.

"It's okay, you're safe now," he murmured in her ear, his arms holding her tight. "Whatever it was, it can't get you now. I'm here, and I won't let anything hurt you."

"I hope that was a promise you just made," she whispered, but somehow it didn't sound like the joke she'd been trying for. "How did you find me?"

"When I learned from Ralph and Lynn that you'd joined this game, I found the people running it and twisted a few arms," he answered. "I was told that from where you'd entered the maze you'd be coming out here. I was trying to decide whether to go in looking for you, or wait until you came out. When I heard the pounding I opened the door and came in. Can you tell me now what frightened you like that?''

''It was a man with a gun,'' she said, feeling ready to stand alone but not quite wanting to. ''He came out of one of the vaults opening behind me, and I have reason to believe he was the same zombie who directed me to the meeting with David's body last night. He shot at me twice, but missed both times.''

''Stay here,'' he ordered abruptly, and then he had let her go and was striding up the corridor in the direction she'd come from. She wanted to follow him, but her knees were too weak to carry her that far. Instead she let her eyes do the following, and concentrated on gathering the strength she would need if the trouble that had been after her turned on Gray.

Gray slowed to a cautious pace before slipping around the curve. He was out of sight for a couple of minutes, then reappeared looking unhappy. It was odd the way he'd gone charging off, Diane thought, as though he'd be able to handle a man with a gun if he found one. He should have been pleased he hadn't found anyone, but he wasn't.

''Not a sign of him,'' he announced unnecessarily as he rejoined her, the words almost a growl. ''I went back to what looked like a fork, but decided not to get myself lost by going past it. He could be anywhere, and probably knows this maze better than we do. What made you think he was the same man who spoke to you last night?''

Diane hesitated, trying to decide whether or not to be completely honest, but it wasn't a hard decision to make. Gray hadn't doubted her word when she'd told him about the zombie, hadn't tried to say she was imagining things. In return for his unquestioning belief in her, he deserved the truth.

So she told him what had happened in the locker room with the pirate—all but the kiss, of course. He listened to the story with a faint frown on his face, and then he nodded.

''Okay, so you saw the stain on the uniform,'' he said. ''That means we have to sit down and discuss what to do next. Let's go to the restaurant. They'll have coffee to help the discussion along.''

"I don't understand," she protested as he put an arm around her shoulders to urge her toward the doorway. "The thing we do next is tell the police about this. Why would we need to discuss it?"

"When we're alone," was his very unsatisfying answer. Then they stepped through another doorway into a room that held four people. Two of them were watching a board with blinking lights at more than half a dozen spots, one was looking down at a terminal screen, and the fourth stepped forward to begin asking about spirits. Gray waved him off, and he and Diane were able to leave in peace.

By the time they got to the restaurant, Diane was feeling enough better to cringe at the thought of what she must look like. Her hair had to be a mess, her clothes wrinkled and damp, her face as pale as any vampire or ghoul there....

"You have no idea how glad I am to see you sitting here across the table from me," Gray said as he took a chair, after helping her into one of her own. "When I couldn't find you this morning, I began getting this awful premonition that grew stronger and stronger— Well, it's just about over now, and you're still all right."

"Just about over?" Diane asked, the only part of what he'd said she felt able to comment on. The rest...she would have to think about that later.

"We still have to decide what to do next," he said, then paused to order two coffees. The ghoul waiter was right back with the cups and a pot, and once the coffee was poured and the man had left, Gray continued.

"Telling the police is the first thought that comes to me, too," he said, "but only until I start thinking about what happened. The man who shot at you presumably knows how to use a gun, otherwise why would he be the one doing the job? We can assume he knows how to shoot, and yet he fired at you twice and missed both times. I'm not unhappy about that, but it does make me think."

Diane was about to demand what it could possibly be making him think about, when sudden understanding flooded her, drowning the words. The picture wasn't a pleasant one.

"It's making you think he missed me deliberately," she said, slumping back in her chair. "I was supposed to run hysterically to the police, screaming that someone had tried to kill me, and when they went to investigate they might not even find any bullet holes. If he was using blanks they wouldn't, but they would certainly start wondering what I was up to."

"Especially when you told them it was a zombie bellman like the one last night," Gray pointed out. "They'd marvel at the very convenient coincidence that the same man was after you again, and then probably suggest the second man was a different zombie entirely. 'Maybe you're not tipping properly, Ms. Philips, and that's why all those members of the staff are after you.' You know, something cute like that."

"And then I'd look even guiltier, especially if they pulled something else," Diane muttered before raising her cup to her lips. She kept feeling she was getting in deeper and deeper, but still hadn't the faintest idea in what.

"But they might also be counting on you seeing that and keeping quiet," Gray went on as he ran a hand through his hair in distraction. "If their plan is twisty enough, it could reveal the fact that you were shot at and didn't report it, and *that* fact would make you look guiltier. Damn! Now I don't know which way to go!"

"We'll have to think about it for a couple of minutes," Diane said, feeling just as morose and frustrated. "Maybe there's a third option we're just not—"

"So there you are!" a voice exclaimed, and Diane looked up to see Anita Rutledge, who immediately turned away. "Hey, everybody, she *is* in here."

A moment later they were surrounded by a crowd, and once its members had settled into chairs Diane understood. The ones who had been looking for her were Ralph, Bill and Lynn, their numbers increased by the presence of Anita.

"Have we got something to tell *you*," Bill enthused with a grin. "Anita helped with it, so we let her join us."

"I didn't do anything but nod encouragement," Anita said with a laugh. "Lynn was the one who really made it happen, and I wouldn't have believed it if I hadn't heard it myself."

"It's definitely something to think about," Ralph agreed, "but maybe you found out something good, too. What did George have to say?"

"George started to tell me about something, but we were interrupted by the game," Diane admitted. "I'll have to run him down later and ask him, but what did you find out, Lynn?"

"Something that confirms my belief that David Bellamy should have been drowned at birth," the older woman said. Her cold fury dispelled the others' enthusiastic amusement.

They were interrupted again by the arrival of the waiter, and by the time everyone had their coffee and the man was gone, Lynn had control of her anger again.

"There are so many stories that float around about people, and most of them turn out to be partially or completely untrue," she said with a sigh. "The one I heard most often was that David indulged in blackmail as a hobby on a regular basis, but I didn't believe that even of him. In spite of what he tried to do to you, Diane, I just couldn't believe anyone I knew could be capable of that."

She paused to sip at her coffee, her wrinkled face showing pain, and no one made a single sound to interrupt.

"We spoke to Angela Wilkes, asking about her room and its decorations, and then we began discussing David," Lynn continued, giving Diane the impression they hadn't told Anita about the replacement candlestick. "We all agreed we hadn't been able to stand the man, and wasn't it sad there wasn't anyone we could think of who would be sorry he was dead. That was when Angela said *she* was sorry he was dead."

Diane raised her brows at that, and Lynn smiled faintly.

"Yes, the comment was an incautious one, and Angela realized that as soon as she said it. She tried to change the subject, tried to pretend she'd been joking. But, although the rest of us didn't really resist, she found it wasn't working. She needed to tell *someone* the truth, and the opportunity just happened to be there."

"*Lynn* happened to be there," Ralph put in with something of a growl. "She was the one Angela spoke to, the one she wanted to make understand. And, of course, she did understand. Me, I could never understand someone like David Bellamy if I lived to be a thousand."

"It wasn't David I was supposed to understand," Lynn pointed out as she stared down into her cup. "It was Angela. And although I sympathize I can't really say I understand. David blackmailed Angela the way he tried with you, Diane, but unfortunately she didn't have your inner strength. Instead of refusing she gave him what he wanted, hating the need, hating him—until one day everything changed.

"Angela suddenly discovered she was in love with David. It was one of those terrible turns the human mind is capable of. She hated him but she also loved him, and then she made the mistake of telling him so.

"He was absolutely furious," Lynn said with a shake of her head. "He raged around so, Angela was afraid he might kill her. He didn't, of course, but he broke off their 'relationship' entirely, then began attacking her in print. He was with the magazine by then, and Angela was crushed.

"It seemed that David wasn't able to accept love, only hatred. As long as Angela simply hated him he was perfectly happy, well satisfied and well content. When he found out she loved him, his own emotions changed to hatred. She was horribly confused, but she did eventually realize that the only chance she had of getting him back was to make him believe she no longer loved him."

"So she took to challenging him in public." Ralph picked up the tale while Lynn paused to drink. "She taunted him and laughed at him, trying to entice him back, but for some reason he didn't go for it. He just continued to attack her, viciously and with everything he had."

"I tend to think he was afraid of her," Lynn said, setting her cup back down. "If she loved him once she might do it again, and he must have been terrified at the thought. The only kind of woman he could be comfortable with was one who loathed him, one whose hatred would never change to anything else.''

"Don't even think it," Diane said at once, feeling her cheeks go pale. "I don't even want to consider the possibility that he was really attracted to me because I hated him. He was the one who hated me, and I'd prefer keeping it like that.''

"Angela thinks he was attracted," Lynn said with a sigh, reaching over to pat Diane's hand. "That's the real reason she dislikes you so. She considered you a rival, and not just professionally. The poor thing is so mixed up.''

"She's not the only one," Diane said, leaning back in her chair. "And what has all of this gotten us? Deeper into the woods, I'd say, with the wolves getting closer all the time.''

"Well, it gives us a motive for murder and a motive for framing," Ralph pointed out. "If Angela finally admitted to herself that David would never take her back, she could have blamed *you* for that state of affairs, gone ahead and killed him, then tried to make you look guilty. She *is* capable of doing it, you know.''

"But if she had, it isn't likely she would have unburdened herself to me," Lynn pointed out in turn. "We could say that was all part of her scheme, but what possible purpose does it serve? You don't tell everyone the answer to the mystery before you have to, even in a book.''

"It could make people think it isn't the real answer," Ralph replied promptly. "If you present it in just the right way, everyone thinks it's a red herring and simply dismisses it. It's a useful trick I've played with once or twice, but I don't think I'd use it in real life.''

"Even in books, I prefer the KISS principle," Anita put in with a grimace. "You can dangle all the red herrings you like, but when it comes to the actual murder, 'Keep It Simple, Stupid.' The more frills you try to add, the more clues you're likely to leave.''

"That's fine as long as you have the choice," Gray said suddenly, startling everyone. "A planned murder can be done easily and neatly, but what about when you're forced into moving before you're ready? When you have to improvise, you're almost certain to make a mistake."

"Not if you really do stick to the KISS principle," Bill disagreed, coming to Anita's defense. "I can't tell you how many hundreds of manuscripts I've seen over the years, and the ones that really work are the ones that are basically simple. Even if the writing stinks."

"Which all too often it does," Anita said with her nose wrinkled. "The ideas can be great, but the way they're handled..." She shook her head, then looked at Lynn and Diane with a smile. "In case you two aren't keeping track of time we three and Angela have a panel coming up. Since we're already here in the restaurant, why don't we have lunch now? By the time we're finished, it should almost be time for the panel."

Diane saw the others agree, Ralph and Bill enthusiastically, Lynn calmly, Gray with shrugging unconcern. So there was nothing to do but go along with it. She was still too disturbed to be hungry, but she had the feeling she'd better get used to it. If there wasn't even more disturbance in store for her ahead, she didn't know a thing about murder mysteries.

GRAY ATE with Diane and the others, then went with them to deliver the women to the room their panel was in. There were quite a few people in the audience, which meant that when Angela Wilkes failed to show up, they couldn't wait too long before beginning without her. Once the panel was underway, Ralph drew Gray and Bill back out into the hall.

"I don't like the feeling I have," Teak said directly to the other two men. "I think we ought to find out what's keeping Angela."

"Ralph, you're letting your imagination run away with you again," Bill warned, looking more weary than worried. "Angela was really broke up when we left her—or, rather, when she left us—so give the woman some room. She'll need a lot of time before she gets her life together again."

"I just want to make sure she's all right," Teak insisted
He looked at Gray. "What do you think?"

"I think it can't really hurt to show someone you car
about them," Gray said, reflecting that he'd been about t
slide away from the others to check on Angela himself. H
would have preferred going alone, but with Teak as deter
mined as he seemed, it wasn't worth the effort of trying t
talk him out of it.

"See, Bill, we're only showing we care about her," Tea
said, presenting the matter as settled. "If she forgot th
panel we'll remind her, and if she forgot it on purpose we'
leave her alone. Let's go."

Bill shook his head as Ralph took off toward the eleva
tors, but he made no effort to let the others leave him be
hind. They headed to room 337, but that was as far as the
got. Knocking produced no results at all, not even on th
third try.

"You see?" Bill said to a frustrated Ralph. "She isn'
even here. Either she's out doing something to brighten he
mood, or she remembered the panel late and got there afte
we left. Let's go back and see what they all have to say."

"If this was a normal door lock, I could have it open i
no time," Teak muttered, ignoring Bill completely. "Do yo
know anything about these things, Grayson?"

"I know that illegal entry gets you a jail term," Gray of
fered, keeping his amusement on the inside. "Why don't w
go after that cleaning woman we passed coming out of th
elevator? She's got to have a passkey, and that will at leas
let us look into the room."

"Even if we will have to talk her into letting us use it,'
Teak agreed with sudden enthusiasm. "You two wait her
while I take care of it."

He strode away with purpose squaring his shoulders
leaving Bill to sigh as he leaned against the wall and Gra
understanding more than he had. Ralph Teak was willing t
pick a lock in front of witnesses, but bribing a cleaning
woman would be done in private. An odd man, Ralph Teak,
and possibly just as complicated as his books.

Teak was back no more than five minutes later, the cleaning woman with him. Rather than looking guilty, though, she looked determined, and Teak's first words explained why.

"I told her I was worried about Angela," he said. "This lady won't let any of *us* in, but she's willing to take a look herself."

"And then we can get back to the panel," Bill said with a nod. "Where Angela probably already is."

Teak made no answer to that, probably because he was too busy watching the cleaning woman open the door and enter. Or start to enter. They all heard the woman gasp, and then she was backing out again.

"What is it?" Teak demanded, putting a hand on the door to keep it open. "What's in there?"

Instead of answering the woman turned and stumbled away, looking as though she was about to be sick. Gray moved up fast to look through the door over Teak's shoulder, at the same time putting a hand on that shoulder to keep the older man from entering the room.

"You can't help her now, so there's no sense in trampling down whatever evidence there might be," Gray said, fighting the sickness that threatened him. "She shot herself in the head, it looks like, and there's nothing anyone can do. We'd better call the police."

Teak nodded heavily and moved back from the door like a very old man, letting a pale and shaken Bill Raglan come forward to help him. Gray took one last look into the room before letting the door close, then he followed the others in search of a phone. On the surface it looked like Angela Wilkes had committed suicide, but had she really? Or was she actually another victim of whatever was going on here?

THIS TIME Lieutenant Gerard used a small sitting room on the second floor to do his interviewing, probably at the hotel's request. Gray had the feeling the hotel wasn't so much trying to keep the second death quiet as to keep the lieutenant out of the way of the paying customers. Gerard's expression was downright sour when Gray took a seat opposite him.

"Well, Mr. Grayson, here you are involved again," Gerard said, his dark gaze direct. "Do you get in this much trouble back home?"

Gray answered with an amused smile. "I may be involved again, but you can't really call that trouble. We were checking on the woman because she was badly upset earlier today, and our concern proved correct. She *did* commit suicide, didn't she?"

"Whose idea was it to go looking for the Wilkes woman?" Gerard asked, deliberately ignoring Gray's half question. "You and Raglan and Teak were together. Did you all get the same idea at the same time?"

"The first one to make the suggestion was Ralph Teak, but I agreed with him," Gray answered. "Bill Raglan thought we were imagining problems, and came with us just to prove he was right. Too bad he wasn't."

"We all could have used a break like that," Gerard muttered, then looked at Gray. "This time Ms. Philips has an alibi for every minute of the time involved, so I won't even be questioning her. That leads me to ask why you're involved in all this. What's a respectable west-coast attorney doing rubbing shoulders with mystery writers and editors? Especially when he came here on his own, and he knew none of them before he arrived?"

Gray hesitated, tried to make himself look embarrassed, then realized he didn't have to work very hard to accomplish it. The story he was about to tell had enough truth in it that it made him uncomfortable to think of, let alone talk about.

"I happened to...come across...a very attractive young lady when I first arrived at the hotel," he said, groping for the right words. "It might have stayed like that—a favorable impression and no more—but fate or something put me in the right spot to give her a hand when she needed it. That was when I began getting to know her, and realized I wanted to know her even better.

"When she suddenly found herself in trouble, I found that my interest wasn't disappearing. On the contrary, I discovered my concern had increased, and it was shared by those who already knew her. As far as all of us can see she's still in trouble, so we've formed a cooperative group to try to help her out of it. Have you been told for certain that Angela Wilkes was murdered, or do you only suspect it?"

"I can't say you aren't persistent," Gerard responded, studying him coolly but carefully. "What leads you to believe I think the Wilkes woman was murdered?"

"For one thing the fact that honest citizens who find a suicide and immediately report it to the police aren't generally considered as 'being in trouble,'" Gray said. "For another, neither Diane nor anyone else would need an alibi for a proven suicide. Either there's already a question, or you expect that there will be. Would you be good enough to tell me which?"

"In one way or another, the death of the Wilkes woman is tied into yesterday's murder," Gerard said, as though he were making a statement for the media. "I don't yet know exactly how, but I intend finding out."

"Have you been told how she was involved with Bellamy?" Gray asked. When he got Gerard's nod he said, "It's been suggested that when Angela finally had to admit she'd never get him back, she decided to kill him and blame the murder on Diane, who she saw as a rival. Do you put any credence in that?"

Gerard replied with a shrug that looked a little too casual. "It's worth keeping in mind as a possibility. I'm not yet at the point where I'm willing to rule anything out."

"It would be nice if we could find something that *could* be ruled out," Gray muttered, rubbing his face with one hand. "Everything we learn is part of the same puzzle, but as interlocking pieces they make good book ends. Until we find the key we won't know edge piece from center of the puzzle."

"Grayson, let me say this as forcefully as I can—stop playing detective!" Gerard was deeply serious, and apparently more concerned than he'd seemed. "There's more involved here than one simple murder. If the bunch of you keep poking around, one or more of you could end up like Bellamy and Wilkes. Enjoy your convention, enjoy the hotel—but stay out of this investigation!''

"I wish I could oblige you, Lieutenant," Gray said with a mirthless smile as he realized he was almost telling the truth. "Possibly if it was up to me alone— But even so, the people I'm with are finding out things that you and your force aren't in a position to. Do you really want to shut off what could conceivably turn out to be your only source for the truth?''

"Things like what?" Gerard demanded in challenge, now angry. "What do you think you know that I don't?''

"How about the identity of the bellman who took Diane Philips to her suite when she checked in?" Gray responded. "She realized that she left the man alone in the study to get him a tip, so he had access to the candlestick that was the murder weapon.''

Gray had thrown out the information for a reason, and was given a bonus reward when Gerard's expression showed very briefly that he hadn't thought of that line of pursuit. Or possibly hadn't yet been able to learn the name of the man.

"All right, tell me who it was," he growled, reaching for his notebook. "And then you can tell me why you didn't tell me before now.''

"His name is John Dixon," Gray supplied with an inner smile. "Diane only found out earlier today. But part of what she learned was that the man is off for the weekend and therefore probably gone from the hotel. You may have to put out an APB if you decide you want to talk to him.''

"If I have to, I will," Gerard assured him, thereby accomplishing Gray's main purpose. "And the reason this name was held closer than state secrets?''

"Think about it," Gray urged. "If Diane had called you and said she just *happened* to remember that this guy was alone in the study, but she checked and he just *happened* to be away from the hotel right now, how would you have felt? That she was getting desperate and trying to shift suspicion to someone else? That she was giving you a false lead as part of her diabolical plan?''

"All right, all right, I probably would have been suspicious at the very least,'' Gerard admitted grudgingly, leaning back in his chair. "I don't know that I'm not, even now. What else have they found out?''

"Nothing else that concrete,'' Gray said with a shrug. "Everyone had a reason to hate Bellamy, everyone had the opportunity, no one had access to the murder weapon. Why the candlestick from Angela Wilkes' room ended up in Diane's suite was something they were trying to find out, but I got the impression Angela made her confession to Lynn Haverstock before they could ask her. After that, Angela was too upset to question further.''

"I'll bet they knew where that candlestick came from before I did,'' Gerard said with a grimace. "I still don't like the idea of you people poking around, but the only way I can think of to stop you is to arrest you all. I'd do it in a minute, but without bringing charges it would mean my job. Will you at least keep me posted if you learn anything important?''

Gray hesitated, trying to decide whether or not to tell the man about what had happened in the maze. If it was himself he was telling about, he wouldn't have given it a second thought. But things were getting very complicated. If he missed this opportunity, he might not get another.

"Something else did happen, but this time not reporting it was my idea,'' Gray admitted, grudging every word. "It seems to be a 'damned if you do, damned if you don't' situation, and you'll need to consider all the options before coming to any conclusions.''

"Do you want me to swear in blood, or will Scout's honor do?'' Gerard came back dryly. "I try to get my exercise from playing racquetball, not jumping to conclusions. Tell me what happened.''

"I couldn't find Diane this morning, and then I learned she'd joined one of the hotel games,'' Gray answered with a sigh. "I pestered people until they told me which part of the maze she was in, but when I got to the door she was supposed to come out of, I heard muffled pounding. I got the door open and she almost ran me down, that's how panicked she was. Once she could talk again, she said someone had gotten into the maze with her and had shot at her.''

"With a gun?" Gerard blurted, then shook his head. "For some reason, in spite of the Wilkes woman, I'm not expecting real weapons to be used here. It would fit better if she'd been shot at with a blowgun, or a crossbow, or even a specially rigged clock.''

"Then you *do* feel it," Gray said, greatly relieved. "The sensation that this is all a movie production or something. Diane wanted to call you, but that didn't feel right to me. The man fired two shots, and both of them missed. What if she had called you, you had sent in your men, and nothing could be found in the way of bullet holes?"

"I would have decided she was lying, and probably for a special reason," Gerard said thoughtfully. "It might occur to me that blanks were used, but why? And then if something happened that made the incident look even more like a setup, I'd probably forget about the possibility of blanks entirely. What did the man look like?''

"She said she thought it was the same man who sent her to where Bellamy's body was last night," Gray provided. "He was made up like a zombie again and wearing that red uniform. It was at least the same uniform. She recognized a dark spot on it.''

"Handier and handier," Gerard muttered, shaking his head. "An attack in an odd place, done by someone easily recognized but who we can't locate. And what am I supposed to think if there *are* bullet holes?''

"Your guess is as good as mine," Gray said, the trite phrase more of a compliment than the lieutenant knew. "Whatever it turns out to be, it should implicate Diane Philips even more thoroughly.''

"But isn't that too obvious?" Gerard argued, as though thinking out loud. "Everyone's yelling now about how she's being framed. Only a real imbecile would do something to implicate themselves more deeply when they're presently safe behind a very reasonable doubt.''

"That's the way I would see it, Gerard, but you and I aren't writers," Gray pointed out. "If this is being orchestrated by a professional writer, the next step is all figured out and ought to be perfectly logical. If I get through this in one piece, I'll never read a mystery novel again.''

"You and me both," Gerard said, then blew out a deep breath. "And Grayson—''

Gray looked up at the lieutenant's tone, to see that he wore that very serious expression again.

"One of the possibilities we have to keep in mind is that Diane Philips *is* behind all this," he warned. "I've read her stuff, and she's really good. If there's a writer somewhere behind all this, don't let your hormones make you forget it could be her.''

"It's not only my hormones that refuse to believe that,'' Gray said with a quick shake of his head. "I can't explain my reasoning to you, but I'd find it easier to believe that *you* were involved. Diane Philips didn't commit that murder, and if things work out right I'll be able to prove it.''

"And if they don't work out right, chances are I'll have more bodies," Gerard said as he got to his feet and put his hand out. "I appreciate everything you've told me, but I also expect you to keep up the habit. And don't forget: all of you *be careful*!''

"As if it were a matter of life and death," Gray promised with a smile as he shook hands with the man. "Thanks for your help, Lieutenant, and I'll try to keep you posted as things come up.''

Lieutenant Mike Gerard wasn't pleased with the way Grayson put that, but he watched the man leave without saying anything out loud. The background check on Grayson had come back all but glowing, and yet Gerard had the strangest feeling the lawyer hadn't fallen into this mess as accidently as he claimed.

"But he couldn't possibly be hiding anything," Gerard muttered, throwing his pen on the table before sitting again. Oh no, none of the people involved were hiding things, not a single one of them. Everyone with motives and opportunity, most of them used to playing games with the truth—

And the death of Angela Wilkes. So far it looked like the suicide it was supposed to be, but Gerard was reserving his opinion until he got the results of the very detailed autopsy he'd ordered. The incident couldn't just be a coincidence...but what if it *was* a coincidence...or had been made to look like a coincidence...or...

Chapter Fourteen

Diane waited anxiously for Gray to get through the questioning, but when he appeared she was almost afraid to approach him. They had decided earlier, privately, that if the lieutenant seemed receptive, Gray would tell him what had happened in the maze.

All the others were hurrying over to him, wanting to know if he'd learned anything from the lieutenant, but before they reached him he looked at Diane and gave her a small nod. He'd told Gerard, then, so at least that was done. Even if it proved to be a mistake.

"You mean they're not sure yet whether Angela committed suicide?" she heard Ralph asking, a frown in his voice. "Living alone in New York frightened her, so she's had a gun permit for years and went armed whenever she could. How can there be any question?"

Others jumped in with comments and questions for Gray. Seeing that, Diane had to smile to herself. Ralph and Bill had been questioned first, but it was Gray they all asked things of, Gray who they had expected to get information they hadn't been able to. For a quiet man, he was very good at encouraging others to rely on him.

She was discovering she was no exception. She remembered how she'd felt at the end of the maze, when it had been *his* arms she'd taken shelter in. The only way it could have been better would have been if it had been the pirate instead, and maybe not even then. She still wasn't absolutely sure why that pirate kept appearing so mysteriously, but with Gray—

Diane stopped for a moment, and then continued on the same line of thought. With Gray she thought she knew. But did she really? They'd come in on the same van from the station, she'd stepped on him, he'd taken her part against David, and then again during her questioning after the murder. What did that add up to?

"An interest without a real basis," she muttered to herself, but then she remembered what Lynn had said the night before. Lynn thought Gray was attracted to her. Under other circumstances Diane would be pleased with the idea and wondering if it was true. Gray was an attractive man who became even more attractive the longer you knew him, but—

But Diane still had a secret admirer she couldn't forget. She gave a sigh of exasperation, annoyed at herself for trying to find fault with Gray.

Would she really rather think more about taking a chance with someone whose face she didn't even know? And whose motives she couldn't be sure of. Why *was* that pirate sneaking around, and where did he fit in? He seemed to know more than the rest of them did, possibly even more than the police, but he refused to share that knowledge. He wanted her to trust him. But with a murder accusation hanging over her head, could she really afford to do that? Who could he possibly be . . . ?

"Are you coming, Diane?" Anita asked.

When Diane looked up she had the feeling she'd missed something. "Coming where?" she asked, seeing that the others were sort of drifting off while they talked. "Where are we going?"

"Over to the bar-lounge area," Anita answered, linking an arm through hers to draw her along. "In less than an hour, you, Lynn and Ralph have to be at that individual talk thing scheduled in the big conference room. We've decided to have drinks until then, and afterward we'll go to dinner."

"For some reason my appetite this weekend isn't what it usually is during a convention," Diane said with a sigh, letting herself be coaxed into motion. "Murder isn't as much fun as it used to be."

"You'll get over feeling like that," Anita assured her. "Murder *is* fun. Nothing will ever change *my* mind about that."

"It better not, or you probably won't have a job editing mysteries anymore," Diane said with a smile. "But come to think of it, you might have a problem with that anyway. You and I were supposed to talk business this weekend, but we haven't found much time for it."

"There's always breakfast tomorrow," Anita said with a dismissive wave of her hand. "If neither one of us becomes a corpse before then, we'll consider it a date. How's ten o'clock?"

"Morbid," Diane said distinctly while Anita chuckled. "Ten o'clock is fine, but the rest is morbid. Let's catch up with the others."

Catching up wasn't difficult, not with everyone adjusting their pace to Lynn's cane-assisted stroll. The subject was still whether or not Angela had been murdered, and if she *had* been done in, how her death connected to David's. They were *all* being morbid, Diane realized, but it was a question that did have to be answered.

"You ladies take that couch," Bill directed when they reached their destination, gesturing at the sheet-covered object. "We manly he-men can struggle with dragging over those monstrous chairs."

"It isn't that much of a struggle for some, Bill," Lynn pointed out, referring to the way Gray was having no trouble with the chair he'd chosen to bring over. "But I think I need to ask a favor. Gray, my dear, may I trade seats with you? Getting in and out of a chair is much easier for me."

"Of course, Lynn," Gray answered with a smile after setting the chair in place. "I've always preferred couches to chairs anyway."

"And since it's necessary, you'll force yourself to sit next to Diane," Anita said with amusement. "Outsider man-

ners are a nuisance to *us*, Mr. Grayson. We're not set rock
hard in our ways. We all know you like her, so why try to
hide it?''

"As a matter of fact, what I'm trying is the exact opposite," Gray answered with a smile as he seated himself next
to Diane. "Is it working?"

"Look, there's George Lombardy," Ralph interrupted,
saving Anita from having to answer and Diane from the
warmth she could feel in her cheeks. "George, come on over
and join us."

"With pleasure," George called. He paused only long
enough to get a chair for himself. Once he was seated he
said, "I have something to ask you about. What happened
with Angela Wilkes?"

"It looked like suicide, but there's a chance it's murder," Ralph answered. "But let's talk about something else.
Diane mentioned you told her you'd heard a story about
David Bellamy and a writer. Would you tell us that story
now?"

"Why not?" George said with a shrug. "I would have
thought one of you would have heard it— The word went
around that Bellamy had been playing footsie with a well-
known female writer, then dumped her for another female
writer. The first one threatened to kill them both if he didn't
come back to her, but he wasn't having any. Everyone had
their own guesses about who the women were, but nothing
in the way of solid proof ever turned up. Does that help you
any?"

"If it turns out that Angela was a suicide, it does indeed," Ralph answered with a thoughtful nod. "She wanted
David back, but David ignored her to torment Diane. Angela went crazy with jealousy, killed David so no one else
would have him, framed Diane to get even with her, then
grew so despondent she committed suicide."

"I'm afraid I can't accept that," Lynn said, her wrinkled
face thoughtful. Some of the others murmured agreement.
"If one of us tried putting that pat a solution into a book,
we'd get the manuscript bounced back by return mail. And
I think we all know that real life is *much* stranger than the

things we write. I can't imagine events falling into that neat a package.''

"You're suspicious because real life doesn't usually cooperate by being neat?" Ralph asked with a snort. "That's another line of reasoning we'd never get away with in print, Lynn. What's your real reason for not agreeing?''

"You know me too well for me to get anything by you, Ralph," she answered with something of a smile. "I *do* have another reason for believing as I do, but I can't put it into words yet. When I can I'll set it out in front of you."

"Then it's a theory you're working on, and not a reason," Ralph said with a stronger smile. "All right, go ahead and keep it to yourself. And if one of us comes up with it on our own before you say anything, we'll refuse to believe you thought of it first."

Lynn nodded her head regally in agreement to his terms, and Diane noticed that Ralph looked faintly disappointed. He'd probably been trying to coax Lynn into revealing her theory now, but the older woman hadn't fallen for his trick. If someone else came up with her theory, she'd lay no claims to the idea.

But that was *if* someone else came up with the theory. Knowing Lynn, Diane was certain that wasn't going to be as easy as it sounded, not for Ralph, not for her, and certainly not for George. As far as Bill and Anita went, if one of *them* came up with the idea first, they'd probably decide to turn writer. And Gray...

Gray was sitting on her left, his right arm on the couch back behind her, most of his attention on what was being said around him. *Most* of his attention. The rest seemed to be turned inward, and Diane suddenly had the strangest feeling that if anyone was able to anticipate Lynn, he would be the one....

People kept coming over to get the "real" story from those who had had close encounters with the deaths, and soon it was time for the individual talks.

Gray slipped a hand to Diane's back as she began to get up, helping her to her feet, and she smiled her thanks before joining the general exodus. She enjoyed his helping hand, but if that was Gray's idea of showing active interest, there was a pirate he really ought to meet....

ONCE DIANE and the others were settled with their groups of fans around them, Gray slipped out of the room and returned to his suite. He had about an hour before the group reassembled for dinner, and he wanted to call Jack and bring him up to date on the latest happenings. Someone had said something that had given him the faintest, tiniest glow of an idea, one that he wasn't yet able to reach. He didn't know what it was that had sparked the idea, otherwise he would have tried encouraging the thought from the other end.

He sat down in the chair behind the desk in his study, but didn't immediately reach for the phone. For the last few minutes something else had been bothering him, and although he'd been trying not to think about it the disturbance refused to let him be. When he'd finally put his arm around Diane to help her off the couch...the way she'd smiled at him...

"She's just about convinced that's the best you can do, you jerk," Gray growled at himself. "Are you holding back because you don't want to cut in on yourself in that other getup? What is your problem?"

He wished he knew the answer to that one, but he couldn't seem to figure it out. It never seemed to be the right time for Gray to make his move, not even when Anita Rutledge had brought the matter into the open. He'd forced himself to admit his interest. But Diane hadn't said anything, hadn't even looked as if she *wanted* to say something. Under other circumstances Gray might have wondered what she was thinking, but right then he was pretty sure he knew. She was thinking about how much better a certain pirate would have handled things...

"Good grief, I'm *jealous* of myself!" he whispered, not quite believing matters had come to that. "I'm holding back with her because I know there's a man she likes better than me!"

Gray put a hand over his eyes and leaned back in the chair. Diane Philips was attracted to the pirate she'd already met twice, and the proof of that was the way she hadn't told anyone about their second meeting, not even her closest confidants. She was protecting the man, trusting him the way he'd asked her to.

Almost the way she trusted him, James Grayson. Almost, but not quite.

He cursed at himself under his breath, then reached for the phone. He didn't have time to waste on fantasies, not if he wanted to be ready for the enemy's next move. And there would be a next move. He was sure of that.

"Hey, Jack, how are you doing?" he said when his partner answered the phone. "Boy, this is turning out to be a weekend I'll never forget. I may even come back to the city to tell you about it before going home."

"It's all right, the line's clear," Jack responded to Gray's hidden question. "What have we got now?"

"A suicide that might turn out to be a murder," Gray answered. "Here's what happened." He gave Jack all the details, included the incident in the maze, then said, "So you see why we think Diane's being set up for something else. The death of the Wilkes woman may or may not be part of it, but there almost has to be something else."

"You sound like you're hoping," Jack commented. "It's gone from 'the Philips woman' to 'Diane' awfully quickly. You're not forgetting that even if you proved her innocent it would only be half the job, are you?"

"No, I'm *not* forgetting," Gray said, working to keep the words free of anger. "The main reason I'm here is to find out who *is* guilty, to clear my brother. But it won't be Diane. Do you have anything new from your end? If not, I have to be getting back."

"There's one thing," Jack answered with a sigh. "An addition to the background info I gave you. Lynn Haverstock—sometimes called the reigning queen of mystery—she stopped writing about three years ago, and most people aren't sure why. The general opinion is that she finally ran dry, but there was one small column that had a theory of its own."

"Let me guess," Gray said, leaning forward. "David Bellamy was involved."

"However did you know that?" Jack asked sourly. "You must be psychic. Yeah, Bellamy was involved, him and his column. He wrote this piece that supposedly praised her last few books, but what he really did was suggest the plots had been used before, the twists were obvious, and the characters boring. He also very delicately asked if it wasn't time for her to retire before she really embarrassed herself. After the column she pulled the manuscript that had been about to go to auction and never submitted another word."

"So we now have another life ruined because of him," Gray said, digesting what he'd heard. "If the others know, and they probably do, they're accepting her decision by not discussing it. If Diane wasn't on the spot because of his death, I'd be tempted to walk away and forget about it, too. What if it turns out that the murder group had nothing to do with this? What if your friend Ed picked up a whisper of something unrelated, and either assumed or hoped it was connected?"

"Then *you'll* have to make the call," Jack said without hesitation. "There are some people who never break the law, ones who attack the helpless in such a devious way that the law *can't* step in. If one of those finally drives a victim into giving him what he deserves, I won't lose any sleep over it. The law has to prosecute the victim if he or she can be found, but it isn't your job to find them. It's up to you whether or not to turn over any evidence you find."

"Yes, I can see that," Gray said, then added his goodbyes. Once he'd hung up he just sat in the chair for a while, thinking about what he might have to do. He couldn't let Diane be charged with the murder, but how would she feel if he got her free by proving Lynn Haverstock guilty? Assuming Lynn *did* have something to do with the murder...

Gray tapped the arms of the chair decisively, then got to his feet. From what the others had said, the convention people wanted all of their attendees at the costume party that night. They had something planned that wasn't on the original schedule, a surprise for all the pros who had so graciously attended.

While everyone was busy with that, the pirate would be going through Lynn Haverstock's possessions, trying either to prove or disprove her guilt. If he came across any proof on the pro side, he could decide later what to do with it.

In the meantime, since James Grayson had to actually show up at the party he'd better rent a costume of his own. And he did intend to be everywhere Diane was until the mystery was solved. After that...

He cursed at himself again, then strode out of the room.

WHEN THE INDIVIDUAL talk session was over, Diane joined the others in going to dinner. Once again they were eating in the restaurant on the lobby floor because they didn't want to be late to the costume party. Maybe after the party things would start going back to normal.

"Never saw anything like it in my life," Ralph announced as he settled at the table. "All they wanted to talk about was my books. Don't they know there was a *murder*?"

"One murder here against fifty or more in your books, Ralph," Bill pointed out with amusement. "And the one here hasn't yet been neatly solved. I'm sure they've talked it out among themselves. But since they can't come up with the answer, they'll talk about books until the next thing happens."

"What if there isn't a next thing?" Diane suddenly found herself demanding. Books were not what *her* group had insisted on talking about, and she felt strung out almost to the breaking point. "What if nothing more happens, and tomorrow afternoon we simply all go home?"

"I don't see how the murderers can allow that," Ralph answered for Bill, reaching for the coffee that had already been brought and poured. "The police won't stop investigating until they have someone to blame the murder on, and it looks like poor Angela won't serve the purpose. If she had left a note confessing, they might have given in to the temptation and closed the case. But, without a note...what do you think, Lynn?''

"I agree," Lynn said. The older woman seemed more quiet and introspective than usual. "If they don't have someone to arrest or blame, they'll just keep digging. That's been clear from the beginning."

"So that means there *is* a next thing on the schedule," Ralph stated, now picking up his menu. "What it will be is anyone's guess, so we'll just have to wait and see. And speaking of guesses, does anyone know what this surprise the convention people have for us will be? Bill? Anita? George?"

Everyone agreed they hadn't any idea, and then settled down to decide what they wanted to eat. Everyone, that is, but Diane. She couldn't argue with what Ralph and Lynn had said, and that meant there was more horror in store for her. If she'd had anything of an appetite earlier, that realization killed it entirely.

"Don't let it get to you," a quiet voice murmured from her left. And then Gray's right arm was around her shoulders, his left hand patting hers. "You won't have to face whatever's coming alone. And just remember, the more they do, the more of a chance there is that they'll make a slip."

She turned her head to look at the calm man regarding her, and suddenly she could feel that he was right. She wasn't alone, not with him there, and that did make all the difference.

"Thank you," she whispered back with as much of a smile as she could manage, briefly squeezing his hand. "You're absolutely right. I won't forget again that I have friends."

His expression flickered at her use of the word friend, but what else could she have said? At that point they were no more than friends, even though she was beginning to wish he'd tried a little harder to make it more than that.

Diane tried ordering very little, but the others bullied her into choosing a full meal. The table talk drifted into discussions of writing and editing and publishing, and when the food came, Diane found she was able to do it justice. Most of *her* thoughts were about Gray, and how good it felt to have him sitting there beside her.

When the meal was over, everyone separated to go to their various rooms and suites to get ready for the costume party. Diane expected Lynn to go with her, but when she turned around the older woman had already disappeared. Possibly she was going back to her own room for something, and would return to Diane's later.

Gray stopped to pick up his costume at the shop, and then he saw Diane to her door. She hoped he would say he'd stop back when he was ready, so they could go to the party together. But all he did was smile and say he'd see her later. Then he went on to his own suite.

Diane was disappointed, but the only one available to tell that to was herself. Herself told her to forget it and get on with taking her bath, but she only accepted half the advice. She went to take her bath, but still kept thinking about Gray.

After the bath she should have put on her costume, but she wrapped up in her robe instead, then lay down on her bed. She was tired after the day she'd had, it wasn't over yet, and she hadn't been wise enough to take time to exchange the harem queen's costume for something else. She almost felt as though the costume was bad luck, since that's what she'd been wearing when she'd found David's body.

But it was also what she'd been wearing when she first met the pirate. Would that make the costume *good* luck? She didn't know, and thinking about it was making her very sleepy...

IT WASN'T a loud noise that woke Diane, but it was a definite sound and it had come from Lynn's room. The clock said she hadn't slept long, and she was still sleepy. But she also wanted to ask where Lynn had gone, so she got up.

The pull cord opened Diane's door silently, and she resettled the robe around her as she padded toward the second bedroom. Odd that Lynn had just left like that, without a word to anyone. Had it been personal business that had taken her away, or was she working on her theory?

Diane reached up and twisted the wall hanger, and only at that minute did her sleepy mind ask, "How did Lynn get in? The door was locked, and she didn't have a key!"

The question was a good one, but it came a little too late. The door was already sliding open....

Chapter Fifteen

Gray let himself into his suite, arranged the new costume on his bed, then ignored it in favor of digging out the pirate costume. He had some looking around he needed to do before the costume party started, and if he hurried he wouldn't be more than a few minutes late.

He'd wanted to ask Diane to wait for him so they could go to the party together, but that wouldn't have fit in with his snooping plans. He'd enjoyed being with her even with four other people around, and somehow he thought she might be enjoying it as well. If he'd called for her, the two of them might have found themselves alone . . . unless Lynn Haverstock had come back from wherever it was she'd disappeared to. The way she'd just gone off after dinner bothered Gray, especially after her silence during the meal. And the older woman hadn't eaten as well as she'd pretended. There was something on her mind affecting her appetite.

Just now, the only possibility Gray could think of was regret over what she would have to do to strengthen the frame around Diane. He didn't like to think that, especially since Lynn appeared to be sincerely fond of Diane, but he couldn't take any chances. He had to check her room to see if there was anything incriminating to be found.

Gray donned the pirate costume in record time, all the while cursing himself for not having checked Lynn's room while she was doing that individual talk thing. Between the conversation with Jack and the need to rent a costume he hadn't had much time, but he should have squeezed it in anyway. If something happened to Diane because *he'd* had too full a schedule...

The stairway to the third floor wasn't far from Gray's suite, and he got to Lynn's door without seeing anyone. He reached inside his shirt for the passkey card he'd liberated from the staff area that morning. He used it quickly, opened the door, and slipped inside.

There was no one there. The older woman's clothes were in the dresser and closet and her toiletries arranged on the wide sink in the bathroom, but there was nothing unusual in those places. There was also nothing taped to the back or bottom of any of the drawers, under the mattress or chair cushions, behind the window drapes, or in the toilet tank.

Gray glanced at the room's ceiling, but even if there'd been a fixture he didn't think Lynn would have been able to reach it. That meant there was only one place left to search: the bag she'd taken to Diane's suite the night before. He'd have to retrace his steps to the second floor, and try to find out if Diane was gone from the suite.

He checked the hall before stepping out of Lynn's room, but the luck he'd had was too good to hold forever. He had barely started toward the stairway when a door opened halfway down the hall, and a woman dressed in a pink costume stepped out. Gray kept going, hoping she would simply think he was someone on his way to the party, but no such luck.

"Hey!" the woman called. "Hey you, the pirate!"

Grey broke into a run, reached the stairway before the woman had taken more than a couple of steps, and took the stairs downward two at a time. The woman in pink was Anita Rutledge, and the last thing he needed was to be cornered by her. The more people who saw him in both guises, the better the chance he would be found out.

Just as he reached the bottom of the flight, he heard the door opening above, and then the clatter of high heels. The Rutledge woman was following him. That meant it was time to disappear for a while. He checked the hall quickly before moving out into it, then headed straight for his own door.

He had just gotten the door closed behind him when Anita Rutledge appeared. Through the peephole he could see she was slightly out of breath and more than slightly annoyed. She'd obviously lost her quarry, and couldn't see a trail to be picked up.

He was able to watch Anita walk across to Diane's door, still looking around. Then she gave up the search and knocked. She waited a moment, knocked a second time, then gave up on that too and walked away. A minute or so later Gray heard the sound of elevator doors opening and closing, and when he risked a look the woman was gone.

He took a deep breath, then eased back into the hall. Getting spotted was unfortunate, but at least he now knew Diane's suite was probably empty. That meant he'd be able to check Lynn's room there, go back and get into the ghost costume he'd rented, then catch up with Diane.

Getting inside was no harder than it had been with Lynn's room and he knew how to find the bedrooms. He stepped into the room he'd seen briefly when he'd brought Lynn's bag to it, located the bag and its contents and began his search.

The mattress landed back on the bed with more of a thump than he'd intended, but it was a good indication of how frustrated he felt. Gray wouldn't have enjoyed finding out Lynn was guilty, but at least it would have been a final answer.

He stood in the middle of the room, mind whirling with dozens of thoughts.

And that was when the door to the passage slid open right in front of him.

"What are you doing here?" Diane asked the pirate, privately trying to decide whether to move closer to him or run. He'd gotten into her suite without the least trouble, and that meant he could have done it before...to get a candlestick...

"Happily demolishing a theory," the raspy answer came. Diane could feel eyes behind the mask fix on her. "I learned that Lynn Haverstock had a very strong motive for murdering Bellamy, and I was trying to confirm or deny her guilt. So far there's nothing to show she was involved in any way."

"Well, of course she wasn't involved," Diane responded indignantly, enough encouraged by the pirate's motionlessness, and his response to her question, to step forward into the room. "I'm not saying Lynn could never kill a man like David. If she had strong enough reason she would do it, but she would never try to blame me—or anyone else."

"For the moment I'll be glad to take your word for that," the man whispered, soft words framed in a rough tone. "Ralph Teak also has a motive, as does his editor Bill Raglan. Is there anyone *you've* been able to add to the list?"

"Everyone seems to be on that list, including George Lombardy, who barely knew him," Diane answered with a sigh. "David apparently went out of his way to make enemies of half the world, and I simply can't understand that. Why would any human being prefer being hated to being liked or loved?"

"Some people have been so twisted, they think hatred *is* love," the pirate answered in a rasp that somehow suggested pain. "People really do want to be loved, so they go looking for what they're raised to think that is."

"That's horrible!" Diane whispered with a shudder, closing her eyes. "Could that be why Angela fell in love with him? Because that was the sort of love *she'd* been raised with? But where does something like that stop? *How* is it stopped?"

"That's a question a lot of people would like the answer to," he said. Then he took her in his strong arms. "Are you all right?"

Diane nodded, and it wasn't a lie. She was pressed tight to the man who had called himself her secret admirer. He seemed to understand exactly how she felt, and even felt that way himself. He'd asked her to trust him, and at that moment there was no question that she did.

She raised her face to look at him, to try to see through and around his mask to the man behind. He reminded her of someone, but she couldn't for the life of her remember who. The feel of those arms was familiar, the gentleness in the way he held her comforting. Was she just remembering the last time *he'd* done it?

It was all so confusing, so close to being overwhelming. Why couldn't she have met him only during the dance at the costume party, instead of also standing over a corpse? Why couldn't they exchange their own names instead of the names of suspects? And when was all this going to end, so they *could* do all those things?

"I'm getting closer to those I'm after," he whispered, almost as though he were reading her mind. "I promise you it won't be much longer, and after that—"

He left the rest of the promise hanging in the air, but Diane didn't mind. He had also lowered his lips to hers, and the warmth in them immediately spread to the hands touching her through the robe. The softness of his lips, the strength in those hands—suddenly she was returning his kiss with passion. It was insanity, pure, unblemished madness; in spite of that it was what she wanted.

Her arms circled the broad hardness of his body so that she too, could touch with her hands. Now his kisses were consuming her as hers were consuming him.

He made a small sound deep in his throat. One of her bare breasts had touched his flesh where his shirt lay open, and he shuddered as though burned by the contact.

"Will you let me make love to you?" he rasped in his whisper, refusing to let the words interrupt his kisses. "If the answer is no, I have to leave *now*."

Diane wanted to say yes, everything inside her screamed that she would be a fool to refuse, but she suddenly discovered she'd been asked for an agreement she couldn't give. Fantasy is wonderful if it somehow appears in your life, but it doesn't do well when it comes into contact with reality. She trusted her secret admirer, but there were no promises between them—and there was someone else to consider.

"No is the only answer I can give," she whispered, hating the words even as she spoke them. "If you don't understand why, I can't explain it."

He hesitated very briefly, presumably looking down at her, and then he nodded wearily.

"Unfortunately, I *do* understand," he whispered back, slowly taking his arms from around her. "I'd love to be able to tell you you're being unreasonable, but that wouldn't be the truth. We'll just have to wait until this is all over. You'll see me again—and soon—but for now, good-bye."

His fingertips came to her cheek to match the last of his words, and then he was striding out without looking back. Diane followed to see that the door closed behind him, then put on the night latch before going back to her own bedroom.

"All right, you did the right thing," she muttered to herself as she lay down on her bed. "It was the only thing you could do, even if your body will hate you for it forever."

I know what would have happened if I hadn't refused, she thought, her hands on the robe that still covered her. He would have carried me to the bed, put me down gently, then opened the robe to let his hands and lips touch me. His kisses on my breasts would make my flesh tingle and harden, the feel of his hands all over my body would drive me mad. I would take his face in my hands and kiss the lips that had been caressing my breasts, and then my hands would reach for his body.

And the feel of it! So broad and hard and wonderful to feel pressed up against me! Kissing and touching we would learn each other, and then he would be free of his clothes and moving to kneel between my thighs. I would be aching for his touch, and then he would be with me and buried deep inside, giving while I took, taking while I gave. Delight without end forever and ever—

Until the perfect ending, the slide down from the mountain top we'd both reached. I would be held in his arms as I also held him, and we'd kiss a final time before he reached to take off that mask. Under it would be—

At that point Diane dissolved into tears. Under the mask would be someone she didn't know, but couldn't possibly be the someone she *wanted* to know. She hadn't insisted on seeing his face, hadn't felt she had the right to do that, but part of that fairness stemmed from cowardice. As long as she put off seeing the pirate, she could dream about it possibly being Gray's face under there. And that made everything a thousand times harder...

GRAY COVERED the short distance to his suite in about a jump and a half, got himself inside and stopped only long enough to put away the pirate costume before getting into the shower. He had to get the makeup off, but even more than that he had to wash away the memory of what he'd almost had with Diane. He *did* understand why she'd refused him. She was a woman with standards, principles...

He wanted her so badly he would have torn down walls to reach her, but the one wall he couldn't touch was that of time. It was the wrong time for both of them, even though the desire was there.

Desire. Gray put his face into the stream of water as he laughed silently and mirthlessly. Diane wanted him as much as he wanted her, that he knew without doubt. If not for all the nonsense around them they could have done as they pleased, gone as far as they cared to.

And I know exactly what it would have been like, Gray thought to himself, the water falling on him almost forgotten. I would have picked her up in my arms and carried her to the bed, and then I would have been able to get rid of that robe. Her body was so soft and beautiful, curved and rounded and calling out to the fire in my blood. My hands would have stroked that softness before my lips and tongue tasted it.

And she would be joining me in that, moaning as she ran her small, delicate hands over me. Her touch would drive me onward toward that uncontrollable moment, the time I would have to have her, but at first it would just bring my lips to hers. How soft and yielding her lips are, but her kiss is as demanding as my own.

The only thing I can think of is getting closer and closer, and then my clothes are gone and her body welcomes me as I begin moving into her—a welcome unlike anything I've ever experienced. I gather her to me as our souls start to merge...but is it the souls of two people in love, or the souls of two strangers? She wanted the love of her secret admirer, but what about the love of the quiet man who had been following her around...?

Gray didn't know how long he'd been standing there, which meant he now had to hurry in order to get downstairs before Diane did. If he arrived *after* her, she would certainly start wondering why.

As he rushed to dress, he flatly refused to listen to the part of him that demanded to know why she hadn't already recognized him. The pirate and Gray were the same size, the same build, the same— Hell, they were the same man! She'd seen the pirate three times now and been with Gray most of the rest of the time. Why hadn't she connected the two?

"Probably because James Grayson doesn't really interest her," he muttered to himself as he struggled to get his ghostly drapery straight over the white pants and shirt meant to be worn with it. He also had a hood-type mask for his head, but he would carry that for a while.

And he had to ask himself why he hadn't told her who he really was? To protect his working identity? Since he didn't believe he had to protect it from her, why hadn't he let her know? Because then he would never know if it was James Grayson she wanted, or a mysterious pirate? Could he be that insecure? Well, to hell with guesswork. Once the murder ring was straightened out, he'd ask Diane about her interest in James Grayson.

With that decision made he was finally able to get himself out of the suite, over to the stairway and down to the lobby floor where he intended to wait for Diane. He took a moment to peek into the ballroom, just to make sure she hadn't gotten down before him, then he went back to stand near the elevators.

"The most appropriate costume possible for James Grayson," he muttered to himself. "A ghost...."

DIANE STEPPED into the elevator knowing she was late, but she hadn't been able to rush. Or, more accurately, hadn't wanted to. It was so much nicer to be thinking about plea-

sure rather than death, but now that she was out of her suite
the real world had the chance to intrude again. Part of her
wanted to leave, simply admit defeat and run away, but the
rest of her wouldn't allow it. And it wasn't just that the police would never allow it either....

When the elevator doors opened on the lobby floor, the
first thing she saw was what looked like the back of a ghost.
Then the ghost turned and it was Gray, waiting patiently for
her to come down. Why hadn't he stopped at her suite when
he was ready, and checked to see if she was, also?

But maybe he had. Diane felt a stab of guilt and possibly
even a small twinge of regret. If he'd gotten to her suite *before* the pirate, it might have been he that she'd gotten to
know a little better. Not that she would have gone to bed
with him, or even would have expected him to ask her. He
was being so careful not to insult her or chase her away....

"Oh, Gray, I'm so sorry I kept you waiting," she said,
meaning every word. "If I'd only known..."

"But you couldn't know," he said with a smile, coming
forward to offer a sheet-draped arm. "It was my fault for
not arranging something with you before we went to dress.
Shall we go in?"

She took his arm with an answering smile, but there was
no smile inside her. When she was with the pirate she remembered no one else, and when she was with Gray she
didn't *want* to remember anyone else. What could be wrong
with her that she felt like that toward two completely different men?

Gray was calm and warm and supporting, but he didn't
command an entire room simply by being in it. The pirate
was exciting and strong and protective, but he couldn't
possibly be considered comfortable. In a distant, physical
way the two were almost alike, but in more important ways
they were totally different.

And Diane didn't know how—if it ever came to that—she
would choose between them.

Reaching the ballroom, Gray put on his hood, and they
joined the other costumed revelers. The room was abso-

lutely packed with people, and they had to move all the way into the center of it before they could dance.

Not more than ten minutes went by before the music was stopped, and a male voice came over the PA system.

"Sorry to interrupt your fun, people, but it'll just be for a little while," the jolly voice said. "We're ready now to unveil the surprise we have for our valued pros, so will the writers please come to the front of the room."

The crowd began shifting around a little, trying to get out of the way of those who'd been summoned forward. Behind the portly vampire holding a microphone was a large, screened something that had just been rolled in by three members of the staff. Everyone was watching it with curiosity.

"I'm suspicious," Ralph stated as he came up beside Diane. He was in his devil's costume, his red-rimmed eyes narrowed. "If they tell us we have to guess what it is before we get it, I'm for turning around and leaving."

"Let's wait until they say that before we decide to leave," Diane said with a smile. "Otherwise we may miss out on something good."

"I'll believe that when I see it," Ralph returned with a shake of his head, and then he looked around. "And where, by the way, has Lynn disappeared to? I didn't see her when you got here, and now she isn't part of our forward-standing subcrowd. Doesn't she want her share of the surprise?"

Diane was about to say that Lynn hadn't come in with her, but the jolly man with the microphone chose that moment to interrupt.

"All right, we're ready now," he said, the amplified words cutting into all conversation. "This is a special Haunted House, thank you for those who helped make this convention work. Gentlespirits?"

The zombie and ghouls who had brought in the surprise began to remove the screening, but then one of them jumped back with a shout, knocking down what he'd been helping to remove. The portly vampire looked at him with a frown, then transferred the frown to what lay behind the flattened screening.

"Damn," he said, apparently forgetting that he was still holding a live microphone. "There's a dead body in our coffin-cake."

Half the people in the room surged forward as the other half drew back, but the scene of the newest occurrence wasn't overrun. Police officers seemed to materialize out of thin air, and a line of them held everyone back while Lieutenant Gerard and some of his people went for a closer look. It was clear the police had been ready for something to happen.

"Do you see that?" Ralph asked Diane. "A red sleeve. I'll bet anything you name we've finally found the zombie bellman who sent you to find David's body."

Diane couldn't speak, but soon there was a ghost beside her who provided a very welcome supporting arm.

"If it is that bellman, he should supply some answers even in death," Gray said, obviously having heard Ralph.

Those answers could be enough to get them to the bottom of things, Diane realized. They were due a break, and if there was any justice at all in the world . . .

"Lieutenant Gerard seems to be coming this way," Ralph observed. Bill and Anita and George Lombardy were now clustered beside Ralph. "What's that he's carrying in his handkerchief?"

"A small leather case of some sort," Bill supplied as he craned his neck. "Possibly a wallet."

"Good evening, Mr. Grayson, Ms. Philips," Gerard said when he reached them, ignoring everyone else. "I thought you might like to know that the uniform the corpse is wearing has a dark stain on the front of it—in addition to the other, newer stains."

"And if that's the man's wallet," Gray said, "it hopefully contains something with his name on it. Could the name possibly be John Dixon?"

"As a matter of fact, it isn't," Gerard said, looking first at Gray and then at Diane. "It's a name I'm not familiar with, but maybe one of you will recognize it. Do either of you know a—"

Gerard flipped open the wallet and glanced inside, but Diane was already in the grip of the coldest of chills. That wallet. It couldn't be. It couldn't possibly be.

"Richard Anderson?" Gerard finished.

"Call him Rick, Richard is much too stuffy," Diane mumbled, and then everything went black.

Chapter Sixteen

Everyone told Diane she didn't actually pass out. She had to be helped to a chair where Anita rubbed her wrist and gently slapped her cheeks, but her eyes stayed open the entire time. Diane herself remembered nothing of getting to the chair. Or of saying anything.

"Yes, that's right, everything will be fine," Anita's voice finally came through to her, sounding as though she'd said the same thing many times over "He'll find out who did it, and everything will be fine."

After that Gray helped her to the second-floor sitting room that Gerard had taken over for interviews.

"Unfortunately I now have proof I wasn't wasting my time hanging around waiting for the next move," Gerard said, standing with Gray behind her chair. "I think I would have preferred having to face an unjustified expenditure for manhours."

"I don't believe the nerve of those people," Gray said. "They had to have killed that man under the nose of every cop here."

"Don't rub it in," Gerard responded with a growl. "We tried to keep the major players of this game under surveillance, at least in the public areas, but doing it without letting anyone know is nearly impossible in this place. You don't know the dead man?"

"No, but it's fairly obvious Diane does," Gray said, sounding worried. "And I have the feeling she'll be the only one who does know him."

"We'll soon find out," Gerard said. "I told my men to get that zombie makeup off his face, and then take a couple of Polaroids. They should be here in just a few—"

A knock at the door interrupted him, but a moment later he was making a sound of satisfaction. A corner of Diane's mind knew what that sound meant, and it made her cringe inside.

"It's all right," Gray was suddenly saying to her, his arm around her shoulders. "You'll look at the picture just to be sure, and then you'll tell us all about it. Take your time, there's no need to rush."

Rush. The word made Diane feel like laughing. Of course there was no rush, in nightmares there never was. You might want to hurry, to get past the awfulness as fast as possible, but your efforts always turned into a crawl.

And then the picture was in front of her, a picture showing slack features with traces of white makeup. She would have preferred being unsure at the very least, but there wasn't any doubt. It was a picture of Rick, and there was no doubt he was dead.

Gray and Gerard were sympathetic but firm as they took turns coaxing her for the story. Slowly she gave it to them— from the time she had first met Rick to the time she'd decided to come to the convention to avoid him. Talking seemed to soothe the numbness in her mind, and by the time she was finished she was feeling hurt and confused rather than in shock.

"So he must have come looking for me, possibly even to apologize, and for that he lost his life," she finished in the dull voice that depression had forced on her. "Someone must have overheard him asking for me and decided on the spot that he was perfect for the next victim. He was someone only I would know, and therefore someone only I would have motive for killing."

"That would be a good idea despite its cold-bloodedness, but I'm afraid it doesn't work," Gerard said from the place behind the desk where he now sat. Gray had put a chair beside Diane's, and his arm hadn't left her shoulders.

"My man spent a couple of minutes questioning the available staff before bringing the picture up, and he said he got lucky," Gerard continued. "One of the staff people remembered seeing the dead man arrive yesterday, in the late afternoon. He had no luggage, he didn't inquire about anyone, and he didn't register."

"He got here yesterday?" Gray asked with a frown, before Diane could speak. "Then why didn't he try to get in touch with Diane? What was he doing all this time?"

"It could be presumed that he didn't get in touch with Ms. Philips because he already knew everything he needed to," Gerard answered, his tone now neutral. "He arrived here, got himself a uniform and makeup, helped her kill Bellamy, directed her to the body for the benefit of the audience in the ballroom, then went to hide out somewhere. Or maybe he was the mysterious pirate we were told about."

"No, he couldn't possibly have been the pirate," Diane said at once, absolutely certain. "If he had been, I would have known. Or are you just saying that he was supposed to be seen not only as my victim, but also as my accomplice?"

Diane discovered with a good deal of surprise that her guilt over Rick's death had thinned out since she'd learned he hadn't sought her out. She hadn't been able to cope with the idea that he was dead because of her, but now it seemed likely that she had nothing to do with any of it. In death she was no more than incidental to him, just as she'd been in life.

"He could have helped you kill Bellamy and possibly even Wilkes, before you two had your falling out," Gerard answered. "Then he tried to kill you during the maze game, so you decided to get rid of him before he tried again. You snuck up on him and killed him, and left him to be found in that cake."

"But what if we hadn't reported the attack in the maze?" Diane asked with a frown. "How would you have known I had such a good motive for killing him?"

"They weren't taking any chances," Gerard said with a snort. "My people were going to wait for the maze area to be closed for the day before they went looking for bullet holes, but it turned out not to be necessary. The hotel maintenance people had a call this afternoon from a nameless guest who reported worm holes in one of the maze corridors. When the workmen went to check it out, they discovered the worms were .38 caliber. We were called and given the chance to retrieve the bullets, and then the management was able to give us a list of everyone who had used that corridor today. I guess it was pure coincidence that your name turned up on the list."

"Just like it would be pure coincidence if the newest victim happened to have been shot by the same gun," Gray put in. "And I bet he *was* shot. Am I right, Gerard?"

"I'd been hoping for a blowgun or a poisoned pygmy arrow," Gerard replied. "I've also been thanking my lucky stars I'm as much of a skeptic as I am. A large crop of coincidences will bother any normal cop, but some of the ones we've got here are really subtle. If someone else came in to take over this case right now, they'd probably arrest Ms. Philips first thing."

"That sounds like you're *not* going to arrest me," Diane said, wondering why she wasn't feeling relieved. Then it came to her. "If our guesswork was right and Rick was killed for the specific reason of framing me more tightly, what will they do now that it didn't work? If someone else was killed because of me, and this time it was someone I really cared about, I don't think I could stand it."

"I don't like the idea of someone else getting hurt any more than you do," Gerard told her, compassion now clear in his voice and eyes. "My biggest problem is that I'm ninety percent convinced of your innocence, and the guilty are still walking around out there. I have to give them enough rope to choke on, and the only way of doing that is not charging you."

"You intend to use Diane as a decoy?" Gray demanded, suddenly no longer calm and easygoing. "You hope they'll go after *her* next, and try to make it look like a suicide? Gerard, I won't stand for that, I'm telling you I—"

"Just take it easy, Grayson," the lieutenant said soothingly, holding up one hand. "As long as I don't have to hide from *her*, I can keep a really close watch against anything they might decide to do. With you on the inside and us everywhere else, she'll be perfectly all right."

"And I *want* to do it, Gray," Diane said suddenly, surprising even herself. "Lieutenant Gerard is right. The next try should be against me. This will keep everyone else safe, and still give us a chance to find the killers. You do want to help find them, don't you?"

Diane watched him hesitate, real worry in his light eyes. He seemed unaware of the way she'd taken his hand in both of hers. It felt odd for her to be reassuring him, but there was no doubt he needed it. He looked torn between two different desires, but he really had little choice in how to answer.

"Yes, of course I want to help find the killers," he said at last. "What I don't want to find is them standing over your body. If I'm supposed to be on the inside, that's just where I'm going to be. Lynn will move back to her own room, and I'll take over the second bedroom in your suite."

He said the words almost like an ultimatum, but the look in his eyes told Diane he knew he needed her agreement. She had to smile then. The second bedroom of her suite seemed a particularly appropriate place for Gray.

She nodded. "All right, the inside spot is yours," she said. "If Lynn won't give up the room, you'll just have to share it with her. She told me she was trying to be a dirty old lady."

"She'll never make it," Gray said with a grin. "A lady she is, but never dirty and never even truly old. Is there anything in particular you want us to do, Gerard? Report in at regular times, or some such?"

"No, we'll be best off if Ms. Philips simply goes about her business, giving them the impression they can get to her without any trouble," Gerard answered. "I've been given accommodations here in the hotel, so I'll be around if you need me. And don't forget, if anything unusual happens, let me know right away."

"At this point we'd need a scorecard to spot something unusual," Gray said, urging Diane to her feet as he stood.

"After this weekend, going back to the everyday will be a positive relief."

"Just make sure you don't relax too soon," Gerard said as he also rose. "This weekend isn't over yet, not by a long shot."

Diane felt like shivering at that comment. They would have to keep their eyes open, and hope they saw the trap before they walked into it.

The lieutenant walked them to the door of the sitting room, opened it, then cleared his throat as he turned toward them.

"We may want to talk to you again, Ms. Philips, so please keep yourself available," he said in very formal tones. "The same goes for you, Mr. Grayson."

Diane saw Gray nod as he joined in the game of pretend antagonism with the police, but her part, as she saw it, didn't include that. She simply walked out of the room, too distraught to be bothered with being polite, and was almost immediately surrounded by the mob.

"Diane, child, are you all right?" Ralph demanded, looking down at her with narrowed eyes. "Who was that dead man, and what are the police going to do?"

"Why don't we go somewhere we can sit down?" Gray interrupted before Diane could answer. "The police have decided not to charge Diane, but it was a close thing."

"He's absolutely right," Bill put in, straightening the cuff of his Louis costume. "Let's at least get her comfortable before we begin pumping her unmercifully."

Anita and George added their agreements from their respective places, so the decision was made. They walked to the gathering room and got themselves settled on couches and in chairs.

"You know," Ralph observed by way of opening, "I'm beginning to believe it's a good thing we won't be wearing these costumes again. Twice worn, two bodies. Who was he, Diane?"

"The man I'd been dating for the past few months," Diane said with a sigh. "He was supposed to have come to the convention with me, but we broke up last week so I came alone. I had no idea he'd come up on his own."

"And they just killed him?" Bill demanded, looking outraged. "For no reason other than to make you look guilty? Do the police have any idea why he was here?"

"They're probably checking now to see if Diane called him," Gray put in quickly. "If they can't find that she did, they'll probably have to accept her statement that she hasn't seen him in over a week. Why he came here still isn't clear."

"Probably because someone *did* call him," Ralph stated, his mind obviously working quickly behind his distracted eyes. "Someone who knew enough about you, Diane, to know what you'd been involved with. It has to be the same one or ones who originally planned the frame, who were looking for something no one here could be accused of but you."

"But what good would it do them?" George asked, obviously feeling enough part of the group to put in his say. "Simply providing a dead body would be meaningless even if Diane did know him—unless he could be tied in with the first murder."

"That red sleeve!" Ralph pounced at once. "He *was* the one who directed you to David's body, wasn't he?"

"We can't be sure, but we think so," Diane admitted. "By 'we' I mean Gray and myself. The police are skeptical about the whole thing."

"But that was Friday night," Ralph said, his frown deeper now. "If he was here yesterday he must have been hiding, but why would he hide? Unless..."

"Here comes the waitress," Anita announced, smoothing down the pink skirt of her princess costume. "And just in time. The only person I know who can think clearly without a drink is Lynn Haverstock."

"That reminds me—" Diane started to say.

At the same time Ralph began, "As a matter of fact, I was just—"

And Bill said, "Speaking of Lynn, where *is* she?"

They'd each had trouble hearing the others, but they all knew they were saying the same thing. Lynn still wasn't with them, and by now she certainly should have been.

"All right, let's go at this the proper way," Ralph said, now sounding and looking grim. "Lynn had dinner with us, and that was the last time I saw her. I was expecting her to go to your suite with you, Diane."

"I looked for her after dinner, but she'd disappeared somewhere," Diane said. "Gray and I went to pick up his costume, and then he walked me to my door."

"Am I the only one who saw her going toward the ordinary part of the hotel?" Bill asked, looking around at everyone. "I thought she must have wanted something from the gift shop there, so I pretty much forgot about it. No one saw her after that?"

Not a single head nodded. That *had* been the last time anyone had seen Lynn, and Diane didn't like what that could mean.

"We're going to have to look for her," she stated after a minute's silence. "Assuming her disappearance is just a coincidence would be stupid after everything that's happened, but maybe we'll get lucky and it will be. I'm afraid..."

"Think positive until the negative happens," Bill said when she didn't finish the sentence, trying to sound assured as he leaned forward to pat her hand. "It's possible she *is* just off on her own somewhere, thinking about the puzzle. Unlike Sherlock and Mycroft Holmes, most people think best without distractions."

"Where will we start?" Anita asked, looking bewildered. "How can we possibly find her?"

"Let's start with the most obvious place," Gray said, getting to his feet. "I'll use a house phone to call her room."

He walked off toward the lines of phones sitting on a table in the corner of the room, but no one watched him go. Everyone was afraid they'd see the bad news before he brought it back.

If anything had happened to Lynn, Diane knew she would not rest until she found out who the murderers were. She had been shocked at herself for feeling so little over Rick's death, once she realized she wasn't to blame. But that reaction didn't mean she was without normal feelings. Rick had been someone she'd never really known, while Lynn— Lynn would be avenged, no matter what it took.

Chapter Seventeen

Gray took longer to get back from the phones than Diane had expected. Once he was seated beside her again she found out why.

"There was no answer in her room, so I got in touch with Lieutenant Gerard," he told the group. "Anita was right in saying we had no idea where to look, but Gerard won't have the same trouble. He has enough men here to look everywhere, and they can use members of the hotel staff to help. When they find her, they'll contact us here."

No one made any comment. Diane thought that they all seemed as worried as she felt, and they probably were feeling just as helpless.

Twice Bill tried to restore conversation to their group, but when the second attempt failed he gave it up. They sat in silence finishing their drinks until Gerard appeared, looking very tired.

"We finally found her," he announced, and his grimness caused Diane's chest to tighten. "She'd been hit over the head and dragged into a linen closet."

"She's dead then," Ralph said hollowly. His face looked pale, even under the red makeup.

"No, Mr. Teak, it so happens she isn't dead," Gerard said, looking around at everyone. "She was badly hurt from a blow someone gave her with her own cane. She was covered with blood and undoubtedly *looked* dead to her attacker, who happened to be in a public area and was therefore in a hurry. But she isn't dead yet. The emergency squad people weren't optimistic, though they said she does have a chance. She should be at the hospital by now, and she'll be under guard.''

"Good old Lynn," Ralph said with distinct relief. "Here's to you, old girl, and the way you'll make them pay."

He'd raised his glass in a toast that all the others joined, and once he'd drunk he looked up at Gerard again.

"She figured it out," he stated, almost daring Gerard to disagree with him. "I thought she was behaving strangely during dinner, and now I'm sure of it. She must have figured out who the murderer was, but still needed to confirm her theory. While she was doing it, the murderer noticed and decided to add her to the list of victims."

"You may be right," Gerard agreed without conceding anything at all. "Mr. Grayson, Ms. Philips, I'd like a private word with you over there, please."

He nodded toward a quiet corner of the room, and led the way over. Once there, he stood with his back to the rest of the group.

"As far as anyone else is to know, I'm questioning you about your whereabouts since dinner," he told his two listeners. "Since I'll be taking statements from the others as well, they should have no trouble believing it. In reality, I have something to tell you."

"Please don't say Lynn really is dead, and you were just setting a trap," Diane begged, fear once again replacing relief. "Please—!"

"She's alive," Gerard assured her quickly. "That part of it is true, and also the possibility that she might make it. The thing I wanted to talk to you about is the note we found in her purse. It said, 'He was a blackmailer!' and it was underlined. Do either of you have any idea what it might mean?"

"If it means anything at all, it refers either to the murderer or to David Bellamy," Gray said, while Diane tried to fit the words into the puzzle. "In either event, we'd need to know what the blackmail was about before we could tell who or why."

"No, those aren't the only possibilities," Diane said, drawing their attention. "You two probably don't know it, but Lynn used countless variations on the theme of blackmail in her books, most often disguising it as something else to keep it from being obvious. Her twists were always so intricate, most people never noticed. She could have spotted something that was blackmail, but not the kind of blackmail *we'd* recognize."

Gerard looked unhappy. "You two keep your eyes and ears open, and we'll do the same. If you think of anything else, call me."

This time they both nodded, and Gerard escorted them back to the group then took Ralph and Bill over to the corner. As soon as the three were gone, Anita leaned forward.

"I'll bet he's checking alibis," she said, a sober-looking George listening closely. "Did you tell him we already tried that?"

"All we told him was where we were," Diane said, stifling a sigh. "It's just the way it was with David's murder. Once we all separated to dress, any of us could have done it."

"I love the equal opportunity thinking the police use," George said. "Never mind if a person is *capable* of committing a crime, never mind if his entire life is blameless until that very moment. If he has motive, opportunity and means, he's automatically guilty of whatever crime was committed."

"Or they are," Gray said. "If more than one person fits the bill, they're all considered guilty until the list is narrowed down. What other way is there to look at it?"

"I don't know," George said with a shake of his head. "With more intelligence and less rule book, maybe. I suppose I don't know enough about it to judge. Maybe Bill does, seeing that he's had more experience with them."

"With the police?" Diane asked, frowning. "He was never in trouble."

"No, it had something to do with Ralph," George answered, looking vague. "I remember some story circulating at one of the conventions, but there weren't many details. Did you ever hear the story, Anita?''

"I don't listen to stories like that," Anita said so coolly that it was clear she was closing the subject. Then she smiled. "Ah, here come Bill and Ralph, so it must be our turn, George. Let's go."

As Bill and Ralph arrived, Diane decided she had had enough. Every time she turned around there was someone else being accused—if not attacked or murdered—and she'd had more than she could stand for one day.

"I think it's time to turn in," she announced once Anita and George had gone on their way. "If there are any more murders planned, they can happen without me."

"I can't remember ever feeling this exhausted at a convention," Ralph said. He certainly looked it. "Maybe I'm getting too old for this sort of thing."

"Sure, and Genghis Khan was a nice, easygoing fella," Bill said with a snort before finishing off his drink. "If you're feeling tired, Ralph, it's time to go to bed. But as for getting old—don't make me laugh."

Diane watched the two of them head for the elevators, then put a hand to Gray's arm to lead him the other way. They were already on their floor, and it wasn't that long a walk to their suites.

Once they were out of sight and hearing of the others, Gray asked, "How many different sorts of blackmail *are* there?" Obviously he'd been thinking about what she'd said. "You blackmail someone for money, or you do it to make them give you an inside track to something, or an edge you wouldn't normally have. What other things would you use it for?"

"Have you forgotten how David used it?" Diane asked in turn. "I doubt if he ever asked for money, but he still used it to get what he wanted. And some people do it without ever realizing that that's what they're doing. Haven't you ever heard of emotional blackmail? That's using someone's feelings as a handle to twist them in the direction you want them to go. Moral blackmail threatens to expose you to the disapproval of those around you, even though you probably haven't done anything *legally* wrong.''

''And psychological blackmail is another thing Bellamy made use of,'' Gray said with a distracted nod. ''Twisting people's thinking in order to get them to do as he wanted. What are the chances Lynn did mean him, and not the murderer or murderers?''

''I think the chances are excellent,'' Diane said, beginning to feel depressed again. ''David was blackmailing someone, and that's why he was killed. They must have been trying to frame me so that the investigation will end, but that's something I don't really understand. If what they were being blackmailed about was all that easy to discover, the police would probably have it by now. If they don't have it now, there's an excellent chance they never will.''

''Maybe—maybe it all has something to do with this weekend,'' Gray suggested, obviously groping for words. ''If someone is charged by the time this weekend is over, the investigation won't go beyond this area and this time. If it does go beyond it— I don't know, maybe everyone involved turns into a pumpkin.''

''I think I already have,'' Diane said with a yawn. ''It feels like years since the last time I slept. Who says thinking isn't hard work?''

''Not to mention all the rest of it,'' Gray said with a smile, then gestured ahead of them. ''There's my suite, and yours is right beyond it. We'll get you inside and do a quick search, then you'll lock the door behind me while I go get the things I'll need for staying the night.''

''And by the time you come back, I'll be able to fall right into bed,'' Diane said with a nod, surprising herself that she'd put in words what she'd been thinking. ''Is that the way you had it planned?''

''Well, you did say you were tired,'' Gray pointed out, but the flush in his cheeks was visible against the white of his costume. ''I mean, I thought I made it clear that I was just forcing you into letting me sleep in the suite, not anything else. I've never forced myself on a woman, and I never will.''

"I think you'd better check your definition of force, my friend," Diane said, opening her door. This time she used the word *friend* deliberately. "Something tells me most people don't apply it as broadly as you do. Okay, here we are. Search away."

Gray let the subject drop with indecent haste. He moved past her, opened the secret passage, then disappeared to begin his search.

"Some men need a good shaking," Diane muttered, choosing to wait rather than join Gray. "Here I stand in this costume, and all *he* wants is to be sure I know he won't make a pass at me—without even finding out whether or not I *want* him to. Which, as a matter of fact, I don't."

It happened to be the truth at the moment. There was such a thing as being too gentlemanly, and Gray had managed to find that perfect imbalance. He seemed to be waiting for her to knock him down and take advantage of him, but it wasn't going to happen. She remembered how the pirate hadn't waited for her to make the first move....

"I didn't find anyone hiding under the beds or in the closets," Gray announced as he came back into the room. "Lock the door behind me, and don't open it again unless you're sure it's me. I should be back in about ten minutes or so."

"Yes, sir, boss," Diane answered crisply, noticing that he still hadn't looked at her. "Any other orders, sir?"

"I've insulted you, haven't I?" he said with a sigh, finally bringing his light eyes up to study her. "I was trying to keep you from feeling cornered, but all I did was make you believe I'm uninterested. I'm not, you know. I just don't want these circumstances to force you into something you'll later regret."

As tired as she was, Diane was ready to disregard any excuse or explanation he made. But suddenly she really heard and understood what he was saying. It had nothing to do with whether or not he considered her attractive.

"You were thinking of me," she stated, knowing it to be the truth and feeling terrible for having embarrassed him. "I've never— Gray, I'm sorry."

"It's not your fault, it's simply my bad luck," he answered with a smile. Then he came over to raise her face to his. He brought his lips down to hers with firm deliberation as well as tenderness, and then he lifted his head again. "Tomorrow we'll get the bad guys, and then it'll be my turn. Will you have dinner with me tomorrow night? Just the two of us, alone?"

"But tomorrow I'm going home!" she protested, feeling even worse than she had.

"I know," he said, and his smile turned to a grin. "Come and lock this door behind me, and don't open it again until you're sure it's me."

He left then, pulling the door shut behind him, and Diane walked slowly over to lock up. She still felt terrible for having teased him about his plans and intentions, but something else had occurred to her. If Gray was being this careful to be sure she wasn't simply turning to him out of desperation, he must feel . . . he must be—

"Could he really be that serious?" she asked the room in a whisper. "Serious enough to be willing to follow me home? And he hasn't even made any smooth-sounding promises . . ."

Diane knew she'd never met a man like that before, and she very much wanted to get to know him better. But there was someone else to consider, someone who *had* made promises. She didn't know what to do. Forget one? Which one? Choose between them? How? Run away as fast as she could? She almost wished that were possible, but she'd promised herself never to run away again.

GRAY PACKED his clothes and toiletries in about a minute and a half, then went to the phone to call Jack. He wanted his partner to know what had happened and where he would be.

All he got was an answering machine. "If you have this number, you should know who you've reached," the message said in Jack's sour tones. "Since even dedicated geniuses like me need to sleep sometimes, you'll have to leave the latest after the beep. If you're an associate j.g., just follow the lead.''

Gray laughed as the beep sounded, then said, ''That's the whole trouble, there *are* no leads. Or possibly too many leads. We're having trouble deciding. There's now been another murder and an attempted murder. I'm staying with D, and can be reached there in case of emergency. Don't let the bedbugs bite.''

He hung up then, not wanting to leave too much information in case someone other than Jack heard the tape. ''Associate j.g.'' had nothing to do with a junior grade officer. It referred to him, James Grayson, who was Jack's current associate. And now he could get back to Diane.

Diane. Gray sat back in the chair, trying to decide how he should feel. On the one hand, he was delighted that she'd finally said something to him about his lack of active pursuit. It was an opening he hadn't wasted, and he was already looking forward to the dinner he'd asked her to.

But in another way he was very bothered. Diane had indicated an interest in *him*, but she hadn't said anything about another man in her life. And the other man wasn't just a casual acquaintance, not after what had gone on between them earlier in the evening. It had been passionately intense, a burning need between two very involved people.

Gray got out of the chair to pace, feeling like a peeping Tom who had spied on his major rival. He wasn't a child without experience. He knew women and the way they reacted, and Diane hadn't been thinking about anything casual and unimportant when she'd kissed the pirate. And yet, just a few minutes ago, she'd been encouraging Gray.

''Without a visible thought for the other man in her life,'' he muttered. ''Is she just showing an interest in me to cover what she feels for the pirate? She's been shielding him from everyone, defending him even with the police. . . .''

Gray experienced the most intense stab of jealousy, stronger than he'd ever known was possible. A woman like Diane, intelligent, caring, loyal—but loyal to another man!

''It doesn't matter that he loves her! I love her, too!''

It took saying that out loud to bring Gray back to his senses. It was one thing for Diane not to know there was only one man, entirely another for Gray to forget. He'd been pressing too hard in too many directions, had been running too short on sleep. Another day, and this insanity would hopefully be over.

"And tonight I'll have a talk with her," he promised himself, walking over to pick up his bag. "It's time to tell her who the pirate really is. It's one way of getting rid of him."

He smiled mirthlessly on his way back to Diane's suite. He hadn't gotten close enough to the enemy for them to see him in the pirate costume, so they hadn't been feeling the pressure he'd wanted them to. It had been one large waste of time except in *one* way.

When Diane was certain it was Gray, she opened the door. But there was nothing of the time alone with her he'd been looking forward to. She bid him an immediate, quiet good night and disappeared into her room.

Chapter Eighteen

Diane was up and dressed so early, she had more than enough time to order a pot of coffee from room service. She'd called the hospital and been told that Lynn's condition hadn't changed. That news had made her even more depressed and introspective than the rest of the mess.

She'd thought Gray was still asleep, but soon after the waiter who brought the coffee was gone, Gray stepped out of the passage, fully dressed in a light tan shirt and dark blue pants. She was wearing a dark blue blouse and pale yellow slacks, but he didn't seem to notice the similarity.

"Just coffee?" he asked, coming closer to the desk where the tray had been put. "Why don't we go down to breakfast instead? I need to talk to you."

"I have a breakfast meeting with Anita at ten," she answered distractedly. "Can we talk later? I really need to do a little thinking."

"What did you intend to think about?"

"Everything that's been going on around us," she said, handing him the cup she'd just filled. "With everything that's happened we ought to be able to make some pretty accurate guesses, but so far we've come up blank. Now's the time to think about that."

"All right," he agreed, adding cream and sugar to his coffee while she did the same with a second cup. "Why don't you think out loud, and I'll try to tear down any theories you come up with."

"If someone's going to play devil's advocate, we should get Ralph in here," she said with a smile that faded quickly. "But we can't get *anyone* else in here, because I'm very much afraid one of my friends is the one who's been doing all this."

"I can see you've already done some thinking," Gray observed as he sat opposite her. "What have you come up with?"

"There has to be a writer behind all this," Diane said, sipping from her cup. "The murderer's moves haven't been planned, they've been plotted, carefully thought out to produce maximum confusion and provide minimum information."

He nodded in encouragement, and she continued.

"Friday night David's body became available to be found just when I'd finished autographing. Coincidence? The man who directed me to it immediately disappeared and couldn't be found for questioning. Another coincidence? The murder weapon came from my suite. I'd had a public argument earlier in the day with the victim. And there had been bad blood between us for quite some time. I had motive, opportunity and access, and I was found standing over the body."

"Which should have gotten you arrested on the spot," Gray added. "The only problem was someone else was seen standing over the body, a someone else who ran. That produced a reasonable doubt."

"Which led people to think I was part of a small group, and had at least one accomplice. The zombie who had directed me into the corridor could have raced around to the other side, pulled off the uniform and put on a mask and wig, appeared as the pirate, then run off. I'm found near the body, but I've made it look as though someone was trying to frame me. I did it that way, you understand, just in case I missed cleaning up a clue that would lead directly back to me."

"And no one mentions the fact that the pirate is tanned, while the zombie is in white makeup?" Gray asked. "But I see what you mean. Your accomplice helps to make you look like an innocent victim, and then you two argue. He's the only one who knows you're guilty, and his trying to kill you in the maze helps you decide what to do. You kill him and leave the body to be found someplace where you'll be, and the fact that he's your ex-boyfriend becomes just another attempt at framing you that no one's supposed to believe.''

"Only by then they should have started believing," Diane said, working to keep her voice steady. "As Gerard said, too much coincidence causes an allergic reaction in most people. Finding Rick's body should have closed the jaws of the trap on me, and so far only blind luck and Gerard's instinct kept it from happening. But Rick's death tells us something else too, something we didn't think of last night."

"What?" Gray asked, watching her take another distracted sip of coffee.

"There's at least one other man of Rick's approximate size involved in this, and he might even have been the pirate," she answered, still feeling sick over the realization that had come to her. "It couldn't have been Rick shooting at me in the maze, for the simple reason that he wasn't stupid. What reason would the other or others have been able to give him for shooting and missing?"

"They could have said they were just setting you up for something else," Gray responded, looking surprised. "They didn't have to give him any details. All they had to do was say it was still in the planning stage. He *could* have set himself up for being murdered without realizing it."

"But that doesn't make any sense," she protested, feeling confused again. "I know now for a fact that I never really meant anything to him, that he was trying to get me here to the convention so that I could be framed. But I can't believe he'd shoot at me with real bullets without having been given a good reason for doing it. No, it was someone else doing the shooting, setting Rick up to be the next victim."

"I see," Gray said quietly, those light eyes on her again. He looked as though he disagreed, but he wasn't pushing the point.

"When Angela turned up dead, I'll bet they held off to see if *she* would be blamed instead of me," she continued. "By that time they were probably willing to take anyone against whom charges could be brought, just to see the thing ended. If she'd left any sort of note at all, that would have ended it."

"Wait a minute," Gray said, leaning forward in his chair. "I'm getting an idea here. Can we assume there's an excellent chance the murderers knew about Angela's involvement with Bellamy?"

"It's not only possible, it's probable," Diane granted him. "What about it?"

"Then they may have been setting up Angela for framing, just in case the frame against you didn't work," he said, even more excited now. "Yes, it definitely fits, especially if it's being plotted. The red herring would be that she killed Bellamy, then tried to frame you. It's a less obvious theory for anyone who didn't like the more obvious."

"If that's true, then she really did kill herself," Diane said, catching Gray's enthusiasm. "If *they'd* done it, they would have left a note of some sort. Without one, there'd be no proof to distract pursuit. But wait—that can't be right."

"Why not?" Gray demanded, certain he had a solid hold on a piece of the truth. "It all fits."

"All but the presence of Angela's candlestick in my suite," Diane responded, sitting back in her chair again. "If Angela was supposed to have killed David, why would she have put the candlestick from *her* room into the place of the one she used as the murder weapon? If the candlestick was used to begin with to point to me, substituting the one from *her* room has no purpose. It's not only crazy, it's stupid."

"I'd forgotten about that," he admitted. "There's got to be a good reason for the second candlestick being where it was, but we don't know it yet. Any more than we know why Lynn was attacked for realizing, 'He was a blackmailer'."

"Ralph was right," Diane said, drinking more of her coffee. "Lynn must have figured out what was going on, so she had to be silenced. Maybe the head of her cane really *is* silver."

"What has silver got to do with it?" Gray asked, suddenly looking faintly panic-stricken. "Have I been missing something important here?"

"No," Diane said with a small laugh, imagining him picturing werewolves or some such. "Lynn's cane was the murder weapon in one of her books, and I had the crazy notion at the time that it *couldn't* have been the real murder weapon because silver is too soft a metal. I think we both know it isn't *that* soft, but I've never been able to get rid of the idea."

"And that's why you think she wasn't killed," Gray said with a smile, finally understanding. "A soft metal doesn't let you hit as hard—"

The phone rang, interrupting them. Diane got up and answered it, her expression faintly wary.

"Diane, it's Anita," a cheerful voice said. "I know it isn't ten o'clock yet, but I woke up early so I thought I'd take a chance and call. You aren't ready early too, are you?"

"As a matter of fact I am," Diane answered. "Would you like to meet downstairs right now?"

"Diane, you're beautiful!" Anita came back with a delighted laugh. "I'm three-quarters starved to death, so I'd *love* to meet you downstairs right now. How's thirty seconds?"

"I'll be there," Diane promised, then she hung up and faced Gray. "Anita is ready now, so we're starting early. If you'd like to join us, I'm sure she wouldn't mind."

"No, I'll survive eating alone," Gray assured her, putting his cup aside as he stood. "You go ahead, and I'll be down in a little while. I left my things scattered all over the bedroom, and I ought to take that costume down and return it."

"I'll see you later then," Diane said with a smile. She still had things she needed to think about, but there would be time for that after she spoke to Anita.

Gray stood in the suite doorway until the elevator doors closed on Diane, and then he went back inside. He was feeling frustrated about not having been able to tell Diane the truth about the pirate without distracting her. But she'd seemed so close to coming up with some answers, and then the phone had rung. And now Gray had to straighten up behind himself before he could leave. And he also needed to call Jack.

"Yeah," Jack's voice came over the line, and happily this time it wasn't a recording.

"You should be careful about answering before you know what the question is," Gray said as he settled down with his coffee cup. "Am I still on for visiting you again after this weekend is over?"

"So far there's no need," Jack said. "Not only is the line still clear, but I even got that message you left. And let me tell you, you had me going for a minute. I know I started that alphabet business, but at least I had the decency to use two initials."

"What are you talking about?" Gray asked. "What did I say that had you going?"

"You said you were spending the night with D," Jack replied. "The first thing that came to my mind was that you were going to the morgue to spend the night with David Bellamy. It took me a minute to understand who you really meant. Now what's this about another death and attempted murder?"

Gray heard Jack's question, but his mind was suddenly much too busy to let him answer. Pieces of the puzzle were finally falling into place.

"Grayson? Are you all right? Can you hear me?" Jack was beginning to get agitated, and Gray didn't want him to get too bothered.

"I think I heard more than you realize," he said at last, speaking slowly while his thoughts continued to settle. "That convention flyer your ex-partner's wife found in his desk—it said D-day was Saturday, and we thought the murder was moved up. It wasn't, Jack, because the murder on Friday wasn't the scheduled one. I think the one scheduled to be murdered on Saturday was Diane."

"What?" Jack yelped. "Say that again, and add some reasoning to back it up."

"The reasoning covers just about everything I've learned until now," Gray said, then filled Jack in on the happenings he didn't yet know about. Then he started over from the beginning.

"As I see it, the phrase 'He was a blackmailer' tells it all. David Bellamy *looked* for things he could blackmail people with, and somehow stumbled across the murder ring Ed was investigating. If we're right about writers being involved, he was in the ideal position to nose out the truth."

"You mean he tried to blackmail *them*?" Jack demanded. "I can't imagine anyone being that stupid. You take money away from killers, you don't live long enough to spend it."

"But that's the whole point," Gray said. "Bellamy usually didn't ask for money, and this time was no exception. He blackmailed them into giving him a murder."

It all fit, all of it, but Gray wasn't sure whether or not it was too soon to feel relieved.

"You have to understand how much Bellamy hated Diane," he went on. "He tried to show her his version of love, and she not only rejected him she made him lose a very good job. She was supposed to hate him back while doing everything he demanded, only she ruined him instead.

"And then he had a problem with Angela Wilkes. *She'd* responded properly to begin with, but then she'd fallen in love with him. He couldn't handle that and he threw Angela out, but she refused to go away. She hung around pretending to hate him again, but he wasn't fooled. She still loved him, and that made him afraid.

"But then he stumbled across the murder ring, and his problems were both solved almost by magic. They worked by killing someone while at the same time throwing the blame on someone else, and that was exactly what he wanted. If he couldn't have Diane he wanted her dead, and if Angela was convicted of the murder he would finally be rid of *her*."

"My stomach isn't as strong as I thought it was," Jack muttered, sounding ill. "That Bellamy must have been pure sicko slime. Eliminate two women, because one won't hate you in the right way, and the other loves you."

"I'm very happy to say I can't relate to that, either," Gray responded. "It may take all kinds to make a world, but I think we can do without Bellamy's sort. And on top of that, he was stupid. Diane was scheduled to be killed Saturday, but he couldn't keep from poking at her with a pin the minute he saw her. He was probably supposed to stay away from her entirely."

"And let his history with her be covered by something almost as hot but more recent," Jack guessed. "Do you know what they had in mind for that?"

"Probably a fight with Angela Wilkes," Gray tried his own guess. "They were supposed to be on two panels together. I heard Diane discussing her with someone, and it was mentioned that Angela hated Diane because publishers were more interested in Diane's books. Combine that with her belief that Diane had stolen David from her—which would come out later—and you have an A-one motive for murder."

"So how do we go from there to Bellamy's getting it on Friday?" Jack asked. "If they had it all set up, why change plans?"

"Bellamy must have done something that made him an immediate liability," Gray said, sipping his almost-forgotten coffee. "I think we know he wasn't sane, so he probably demanded something that would have blown the whole game. He wouldn't change his mind, so they went ahead and made *him* the murder victim, Diane the primary suspect, and Angela the backup suspect."

"By using the candlestick from Diane's suite," Jack said. "But why did they have it in the first place, if *she* was supposed to be the victim?"

"They didn't just have it, they substituted it with the one from Angela's room," Gray corrected. "One of them would have killed Diane in her suite with her own candlestick, then carried it away to clean it almost completely and put it in Angela's room. The police would have decided Angela came to talk to Diane, they had another fight, Angela grabbed the candlestick and killed Diane, then realized she couldn't leave the murder weapon there. If she took it to her room in a panic and substituted the one from there, she might have thought no one would be able to find the murder weapon."

"You're right," Jack said, sounding utterly convinced. "You're absolutely right. And I can see why you think writers are involved. That was a neat shift of the plot, turning the murder into Bellamy's instead of Diane's."

"Not quite *that* neat," Gray disagreed. "They should have gotten the second candlestick out of Diane's suite, but they slipped up and forgot about it. That's one loose end they'll be tripped with, and I think we can make the second murder another of the same."

"That's the murder of the Philips' woman's ex-boyfriend," Jack said, verbally shifting his mental list. "How does that fit?"

"As follows," Gray said. There was a definite growl in his usually mild voice. "There's no doubt the bastard was one of them, so we can bet he got himself introduced to her on purpose. They'd only been seeing each other for a few months, remember, so his job must have been to get her here to the convention.

"At first I thought he was just supposed to back out of giving her an alibi for the time of the murder, but it was more than that. He was bringing her here to be killed, and if he was still alive I'd finish him for that myself. She doesn't even want to believe he'd shoot at her with real bullets, but he was ready to do a hell of a lot more than *that*."

"Then they did start planning this months ago," Jack said after clearing his throat. "Since that was a possibility from the beginning, I got a list of everyone who was involved with organizing the convention, hoping one of the names would eventually ring a bell. Bless computers, the fact that so many people now use them, and what a simple thing it is for someone with talent to open just about any file."

"Okay, let's hear the list," Gray said, knowing, but not minding, that Jack was changing subjects. Danger to Diane was one subject that threw him right out of control. "If I can't recognize an involved name by now, I never will."

There was a muffled rattle of papers, and then Jack began pronouncing names. When he got to the bottom of the list there was another heavy silence.

"So that's it," Gray said softly. "I have to admit it would have taken me a while to get to that name. But it's so obvious! And that's why Lynn was attacked. She didn't figure it out—she remembered."

"What are you talking about?" Jack asked, now sounding confused. "One of those names meant something?"

"More than meant something," Gray said, really excited now. "It gave me the ringleader here at the convention. And I also think I know where Lynn was going last night before they caught up to her. I'm going to check on my theory and then tell Diane. If it works out, we'll have concrete proof rather than guesswork. Bless that sweet old lady, she can think better than all the rest of us put together. Talk to you later."

Gray hung up on Jack's angry protests, too excited to care. He was one step away from breaking the whole thing wide open, and finding what he needed to clear his brother.

And Diane. He smiled as he headed out of the suite, knowing that their dinner that night was now on for sure. She was safe, out in the open where Gerard's men would be keeping an eye on her. Gray was free to do the necessary digging. After that he and Diane would visit Gerard, explain everything, and then it would be over.

And after *that* . . .

Chapter Nineteen

Diane tried to shake off her depression, but it wasn't working.

The thought she'd had about the pirate being one of them now seemed the most obvious conclusion, no matter how painful it also was. Real bullets had been shot at her, and if Rick hadn't been the one doing it, then it must have been someone else. Strange, though, how Gray hadn't agreed with her.

The elevator doors opened on the lobby, and once she stepped out she could see Anita already waiting for her in front of the restaurant. She really *must* be hungry. As hungry as Diane was for the truth. Trust me, the pirate had said, and Diane *had* trusted him. Had she been wrong?

"It took you thirty-*five* seconds, so you're late," Anita announced with a grin as soon as she saw Diane. "I don't know what it is, but I haven't felt this hollow in years. Hey, did you know it's snowing out?"

"Is it?" Diane asked, still trying to pull out of her deep mood. "That should make for fun when everyone starts going home. Is it supposed to get deep?"

"Beats me," Anita said with a shrug. "I don't listen to weather reports when I'm at a convention. Under other circumstances I'd probably stay another night to avoid trouble, but I think at this point I'd rather take my chances with the snow."

"Even if we have to leave on foot," Diane agreed with a grimace. "I've had enough of close-up murder to last a lifetime."

"I'm glad you said *close-up*," Anita responded. "If it was all murder you were giving up on, I wouldn't be able to put this breakfast on the expense account."

A ghoul came over to seat them then, and they ordered immediately. By mutual consent they avoided the topic of murder while they waited for the food, and by the time it came Anita had shifted to listing all the benefits Diane would get if she published with their house.

Using chewing and swallowing as a reason for keeping quiet, Diane let Anita's words flow past as she thought her own thoughts. Why had Gray been so willing to believe that Rick was the one who had shot at her? Did he know something she didn't, or was it just that he didn't know Rick?

Come to think of it, how well did *she* know Rick? She'd *thought* she knew him, but hadn't he tried using emotional blackmail to get her to the convention? If he was involved, and that now seemed impossible to deny, David's murder must have been planned in advance with her as the major suspect. That meant Rick had known what was ahead for her, but had still tried to get her there. Wasn't that worse than simply shooting at her with the intention of missing?

Yes, it *was* worse. So even though the idea hurt, Diane could finally admit it was very possible that Rick could have done the shooting. And he was most likely the one who had directed her to where David's body was, too. And that meant ... the pirate hadn't!

"Well, I'm glad to see you're finally looking happy about *something*," Anita said, drawing Diane back from the world of thought. "I'm used to writers fading out on me while we talk, but you really went deep."

"I'm sorry, Anita," Diane said, really meaning it. "I hadn't thought I was being that obvious. How did you know?"

"Well, when I said our contracts with attractive women writers usually cover permission for selling them into white slavery and you didn't bat an eye, I got the feeling you weren't hearing me. The least I expected was that you'd ask how much your part of the profit would come to."

"Anita, you're terrible!" Diane protested with a laugh that matched the other woman's grin. "I don't believe you really said that. Besides, I thought Phoenix Books wasn't international yet."

"Oh, we have our contacts in the places we need to have them," Anita assured her with a definite leer. "Just try not reading your contract and see what happens."

"I thought you were trying to talk me *into* signing with you," Diane said with a chuckle. "If John ever heard about this conversation, he'd have a fit."

"He'd have five fits," Anita countered, then pretended to look around to be sure they hadn't been overhead. "And now that you have something to blackmail me with, let's start talking business. You have me over a barrel, so I'll have to accept any story idea you come up with."

"Give me a minute to think about it," Diane said very dryly. "After that I should have five or six ideas."

"At least," Anita agreed, going back to her food. But then she stopped. "How about—" she began, cut the words off with a guilty expression, then finished a little too casually, "Oh, never mind."

"Never mind what?" Diane asked as she reached for her coffee. "What were you going to ask?"

"Forget it," Anita said with a sigh. "It's too morbid even for me, but I couldn't help wondering. You *are* better than most, so— Never mind. What's the next convention on your schedule?"

"If your idea was too morbid even for you, you've got me curious," Diane said, lifting a piece of toast. "You might as well go ahead and tell me, or the next time I don't hear it will be because I'm trying to guess about it."

"All right, but don't forget you forced me," Anita said, looking guilty. "You remember last night, and all the times everyone said the murderers would keep trying until the frame around you was tight? Well, considering the fact that you're still walking around on the loose, I was wondering how *you* would handle the next attempt. I mean, if you were them and were doing the planning.''

"That *is* morbid," Diane said with a grimace. "But the question does have its interesting side. What would I do if I were trying to frame me, right? Well, at this point I think I'd have to get 'caught in the act'.''

"Caught in the act of what?" Anita asked, now looking confused. "Another murder? But how would you arrange that?"

"Another murder would be good, but it isn't necessary," Diane said, thinking it through. "Planting or removing evidence would do, as long as there was absolutely no doubt about what I was doing. That's where they've been running into trouble all along. There was always an alternative explanation for everything that happened. If you really want to frame someone, you have to eliminate all other possibilities.''

"You sound so cold-blooded when you say things like that," Anita muttered with a shiver, her dark eyes round. "Now I'm *really* sorry I brought the point up. Let's talk about something else.''

Anita went back to eating in an obvious attempt to throw off the chills, but Diane didn't feel the same. She was glad she'd been asked to look at the problem as a professional, because now she knew what to watch out for. In order to be "caught in the act" she'd have to be lured to some place private, which meant that was what she had to avoid. Stay public and stay safe.

No more than another couple of minutes went by before Anita was back to selling. She didn't get bottom-line specific about advances and royalties, not without Diane's agent being there, but she was making a real attempt to straighten out the points of disagreement Diane and John had had. They were beginning to really get into it, when the ghoul who had seated them came over.

"Excuse me, but is one of you Diane Philips?" he asked, looking back and forth between the two of them.

"That's me," Diane said. "What is it?"

"This envelope was left at my station," the man answered, handing over the cream-colored item he held. "It has your name on it."

Diane took the envelope and thanked him, then looked at it warily. It was hotel stationery, and her name had been printed on it in block letters. It was probably the murderer's next step, and as Diane opened it she realized her hands were shaking.

Inside was a piece of paper that matched the envelope, and the first thing she noticed was that the message was written the same way her name had been: block letters. Then she saw the words.

"Diane," it said. "Join the next group going to tour the Bedlam, and I'll meet you there. I think I have all the answers now, so everything will be fine. The pirate."

"What is it?" Anita asked when Diane drew breath in surprise. "Not more bad news, I hope."

Bad news? Diane wondered. The first consideration was where she'd been asked to meet him, and that was all right. The tour would be public, not private, so she ought to be safe.

But what about the pirate himself? She'd been thinking he might be one of them. Was it still possible? Yes, but not very likely. Having admitted to herself that Rick could very well have been the one to fire at her, it was no longer necessary to believe that the pirate *had* to be her enemy. She had trusted him up till then. If she couldn't trust him one more time, she didn't deserve to learn what he'd found out.

"Diane?" Anita said again. "Did you hear me?"

"Yes, I heard you, and it *isn't* bad news," Diane said with a quick smile, folding the note and stuffing it into her shoulder bag. "It seems to be the exact opposite. I'm sorry, Anita, but I have to go."

"Go? Go where?" Anita demanded, but Diane was already up and leaving the table with a parting wave. Once everything was straightened out, Diane knew she would have to apologize properly, but right now she had an important date. And she had to get to that meeting without anyone following her.

IT TOOK SOME fast footwork, but Diane managed, without anyone appearing immediately behind her, to get to the second floor gathering room where the next Bedlam tour was being put together. She was just in time. The ghoul in the costume shop had told her that five minutes later she'd have had to wait for an afternoon group.

Everyone was herded through a secret passage with vampire guides both ahead and behind. The passage ran straight for about twenty feet, and then they reached a stairway that was imitation brick surrounded by imitation stone—wet-looking imitation stone.

At the head of the stairway was another vampire with release forms, and everyone signed as they passed or they didn't get to pass. Diane couldn't help remembering the last time she'd signed a release for a game. This time would be different. At the first indication that the fifteen or so people in the group were about to be separated, Diane would simply turn around and leave.

Those who had already signed and were therefore descending the steps moved slowly, so no one would be left behind. When the group was all together the pace picked up a little. The stairway had become circular, and they continued to go down, down, down.

When they finally reached the bottom the light grew dimmer, the walls themselves looked positively dank, and soft, creepy music was playing. There were also sounds like faint screams and moans and chilling laughter, but before Diane could be certain of that, the vampire in the lead stopped and turned to them.

"Dear friends, the entrance to the Bedlam is just ahead," he announced in a very greasy, overjovial way. "We're all here to have a good time, I know, but there are certain rules we must keep in mind."

He paused to chuckle in a friendly, familiar way, and then he continued. "We must remember that the inmates here can be laughed at and pointed to, but poking them with sticks and throwing stones or other objects is not permitted. They may look like they're damaged already, but it isn't for us to add to it. And please remember to stay out of their reach. We'd hate to leave any of you behind, but not as much as you'd hate it!''

He laughed heartily then, as though at a really funny joke, and most of the people in the group were laughing with him. It was hard to actually understand that at one time people did go to look at and make fun of the mentally disturbed, but the hotel was doing a good job bringing the point home. Diane, more familiar with the idea than most, didn't join in the general laughter.

They continued up the dank corridor to a heavy metal door. Once the door was open they could hear the sounds they'd heard earlier, but more clearly. There was cackling and laughing, howling and moaning, whimpering and screaming. Diane shuddered and saw several of her companions do the same.

After everyone had passed through the doorway, the guide began pointing out the sights of interest. They'd moved into an area that looked like a very big, very badly lit basement that had a lot of shadows back near the walls as well as dark openings, some of which were barred. Behind some of the barred areas Diane could hear the sound of chains, but it was too dark to see anything clearly there.

"Here we have sweet Henrietta," their guide said, pointing to a filthy woman in long skirts and matted hair who was cackling to herself. There was a heavy metal collar around her neck with a chain that ran to a wall. When the guide pointed to her she tried to reach him with a clawlike hand.

"Henrietta thinks she's a witch," the guide went on. "Everyone else thought she might be one, too, so they had her put away here. If she's going to hex anyone, it might as well be her neighbors in this place. Then no one will care."

Henrietta cackled even louder and tried harder to reach the vampire, but the chain holding her refused to allow it. Everyone looked at her as they passed, but they also stayed well out of her reach.

"And here we have poor Tommy," the guide said, pointing to a young man on the other side of the cellar. "Tommy's been here since he was twelve years old, brought by his loving aunt and uncle. Tommy inherited his parents' estate, but since he was declared insane his aunt and uncle have had to look after it for him. Isn't Tommy a lucky boy to have loving relatives like that?''

The young man was just as filthy-looking as the woman, his hair as long as his straggly beard. He wore manacles on wrists and ankles as well as a collar and chain, and when he tried to reach the guide, the wall his collar was attached to groaned.

"I'm not sure I like the sound of that," the guide said, backing away a little. "The last time Tommy broke loose, we lost some of our group before the attendants could club him back to where he belonged. Maybe we'd best hurry along."

A number of people hurried after the guide, caught up in the spell of the moment, but Diane wasn't one of them. She'd been looking around a little more carefully than everyone else, and she'd noticed that the inmates in the farther shadows weren't people at all, only shapes made to look like people. Most of the horrible moaning and laughter was recorded sound, and Henrietta and Tommy weren't filthy, only made up to look it.

Diane moved along with everyone else, but she was no longer listening to their guide. Just now she was more interested in the game *she* was playing. None of the men with the group looked anything at all like the pirate, and that included the guides. If he was going to meet her, where was he?

She was trying to anticipate what the pirate had found out, and was also wondering what would happen after the murderers were exposed. What if he asked her to have dinner with him? What would she—

Suddenly someone grabbed her from behind, and began dragging her toward the shadows. Diane cried out as she struggled, fear racing through her body. Happily most of the people in the group heard her and turned around.

"Now, now, friends, no need to be upset," the guide called out, still sounding jolly and undisturbed. "I did warn you about what could happen if you didn't keep your distance. Ah well, that's life. Shall we continue on?"

Diane screamed when she saw everyone turning away to leave, but no one paid any attention. They all thought this was part of the game, but it wasn't! The terror inside her *said* it wasn't, not when it was being done like this!

Her attacker dragged her to one of the alcoves. And once she got there she saw it wasn't completely dark. There was a deep red light that couldn't be seen from the outside. Her conviction about it not being a game was soon confirmed. She was pushed roughly toward the straw scattered all over the floor, and she landed hard.

"How good of you to meet me the way I asked," a soft voice said. Diane twisted around to seek her attacker in the dimness. She saw a tall, masked figure in ordinary street clothes, wearing what looked like a blond wig. "Would you like to hear the answers I have?"

"You can't be serious about this," Diane said in a voice that for some reason trembled as much as her body. Had she been wrong about him? "People saw you do this, saw you take me—"

"Really?" the man's whisper interrupted. "Just what did they see? Would *you* like to describe me? What color are my eyes and hair?"

She said nothing to that, the only answer she could give. This was the fourth time she'd seen him, and she still didn't know. It hadn't really bothered her until now.

"Why do you seem afraid of me?" the whispering voice asked. "Have I hurt you before this? I promised to give you some answers, and I'm here to give them. Don't you want to hear what they are?"

"Of course I do," she said, but her voice was still shaky. He was right about not having hurt her, even this time she'd fallen mostly on the straw, but—maybe it was the bedlam surroundings....

"Just wait a little longer," he whispered. "That way we won't have to worry about being interrupted. People are pulled out of the tour group on a random basis all the time. It adds something to their appreciation of the experience, so that's what the staff will think happened. We'll have all the time to talk we need."

Somehow that thought didn't completely stop the pounding of Diane's heart. For the first time since they met, she wasn't sure she wanted unlimited time in the pirate's company. But the man was going on.

"I've managed to find out what the murderers intend to do next," he said, still standing in the deeper shadows. "It's not a bad plan, so we'll have to work to keep it from happening. They're going to send Ralph Teak a message signed by you, directing him to meet you alone in an out-of-the-way place. They also intend to get *you* to the same place."

"Why?" Diane asked with a frown, putting her hand to the straw to help her stand. She touched something metallic, like a length of chain, shifted her hand, then managed to get up. "And why Ralph? What does *he* have to do with this?"

"He's going to become your final victim," the pirate whispered, shifting a little in the shadows. "He'll have decided to confront you, and you'll have tried to kill him. You'll succeed, but in defending himself so will he."

"So we're supposed to kill each other," Diane said, finding it almost impossible to consider the idea except as fiction. "I like my solution better. What about Lynn? If she recovers from being attacked, her story probably won't match."

"A lot of things can happen to a helpless old woman all alone in a hospital," the soft-voiced man said.

Diane sighed, wishing it was already over. "What are we going to do now?"

"We'll stay here for a while, until everyone leaves for their break," he answered. "The next tour isn't until this afternoon, so the staff will be leaving to do other things. Once everyone's gone, we'll be able to go without anyone seeing us. If the murderers can't find you, they can't put their plan into action."

"No, they can't. But that won't be of much help to everyone else's plans." Diane smiled faintly. "I wonder if there's anyone at this convention who *doesn't* have a plan."

"What do you mean?" the pirate whispered softly.

Diane wondered fleetingly why his voice wasn't as raspy as usual.

"What other plans are there?"

She heard him start to walk quietly toward her and was disappointed when he stopped some paces short. She wished he had come all the way over to put his arms around her. Being held by someone in a place like this should have been a requirement. She turned away from him and went to stand by the wall.

She didn't answer his question, but knew he would understand. He'd never asked her to betray a confidence before, and he didn't now. He simply started walking toward her again, very quietly. . . .

Chapter Twenty

Gray went immediately to the normal part of the hotel. The desk clerk there wore a neat gray blazer over a white shirt, black pants and a medium blue tie. At first he looked totally out of place to Gray. Then things dropped back into the proper perspective, and he was able to get on with what he'd come for.

Luck was with him. The clerk who had been on duty the night before had just arrived to start a twelve-hour shift, a little overtime she'd been delighted to accept. A twenty-dollar bill offered discreetly got the clerk to admit to Gray that she had indeed spoken to Lynn Haverstock the night before, and also what the writer had inquired about. It took another ten before he was given the answer as well, but it did confirm his guesswork.

Armed with the proof he needed, Gray headed back to the restaurant to get Diane before hunting up Lieutenant Gerard. If he left her out of the wrap-up of that mess, she'd probably never speak to him again. He stopped at the door, looking around at the occupied tables, but he didn't see her. That was ridiculous, of course she was there. . . .

"May I help you, sir?" a ghoul asked, coming up on his right. "Did you want to be seated?"

"I'm looking for a woman, one of two who were here eating together," Gray said, hoping that at least they'd been there. "One of them had red hair, and the other dark. Did you see them?"

"Oh, yes, Ms. Philips and her friend," the ghoul answered with a gruesome smile. "They were here, but they've left."

"Together?" Gray asked, beginning to feel cold. "Was anyone else with them?"

"No, no one else was with them, and they left separately," the man said. "Ms. Philips left first, after reading the letter that was left for her."

Gray wanted to shout "What letter!" but he wasn't likely to get the rest of the story that way. Forcing himself to stay calm he pulled the balance of the details out of the man, tipped him, then got out of there.

He stopped in the middle of the lobby, trying to decide which way to go. There was no knowing *what* that letter had contained, but it had certainly gotten Diane to move in a hurry. Gray was relieved to remember Diane was supposed to have been covered by Gerard's men. He headed for a house phone.

"It's about time you let me know where you are," Gerard growled as soon as he heard Gray's voice. "We've lost Ms. Philips, and my men claim she did it on purpose."

Gray cursed softly for a moment, then told Gerard about the letter that had been left for Diane. It was something that had made her go off alone on purpose, despite all the warnings she'd been given.

"Which probably means there's another murder scheduled," Gerard said sourly. "I wish it wasn't anything more than her sneaking off to meet her boyfriend, but there's not much chance of that. Her boyfriend's dead."

Gray promised to call Gerard if he learned anything, then hung up. An awful idea had come to him, one that made him feel sick to his stomach. Diane *did* have a boyfriend, one she didn't want the police catching, so she would naturally try to lose any followers before going to meet him. If that was what had happened and she got hurt, he'd never forgive himself for not having told her—

He stood with his fists clenched tight, looking around as he tried to think. Suddenly an idea came to him. The costume shop. People who wanted to be directed to something around the hotel would ask a desk clerk or a roving staff member. But only if they didn't mind others seeing them do it. If they wanted directions without people finding out . . .

Gray didn't quite run to the costume shop, but his controlled hurry didn't waste time. And Diane *had* asked the clerk behind the counter about the Bedlam tour before using the shop's alternate entrance to leave. That was all the information he needed. He knew where she'd gone, could only pray she was still there and still all right.

He took the stairs to the second floor, found the secret passageway by counting five from the corner, then started down. He was giving himself good marks for having located and watched a Bedlam tour leave from the gathering room on Friday, but that wasn't full marks. Only if he located Diane safe and sound would he get those, so he'd damned well better hurry.

Gray stopped briefly at the bottom of the steps to catch his breath from the plunge, fighting not to let pressure rush him. He had to be certain he didn't miss anything. If he missed Diane, he might as well not have come.

The door to the Bedlam opened easily and for the most part quietly. The sound effects were still going on, insane laughter and screams and howling.

As he began moving along, he discovered that most of the human-appearing forms he saw weren't real. They were props of some sort, but there were also live actors used there. There was a clearer section to the right, where some-one might have been sitting or lying down, and another a few steps farther along on the left. No one was there now, but—

And then he saw it, back in a section of dark on the right. Shadows reflected in red, one holding its hands up in front of it.

He moved soundlessly but swiftly through the junk scattered on the floor, coming up to the alcove with the shadows in it. He'd been right, she was there—but so was a male figure in a mask and wig, and he was slipping up behind Diane's back with his hands up . . . reaching for her throat.

Gray launched himself at the masked shadow figure.

DIANE HAD BEEN waiting for the pirate to come to her, but instead someone had rushed in to attack him. She backed to the far corner to get clear of the fight.

They grappled on the ground for a moment, each apparently struggling for a hold, and then they surged apart and rolled to their feet. Both men moved faster than Diane would have expected, and when the newcomer straightened she almost gasped. It was Gray who had attacked the pirate, and the fight wasn't over yet.

It took only seconds for Diane to realize that both men were standing in martial arts ready positions. And then the pirate kicked. It was so fast. As fast as those silly, speeded up movies, but Gray wasn't taken by surprise. He got an arm down to block the kick, blocked another from a different direction, then launched a kick of his own.

Hands weren't forgotten, punches and knifehand blows, but most were blocked or deflected. The fight took the two of them out of the alcove. There was more debris on the main floor to trip them, but also more room to move. Both men seemed eager to reach each other, and simply watching them turned Diane's throat dry.

As she moved to the arch to keep them in sight, she looked for something she could do to stop the fight. She didn't want to see either one of them hurt, but the way they fought said neither one would hear her.

And then something happened that made her insides churn. Suddenly the pirate went down; before she could wonder if the fight was over he was up again, but not empty-handed. He obviously hadn't liked the way Gray was besting him, so he'd brought a sharp-pointed length of pipe back into the fight with him.

At the pirate's first swing with it Gray jumped back, but not far enough. The jagged end of the pipe slashed across his arm, and Diane was certain she saw blood.

Gray had been hurt and the pirate had done it.

To her own surprise Diane had no doubts about what to do. She acted immediately, turning back into the alcove to search for the length of chain she'd felt. It wasn't attached to anything.

Panting more with fear for Gray than for herself, she scrambled back to the arch. Gray was still trying to keep from being hit or cut, but he didn't seem prepared to leave her in order to do it. The pirate was swinging the heavy pipe and stabbing with it, and he radiated the most cruel delight Diane had ever sensed.

Diane began heading out toward where the men fought. They weren't far away, no more than four or five feet, but neither of them seemed to see her. They were completely engrossed in each other, held by the game of death they played. Gray defended and the pirate attacked, and Diane began to swing the chain.

Gray tripped over one of the props on the ground, losing his balance for an instant, but that was enough for the pirate. He immediately stabbed forward, intending to spear Gray—but it never happened. Diane swung the chain down on the pipe, knocking it away from Gray.

Then it was Gray's turn. He came in fast with a yell and a high kick of some sort that caught the pirate in the head and sent him crashing to the floor.

Diane stood where she was until it was clear the pirate would not be getting up again soon, and then she stumbled over to Gray.

"Are you all right?" she asked Gray, not caring *how* foolish a question it was.

"Couldn't be better," he said, drawing her close with his unwounded arm. "Give me just a minute to get my breath back, and we'll have a look at our friend over there. After that, we can leave all this rock behind while we go for Lieutenant Gerard. I find this place very depressing."

"It's stone, not rock," Diane corrected automatically. "Rock usually comes in smaller chunks—"

And just that easily she knew the answer she'd been searching for. She'd known it since the day before, only she hadn't realized it. And that could have been what had given Lynn her clue, showing her the trail that had led to near death from a blow to the head that also fit.

Diane was shaken. She'd trusted two men, she'd given them her love, and both had turned right around and betrayed her. The pirate had lured her here to hurt her, just as Rick had plotted to hurt her.

"Okay, I'm ready," Gray said, beginning to urge her forward. It was true. His breathing had already returned to normal, and he was standing straight.

Gray kicked the pipe away, muttered something as he went down to one knee, then put a hand to the pirate's throat. He held very still for what seemed like a long time to Diane, and then he turned to her with a sigh.

"I was afraid of that," he said. "That kick is dangerous, and I *thought* it caught him straight on. His neck is broken. He's dead." There was no hidden triumph in the words.

Diane wept a little on the inside, but there was nothing to say out loud. The way the pirate had fought showed what a low-life he really was, without any trace of honor. Fool that she was, all Diane could remember was the way he'd held her, the way he'd kissed her, the way he'd asked to make love to her. Quietly, the tears rolled down her cheeks. She *was* a fool, but she'd been more than a little in love with a man who had wanted her dead.

"This isn't the way I planned it, but now that it's done let's see who he is," Gray said, light scraping sounds accompanying the words. Diane had her eyes closed in a feeble attempt to push the world away. But Gray's next words dragged her right back.

"George Lombardy."

Diane opened her eyes as Gray straightened, beginning to feel really ill and even more confused. George? The pirate was George? That felt so strange, so... wrong. She pushed her grief away. There were things to be taken care of.

"And I know who his boss is," she said, swiping at her face again. "Let's go get your arm taken care of, and then pay a call on the brains behind it all. I have a few editorial comments I'd like to make and I'd like your help."

"I have one condition to make first," Gray said, trying to look stern. "We go get my arm taken care of, then get in touch with Gerard. Calling on brains comes only after that."

"If you insist on doing it the easy way," Diane said lightly. But there was no humor inside to match the outward joking. It was almost over. Soon she could go back home and wait for everything to go away.

Chapter Twenty-One

What was left of their group gathered, appropriately, in the nearly empty second-floor gathering room. The convention was still officially going on, but right now most of the attendees were either having lunch, packing to go home, or had already left. Ralph sat in a chair looking weary, Bill paced not far from him looking for a waitress, and Anita sat in the chair to the extreme right looking puzzled.

"Ralph, if we delay much longer, that snow will get too deep to travel through," Bill warned as he paused in his pacing. "We have to get you to the airport, you know, and airports close in really bad weather."

"But we still don't know the answer, Bill," Ralph said, making an obvious effort to pull himself together. "We can't leave without that. And I don't see how I can leave at all with Lynn lying in a hospital bed. I called a few minutes ago, and she's still in intensive care."

"No, she isn't," Diane said from where she sat beside Gray on the couch. She caught Gray's eye and he nodded. "Earlier today I got Lieutenant Gerard to admit that she came around briefly, and now she's simply sleeping. They expect her to recover completely, and they're just saying she's in ICU."

"To protect her," Ralph exclaimed, seeing the point immediately. "Good for the old girl, she *did* do them dirty. What did she have to say when she woke up?"

"Nothing about the murders," Gray contributed, crossing his legs as he continued the tale he and Diane had discussed with Gerard. "At first she was too logy and confused to remember, and then she was asleep. They expect to get a full statement when she wakes up."

"Well, that's a relief," Anita said comfortably. Bill nodded in agreement. "I think we would all have missed her terribly. What happened to your arm, Gray?"

"An almost accident," Gray responded, raising his left arm to look at the wide bandage. "Nothing but a scratch, but you know how overcautious these doctors are. He also seemed to think Lieutenant Gerard would want to know about it, so I had to promise to tell him as soon as I could."

"So there *has* been more trouble," Bill said, slumping back in his chair. "Isn't it ever going to end?"

"I'd say it was just about to," Ralph remarked, looking steadily at Gray. "You have it all figured out, don't you? And you've asked us here so you can tell us about it."

"That's right," Gray said, looking around at all of them. "They just made a try for Diane, and this time she was supposed to die. Do you want to tell them about it, Diane?"

"Certainly, but I have to correct you about something," Diane said, also looking at all three of them. "I wasn't supposed to die right then, but later, when Ralph was available. You had a panel this morning, didn't you, Ralph? Well, that's why they had to wait."

"So there wouldn't be a disparity in the time of death," Ralph said automatically, showing a small frown. "But what was *I* supposed to have to do with it? Did they expect the police to believe I was the one who killed you?"

"Probably. A dying effort as *I* killed *you*," Diane said, nodding approvingly. It all still so seemed distant. "The pirate told me about it while we were supposedly waiting for the Bedlam area to clear out so we could get away safely."

Bill was studying Diane worriedly. "Diane, are you sure he didn't hurt you?"

"No, he didn't have the time," Diane answered. "The first time he lured me to where he and his friends wanted me, and that was all he was supposed to do. The rest of it was assigned to someone else, but the second time the job was all his. Only, Gray came along in time to distract him. It was our friend George Lombardy.''

"George!" all three of the others said together, heavy shock in their voices. They were all having trouble understanding—all, naturally, but one, who was only pretending not to understand.

"Yes, we've figured out that he came up to our group yesterday with the specific intention of luring Diane into the Hungry Crypts game," Gray said. "It worked out beautifully when Lynn volunteered Diane to go with him, not knowing he had plans of his own. He even had the excuse of a story he'd heard about David Bellamy to use, just in case Diane needed to be coaxed.''

"I can't believe George was part of this," Bill said, running a hand through his thinning hair. "What has he been able to tell the police?''

"Wasn't it a mystery writer who first made the statement?" Gray said, looking around. "Dead men tell no tales?''

"But how did he get to be dead?" Ralph asked, the words very quiet. Bill looked even more shaken, and Anita was downright pale.

"I was a little too rushed to be careful," Gray answered, "and you have no idea how I regret it. He deserved to live long enough to be brought to trial, and to be given the chance to turn on his confederates. Or confederate, since I'm fairly certain there's only one left.''

"And you're here to name that one," Ralph said, his eyes fixed on Gray's face. "Go ahead and get it done.''

"I think you need to hear first how we figured it out," Gray said. "Diane and I and Lieutenant Gerard all noticed that the murders and attacks all seemed plotted in the sense of a novel rather than planned in the way of a crime, so a writer was most likely behind the doings. As it turned out, we were right.''

"You mean George Lombardy," Bill said, and this time it was Ralph who sat silent. "He did the plotting, and everyone else followed along."

"No," Gray denied, shaking his head slowly. "I have a friend who's very good at finding things out, and he researched George Lombardy a couple of hours ago. The man never wrote so much as a letter before his novel came out, and also hasn't done anything since."

"And I noticed something strange about him as well," Diane said. "When he and I were talking about his writing, he mentioned something about an outline that wasn't working, then changed the subject. If there's one thing writers like to do it's talk about their work, especially to other professionals. You don't have to give away the gimmick you've thought up, but it *does* help to bounce the rest of it off someone who may know how to solve your problem."

Her three listeners nodded. It was a truth they were all familiar with, but Ralph understood the unspoken part first.

"You think George wasn't a writer," he said, now looking a bit pale behind his quiet calm. "Either you believe David found out he'd stolen someone else's work, tried blackmailing him, and that's why he was killed, or—"

"Or that another writer entirely was involved," Gray finished when Ralph didn't. "And since the only writer left in this group who hasn't been accused or attacked is you, Ralph, you're probably beginning to feel the least bit—cornered."

"That's ridiculous!" Bill said sharply, sounding a little frightened. "Ralph would never get involved in something like this! He saves his murders and attacks for the pages of his books."

"The way most writers do," Gray said with a pleasant nod. "They create a reality that satisfies them so thoroughly, they don't *have* to act in the real world. And Diane tells me that bringing their creations into the real world might very well ruin those creations for a writer."

"But . . . then— I don't understand," Bill stumbled while Ralph suddenly frowned. "What are you saying?"

"He's saying that it *wasn't* a writer who was responsible for all this," Ralph interrupted, strong curiosity bringing strength back to him. "It had to be a writer, and yet it wasn't. I have to hear how that can be."

"It's like that old puzzle question, Ralph," Diane put in, giving him a faint smile. "What's a dog and yet not a dog? Two dogs."

"You mean more than one writer?" he demanded, now looking outraged. "How could they possibly get a group of writers involved like that?"

"It isn't difficult at all—if the writers don't *know* they're involved." Gray took up the explanation again. "You said it yourself—writers are the creative ones, and their creativity is taken advantage of by others. Do you remember what group you were talking about when you said that?"

Ralph paled again without answering, but his gaze followed Gray's and Diane's to fix on Bill and Anita.

"I don't understand," Anita said, tones of confusion making her voice sound small and bewildered. "You can't be saying an editor had something to do with this?"

"Who else would be in so perfect a position?" Gray asked. "Editors read hundreds of manuscripts, and only a fraction of them get into print. As Bill said yesterday, the plots that keep it simple work, even if the writing isn't always good enough to carry the book. And it's the ideas that are being used, not the writing."

"There's something you aren't saying," Ralph put forward, his eyes narrowed. "You said *ideas* as in more than one, and I get the feeling you mean more times than this weekend. What's going on?"

"A bright idea is going on," Gray answered, not surprised at the speed with which Ralph had understood. "Someone has noticed that conventions happen all the time, in hundreds of cities. Going to those conventions is a flawless reason for being in those cities. If something else happened to occur in those cities at the same time, why—it was just a coincidence."

"Something else like a murder," Ralph said grimly. "Yes, I can see that. If a murder is committed while a convention is going on, and the people involved aren't in any way connected to the convention, who would notice? But this time the murders *happened* at the convention. Why would they want to jeopardize such a good cover?"

"I doubt if they *did* want to," Gray said. "David Bellamy was probably the one who insisted, so that everything could happen in front of the only group of people he cared about. He found out about the arrangement, and blackmailed the principals into doing a murder for him."

Gray explained the solution that he and Diane had reached.

Diane kept her silence. To find out that someone had meant to kill her had been horrible, worse than anyone could imagine. The only way she could handle hearing it discussed was to put it out of her mind, to save her reaction for a time when she could tremble and be ill without anyone around to see.

"So you can see that they had to change their plans rather quickly," Gray continued. "The initial change was simple in that Bellamy was killed instead of Diane, and Diane was made the major suspect and Angela the backup in case it didn't work. We may never know what Bellamy insisted on that caused his death, but he'd apparently never noticed how easily roles could be reversed in the particular plot the group was using."

"That had to be the start of their problems," Ralph said. "Diane wasn't immediately charged, and then Angela killed herself. I'm willing to bet now she *did* kill herself. If *they'd* had a hand in it, they would have used it. Killing one of their own was an act of desperation, and when it didn't work they grew frantic. They should have known killing Diane and me together wouldn't work either—but they didn't."

"Because they were desperate and frantic," Gray agreed. "They'd had to leave the preestablished plot, to improvise. And since they weren't used to doing the constructing, the thread of logic began falling apart. One person had already spotted the plot they were using, and they were terrified it would happen again."

"Lynn," Ralph said at once, his face darkening. "So that was it. She recognized the plot, and because of that the answers began falling into place for her. But why didn't some of the rest of us also recognize it?"

"Because the rest of us hadn't seen the book," Diane said, bitterness edging her voice. "I'll admit this part is guesswork, but it fits in really well. Do you remember when she pulled back that manuscript from auction, Ralph? That was three years ago. Apparently it was David's poisonous doings that caused it, but not before a number of editors got to read it. We think the murderers used it without remembering where it had come from."

"But Lynn *knew* who could have read it and who couldn't," Ralph said with another nod. "She disappeared for a while, probably to rethink her logic, then confronted the guilty."

"No, she didn't disappear to think," Gray said at once. "She went to check on a story point that they might have been stupid enough to use—and they had. I followed her trail, and was told both what she asked and what she found out. Richard Anderson, the man found dead in the zombie costume, had been preregistered here in another name and there were two clues there. The reservation had been made Friday afternoon by someone already here. And I'd be willing to bet he'd been registered under the exact name Lynn used in her book. At least, she'd asked for him by name."

"And that means he wasn't originally meant to die!" Ralph exclaimed, enthusiastic again. "Otherwise the reservation wouldn't have been traceable that way. Sloppy doing from sloppy thinking."

"Only partially sloppy," Gray corrected. "Since he had to be here anyway, giving him an alias should have kept him in the background. And he'd been put in the normal part of the hotel, where no one should have connected him with the convention."

"It's too bad you weren't able to get a description of the person who made the reservation for him," Bill said, his voice still rather faint. "That would have settled the matter rather thoroughly—even though I find it impossible to believe any of this.''

"Oh, but I did get a description," Gray said, looking straight at him. ''You'd be surprised how good some hotel people are at remembering individual guests, even without having gotten special tips to jog their memories. The girl I spoke to was able to go into detail.''

Silence descended on all of them again, an awkward, heavy silence that Diane decided to break.

"People who travel a lot tend to find hotel staff faces running together in their minds," she said. ''Because of that they start believing that *their* faces do the same for the various staffs. Sometimes that happens, but not always, so it's a bad habit to get into. Isn't that so, Anita?''

Chapter Twenty-Two

Diane saw Bill start, as though the ax he'd expected to land on him had hit the next person instead, and then he turned to look at Anita as everyone else was doing. Anita, though obviously more than aware of all the stares, showed nothing but greater confusion.

"I don't understand," she said again, shaking her head just a little. "Why are you asking *me*? They couldn't have described *me*, because I wasn't there. I've been nothing but a spectator in all this."

"That's not what the evidence says," Diane countered, knowing some of the anger she felt was showing. "Once I had the right direction, I began tripping over things I'd noticed earlier but just hadn't seen. And you won't believe what finally gave you away."

"I still don't know what you're talking about," Anita said very reasonably, and then her expression grew concerned. "Diane, you and Gray have been under a lot of strain this weekend. Once you calm down—"

"It's strange you should mention Gray," Diane interrupted, still looking straight at her. "It was remembering your comment to him that finally started me up the right path. Do you remember when we were here in this room for drinks, and Lynn exchanged places with him? The change put him next to me, and you said something about his not needing to hide the fact that he liked me. You said we weren't as rocklike as those of the outer world."

"So?" Anita returned with a shrug. "How does the fact I said we were different from the rest of the world mean I'm guilty of murder?"

"It means you're guilty of using the back corridors of the second floor at some time," Diane countered, seeing the tiniest change in her expression. "There are two signs to warn you off if you turn the wrong way. Beyond the first sign is the staff area. Beyond the second sign, the one warning about falling rocks, is an access to the ordinary section of the hotel. The sign was probably put there to keep costumed people from bothering those who don't like costumes, and is the staff's idea of a joke. Falling rocks—and normals—are nuisances. What were you doing walking around on the second floor near that sign, Anita? Your room is on the third floor."

"Why, I just got curious and went to see where the corridors led," Anita answered with a smile that was too bland to be anything but smug. "The last time I looked, there wasn't a law against *that* either."

"But there *is* a law against being involved with murder," Diane said, rolling over the smooth explanation. "How much blood did you actually get on the angel costume you wore, Anita? It couldn't have been much or something would have showed after you washed it out, but it was certainly enough for a police lab if they knew enough to check. That's why you switched to the princess costume on Saturday. Just to get rid of the original costume."

"That's ridiculous," Anita said, but her smile had faltered. "I changed costumes because I didn't like the original one. It didn't fit right."

"It seemed to fit right enough for you not to complain about it to the rest of us," Ralph put in, his dark eyes glittering. "And you took the trouble to get another costume enough like the first that no one was supposed to have noticed the switch. But Diane noticed, so did I, and I'll bet Lynn would have, too."

"And speaking of Lynn," Diane resumed, wondering if her voice really had turned as growly as it sounded in her own ears. "You're the one she went to talk to, and you're the one who hit her with her own cane. That's why she didn't die. You couldn't strike as hard as your male accomplices, not with something that wasn't as heavy as a brass candlestick. The head of the cane was too light, so she lived through the attack."

"And now you won't be able to get to her to finish the job," Ralph said with relish. "She'll wake up and remember everything, and that will be the end of *you*."

"People with head injuries often lose the memory of what caused those injuries," Anita said, showing a small, confident smile. "I certainly do hope Lynn remembers so I can be cleared, but she probably won't."

"What about people *without* head injuries?" Diane asked, determined to do something about that smile. "I haven't been injured at all, so I've been doing some time-table juggling. What made you so hungry this morning that we had to start our breakfast meeting early?"

"What makes anyone hungry?" Anita asked with a shrug, but the smile seemed a little less confident. "I was ready early and so were you, so we started early. How does that become sinister?"

"It becomes sinister when you realize that the note from the pirate was delivered during that earlier meal," Diane answered. "If we'd started later, as we'd arranged, the note would have been delivered too late for me to catch the morning Bedlam tour. I only just made it. Timing is tricky in things like that, so you moved our breakfast up to be sure."

The smile was completely gone by then, but Anita still wasn't admitting anything. You're just guessing, the look in her eyes said, so Diane brought up another point.

"That touch of asking *me* what I would do to frame me in a workable way— I really admire that," Diane said. "You already had something planned, but just in case it didn't work you wanted another option. And one that was creatively solid, not full of holes like the ones you'd *been* using. I thought you handled that very well."

"Now you're imagining conversations?" Anita asked, back to looking bland. "I never asked anything like that, so you must be making it up. Maybe it will turn out to be something Lynn remembers when she wakes up.''

"There are some things Lynn doesn't *have* to remember,'' Gray said when Diane simply glared at the woman. ''Certain names, for instance, that are on certain lists. Did you have fun helping to organize this convention, Anita? I didn't know editors got involved in things like that.''

"Who told you I helped organize the convention?'' Anita demanded, her face paling as she leaned forward in her chair. ''If you're guessing, you're out of luck. I had nothing to do with it.''

"I enjoy the way you lie with absolute confidence, expecting people to believe the lie and not check any further,'' Gray said with a faint smile. ''My friend, the one who's so good at checking things, found your name on the list of those who promoted this convention. Right now he's looking to see how many more conventions you've helped to get started . . . in places where there were also odd murders.''

"So that's why the program book was so cheap looking,'' Diane said. ''It wasn't done by a group hoping to make a profit on the convention. And that's probably why all of my panels were scheduled for Saturday. By Sunday I was supposed to be dead.''

"It works out as follows,'' Gray said, his light eyes hard despite the smile he continued to wear. ''Diane met you at registration, and you were surprised to see her. Rick Anderson had told you she was refusing to come, and you were worrying about how to get around that.

"As soon as you learned she was here, you called Anderson and told him to get up here, that everything would go ahead as planned. Anderson arrived, and by that time you'd managed to switch the candlesticks, but there was a terrible problem. Bellamy was insisting on something that would ruin all your plans and possibly even expose you, so something had to be done about him.

"You arranged to meet Bellamy, and used the wide skirts of your costume to hide the candlestick you were carrying. You hit him in the front of the head. Anderson, who was also there, finished him off, then stayed while you left. When it was time to call Diane to find the body, you used the other entrance to the tunnel to tell him so then went upstairs to wash the blood out of the angel costume.

"Afterward you used George Lombardy to keep an eye on people and things when you couldn't. You had him pass on information about certain happenings that made it look like you were in one place while you were actually elsewhere. I expect we'll find he'd done it for you before. As a 'writer' he was able to attend a lot of conventions without anyone getting suspicious, which has to be why you arranged a book in his name in the first place."

"There are enough people who know you were his editor, Anita. We had no trouble finding that out a little while ago," Diane put in, still digging at Anita's lack of expression. "Maybe the real author of the book died while you were trying to buy the manuscript, and you discovered he or she had no relatives or friends who knew about the book. That way it could become George's, and no one would know any better."

"In any case, Lombardy was certainly a professional of another sort," Gray resumed. "You had him lure Diane into the Crypt game so that Anderson could shoot at her, probably intending to have the attack blamed on Angela Wilkes. Too many people were defending Diane and even the police weren't charging her, so it was time to shift back to the original script and blame the one who was supposed to have murdered her. Angela didn't have as many friends, and she did have a couple of very good motives.

"But then Angela committed suicide. The three of you were probably devastated, but there was nothing you could do. Your best suspect was gone, but you still had to get the investigation stopped. Bellamy would have left something in writing about what he'd learned, and if the police started digging they'd be bound to find it wherever he'd hidden it.

"That was probably when you and Lombardy decided to sacrifice Anderson. In a way he was a definite liability, since I doubt that Diane was the only potential victim he'd romanced. If someone ever spotted his connection with previous murder cases..."

That time there was a real flicker in Anita's eyes, which didn't give Diane as much pleasure as it should have. Rick and his charm, all practiced, well practiced...

"So Anderson had to go," Gray went on. "One of you told him some story or other, got him over to the cake that would be served to the pros and everyone else, and shot him. With Diane the only one in the hotel who could be proven to know him, you figured she couldn't get out of *that* one.

"But she did get out of it. It was another coincidence too large for the police to swallow, and again she wasn't charged. You and Lombardy must have spent hours trying to decide what to do next, and only one possibility came to mind. Diane had to die in a way that absolutely proclaimed her guilt, and then the case would be closed."

Diane knew what was coming next, but she made no attempt to interrupt Gray's reconstruction. He would talk about the pirate's betrayal, she would bleed a little more inside, and then it would be over.

"So you decided to lure Diane to a place where she could be held for a while and then killed," Gray said. "The problem was how to do that luring, but you happened to have come across the answer.

"When all this first started, a pirate was seen standing over Bellamy's body with Diane. He was one of the reasons she wasn't charged then, and you happened to catch sight of him before the costume party Saturday night. You tried to follow him, but lost him somewhere on the second floor near Diane's suite.

"After Anderson's body was discovered, Diane was in shock. She kept saying something about how 'he' would find out what was happening and would save her, and everything would be fine. You suddenly understood she'd been seeing more of the pirate than she'd mentioned, and *he* was the lure you could use to hook her.

"Sunday morning, knowing she would be having breakfast with you, Lombardy left a note for her, then went down to the Bedlam to wait. He'd gotten a wig and fixed up a mask like the one you'd seen on the pirate, and he pretended to *be* the pirate. He was supposed to get Diane out of the way until Ralph Teak was also available to die, then kill them both. But unfortunately for you I happened along. That was the end of him, and now it's your turn.''

"So *you* say," a white-faced Anita snapped while Diane floundered in confusion. Was Gray right? Was George Lombardy *not* the pirate?

"No one in their right mind would believe a story like that, and you can't prove a word of it." Anita went on, "as a matter of fact, I think I'll get my lawyer to sue you for defamation of character.''

"Getting your lawyer would be a very good idea, Ms. Rutledge,'' another voice said, and everyone looked up to see Lieutenant Gerard and some of his men behind Anita's chair. "Someone in his right mind *does* believe that story, and right now he's in the process of checking to see when you or your accomplices were in this hotel before. With as much information as the bunch of you had about this place, someone must have been here and taken a good look around. Since you planned all this, my money is on you being the one. You've already been identified as the woman who made Richard Anderson's reservation on Friday.''

Anita hadn't moved at all while Gerard spoke, and Diane could almost feel sorry for her. From then on she could lie from morning to night, and it would do her not one bit of good. She seemed to understand that, and something inside her crumpled and collapsed.

It took only a few minutes for the police to charge Anita, read her her rights and take her away, but the four remaining members of the group sat silently until it was done.

Then Bill Raglan took a very deep breath, and let it out slowly. "You have no idea how certain I was that that would be me who was taken away," he said. "I'd *also* come to the conclusion that an editor was behind this madness, and I was one of those who had read Lynn's last manuscript. The only problem was, I thought I was the only editor here who fit that description. I hadn't known Anita'd seen the thing, too.''

"It's fairly obvious Lynn knew," Gray said with a smile. "It probably took her time to see the connection because they'd been forced to change the original plot. But once she did see it she also saw all the rest, including Anita's change of costume."

"Well, I'd been waiting for everyone to find out how I'd threatened David Bellamy," Ralph said with a shake of his head. "Everything that happened seemed to have a professional touch, and as someone who presumably had a connection to professionals—"

"You thought *you* would get tapped," Gray finished for him with another smile. "One of the sour notes in this was how George Lombardy kept coming up with stories about everyone concerned, all suggesting an involvement with Bellamy. He was throwing them in all over the place just the way he'd been supposed to, but he had no sense of timing. He was in the middle of sliming you and Bill when Anita cut him short, knowing he was overdoing it. Too much of a pointing finger makes people look the *other* way."

"It looks like he was only professional at killing people," Ralph said. "An all-around professional knows when to keep quiet."

"And he may not even be as high-quality a professional at killing as he would have liked to think," Gray said. "Gerard has already started sending telexes to all other state jurisdictions, telling them what we learned and recommending that they check convention dates in their cities. All murder cases during those times that seem to fit the pattern will be reopened."

"And that way they should pick up all the witnesses they need," Ralph said with a sudden grin. "When you catch amateurs by surprise, they tend to spill their guts. Was that what you were trying with Anita?"

"It was worth a shot," Gray agreed with a shrug. "With both of her accomplices dead she might have been rattled enough to break, but since she didn't, the directional mike the police were using was wasted. Gerard thinks she was the one who started the ring, and I tend to agree with him."

"She was always dedicated to her work," Bill said as he stood and stretched. "Come on, Ralph, I want to check on that snow. If it's still falling, we'll both stay over until tomorrow."

"We'll stay over anyway," Ralph said firmly as he got to his feet. "Lynn needs friendly faces there when she wakes up, and for that even you qualify. Although how anyone can consider an editor friendly, *I'll* never know."

"Not every writer includes a pound of flesh and a pint of blood in their contract demands, Ralph," Bill explained patiently as they began to move away. "With those who don't, we can afford to be friendly. . . ."

"Do they always go on like that?" Gray asked with a chuckle as the two moved out of earshot. "You'd think one or the other of them would get tired of it, if not downright insulted."

"It's the way they express affection for one another," Diane said with a sigh. "They know it, everyone around them knows it, so no one minds. They're so funny together, they've become one of our favorite forms of entertainment."

"You don't look terribly entertained," Gray said, moving closer to put his uninjured arm around her. "If you're still bothered by everything that's happened, don't be. It's all over now, and soon you'll be able to forget it."

"I don't think it's going to be quite that easy," Diane said, not looking at him. "One of the things you said—about George not having been the pirate all along— I just remembered that George was at a table signing books when I first met the pirate, so I don't understand. Before, I thought he refused to tell me who he was because I'd never have believed George was that concerned about me."

"And yet the pirate *was* that concerned about you," Gray said, his fingers suddenly at her face to gently turn it toward him. "Just as *I'm* concerned about you, and more than concerned. Do you remember that we have a date for dinner tonight?"

"Dear Gray," she said with a smile, seeing again how really attractive he was. "If only we could have met somewhere without all the insanity intruding. Do you really want to go on with this? Right now I feel as though I'll never be able to trust anyone again.''

"You just need a little *lack* of insanity," he assured her, returning her smile in the most wonderful way. "It's *my* turn now, you know, and I don't believe in letting opportunity slip past. Will you give me the chance to convince you I'm right?''

Diane wanted to, she really did, but she still hurt so very much. Loving Gray would be beautifully warm and comfortable, but she'd remember her love for the pirate until the end of her life. How fair would *that* be for the man who sat next to her?

"Will you consider that dinner as opportunity enough?'' she asked, intending to pretend an interest that would at least give him the chance he wanted. After that he would certainly give up, and then go home suffering only from disappointment. The tears were running quietly down her cheeks again, a final goodbye to the pirate.

"I'm not used to having women cry when they agree to go to dinner with me," Gray said, one finger coming up to wipe at the small, damp stream. "Are you grieving for the pirate? You took my side against him.''

"When he saw he was losing the fight he didn't try harder, he turned to cheating," Diane said with a vague gesture of her hand, trying to explain a feeling in words. "It wasn't what I'd expected him to do, and it turned him small, and petty, and vicious, and he didn't deserve to win. Especially against you, who hadn't done any of that. Does that sound too melodramatically stupid?''

"Not to me," Gray said, a small laugh of pure delight coming out with the words. "You choose *me* over *him*, and you have no idea how happy that makes me. Some day I may even explain it to you, but— Diane, George Lombardy *wasn't* the pirate. He would have made a lousy secret admirer.''

Diane suddenly found herself staring at him, the confusion back and increased. How had he known about that?

"What's the matter?" Gray asked gently with a grin to match. "I thought you believed in secret admirers. Some of us *can* be trusted, you know, and I did say you would see me again. What I *didn't* say was anything about a mask still being between us."

"It was *you*?" Diane demanded incredulously. "How could it have been? The two of you are so different—! Wait, I know, you're just trying to make me feel better. Somehow you found out about that, and you're just trying to..."

Rather than answer or interrupt in words, Gray took her in his arms and kissed her. For an instant Diane was in shock, and then the shock was past and she was kissing him back, knowing beyond doubt that it was true. It *was* him, and she hadn't lost him!

"Diane, I'm so sorry," he said at last, holding her tight while her arms around his neck nearly choked him. "I never once stopped to realize how you must be feeling, even though I knew you believed Lombardy really was the pirate. Can you forgive me for hurting you like that?"

"This makes up for any other hurt," she whispered with a laugh as she hugged him tighter, her tears this time ones of happiness. "Oh, Gray, no wonder I couldn't choose between the two of you! But why didn't you tell me? You're not wanted by the police, are you?"

"No," he laughed in answer as he looked into her face. "The police don't want me for anything but cooperation in tying up all the loose ends. Why I couldn't tell you sooner involves my brother, but there's no reason why I can't tell you all about it now."

"I can't wait to hear," Diane said with a matching laugh bubbling up inside her. She had them both, the two men she'd fallen in love with, and she'd never have to worry about trusting someone again.

But then she realized there might be something *she* couldn't tell *Gray*. When they'd spoken that morning over coffee, he'd said something about the pirate being tanned and the zombie being in whiteface. That was something else he shouldn't have known, and it must have been a clue for her. That and the fact that George's whisper hadn't been raspy enough. On some level she'd *known* George wasn't the pirate, so she *hadn't* chosen Gray over him.

Unless, of course, her subconscious had already figured it out. Yes, she believed it had, so she hadn't chosen *anyone* over anyone else. She'd wished for the man of her dreams, and her wish had come true.

Now it was time to wish for a blizzard to end all blizzards, one that would keep them there long enough to really get to know each other.

"After I tell you my story," Gray said, smoothing her hair, "will you marry me? No rush in deciding, take all the time you like, the weekend isn't over yet."

"And it might not be for quite a while," she said with a laugh, hugging him again. "But I think I already know what my answer will be. We writers tend to figure endings out first, you know."

"I think I'll skip to the end," he said, grinning, and then they were kissing again. If anyone was watching, Diane couldn't have cared less. It was time to celebrate.

Harlequin Intrigue®

COMING NEXT MONTH

#153 WHEN MURDER CALLS by M. L. Gamble
Megan Summers, TV ratings coordinator and
mother of two, was just getting her life in order when
a serial killer—dubbed the Grim Reaper—caused
chaos in the cozy hamlet of Melbourne, Florida. All
became suspects except for attractive Jack Gallagher,
who despite his odd obsession and hidden agenda,
gave Megan support, shelter, love.... But could he
shield her from the Reaper's scythe, which by the
hour whispered closer and closer to home?

#154 THE JAGUAR'S EYE by Caroline Burnes
Hard work on the Maya excavation wasn't all that
distinguished Celeste Coolridge. The villagers
claimed a mystical tie to the fiery-haired stockbroker.
Archaeologist Mark Grayson's passion had been
reserved for the legendary ruby known as the
Jaguar's Eye. Now he tasted both love and fear for
Celeste as the Maya whispered of strange omens and
an ancient prophesy. Somewhere in the ruins of an
age-old civilization lay the bloodred stone that was
the key to Celeste's fate....

Take 4 bestselling love stories FREE

Plus get a FREE surprise gift!

Harlequin Superromance®

THEY'RE A BREED APART

The men and women of the Canadian prairies are slow to give their friendship or their love. On the prairies, such gifts can never be recalled. Friendships between families last for generations. And love, once lit, burns hot and pure and bright for a lifetime.

In honor of this special breed of men and women, Harlequin Superromance® presents:

SAGEBRUSH AND SUNSHINE
(Available in October)

and

MAGIC AND MOONBEAMS
(Available in December)

two books by Margot Dalton, featuring the Lyndons and the Burmans, prairie families joined for generations by friendship, then nearly torn apart by love.

Look for SUNSHINE in October and MOONBEAMS in December, coming to you from Harlequin.

MAG-C1R